A Tale of
Two Families

Published by Hesperus Press Limited

28 Mortimer Street, London W1W 7RD

www.hesperuspress.com

Copyright © Dodie Smith, 1970

First published by Hesperus Press Limited, 2015

Typeset by Roland Codd

Printed and bound by CPI Group (UK) Ltd, Croydon, CR0 4YY

ISBN: 978-1-84391-557-7

A Tale of
Two Families

DODIE SMITH

1

As the taxi neared the signpost saying 'To the Dower House only', May told the driver to stop. 'We'll walk the rest of the way.'

The driver stopped but said he could easily drive them. 'The lane's narrow but the surface is all right. I often came here when the old ladies were still alive.'

May said she would rather walk, then turned to her sister, June. 'I want to sort of sneak up on the house.'

June, conscious of unsuitable shoes, asked the driver how long they would have to walk. He said not above five minutes, on which May briskly got out of the taxi, to be followed, less briskly, by June. Then May, having discovered on the way from the station that the driver had missed his lunch, told him to drive to the nearest village and get some. 'I'll treat you. And you can take at least an hour. I shall need all of that to explore the place.'

'Okay and thanks,' said the driver. 'And when I come back I'll drive up to the front door. Might be raining again by then. Well, February Filldyke, as they say.'

'Nice man,' said May as the taxi drove off. I haven't heard February Filldyke since I was a child. What ages it is since I was last in the country.'

'Yet of course you have the right clothes for it,' said June. 'But you would have even if you were suddenly asked to go yachting or cross the Sahara.'

'Well, I dare say I could rig up something. Here, hold up!' She shot out a steadying hand. 'You'll need some proper country shoes when you come to stay with us here. I'll treat you.'

'Don't be so sure you're coming here. The house may be a horror.'

'But I told you, George *liked* it when he came to see the old girls about their investments. And it's so miraculous to get the chance of renting such a house. It could be sold for an enormous amount if it wasn't entailed. I do love this twisty lane. And there are signs of spring already. Those dangly things are lambs' tails, later on they get all furry yellow and come off on you.'

'This is going to be a long five minutes' walk,' said June.

May thought this possible as there was still no sign of any house, but she continued to find things to praise: the overgrown hedges, the tall, still-dripping trees, the brilliant green of the grassy verges, the freshness of the air. And after several more bends in the lane they saw a white wooden gate standing open. Once through this they looked across a large, circular lawn surrounded by a gravel drive. And now at last they were face to face with the house.

'Much too large,' said June.

'Not at all. If you knew how I'm longing for space, after that poky flat.'

June laughed. 'You can't call that fabulous flat poky.'

'I can and do. The fact that it's expensive doesn't make it spacious.' May stood still, gazing at the house. 'Georgian, I think – no, the roof looks Queen Anne. I'd say Queen Anne refronted in the late eighteenth century.'

'The things you know about architecture!'

'I told you, I've been reading up about country houses. Those downstairs windows look Victorian.'

'So does the conservatory. That's pretty hideous.'

'I don't agree. It could be amusing if one got the right line on it. And that big room on the left balances it. That could be an orangery, with those tall windows, except that it looks fairly new. Well, come on. Shall we go across the lawn or by the drive?'

'The lawn will be wet. And I bet the whole house will be damp. We're in a hollow here.'

'We are *not* in a hollow. I shall strike you if you go on disparaging everything.'

They crunched along the gravel drive to the front porch, which suggested the lych gate of a churchyard.

'A bit ye olde, this,' said May. 'Porches so often spoil houses. But we can grow things up it. Now the key should be hanging on the right of the door. Well, it isn't. I'll read the letter again.'

There were wooden seats on the inside of the porch. They sat on them and May took a letter from her handbag and read it aloud:

Dear Mrs Clare,

I'm so sorry but I shan't be able to meet you on Thursday, as arranged. I have to represent my grandfather at a family funeral – they keep on happening, I'm sure they're taking years off my life. I'll be home on Friday but I'm not sure what time. Perhaps Saturday would be a good day for you? But you may still prefer Thursday and to be on your own. You'll find some of my great-aunts' furniture in the dining room and drawing-room. It goes well with the William Morris wallpapers (original and still in almost perfect condition). But of course you may loathe the furniture and the wallpapers. I'll leave the central heating on.

Just one thing: If there's anything you want to know please don't ask at the Hall. Though my grandfather has agreed that the Dower House shall be let, it's best not to remind him that it's going to be. Perhaps you could leave a message – I'll put paper and pencil in the hall – and

*then I could telephone you. And if you do decide to come
on Saturday, I'll be here.*

*Yours sincerely,
Sarah Strange*

*P.S. Key on nail right of porch – outside, hidden under
the overhang. Key of the staff cottage under its doormat.*

May handed the letter to June. 'Curious handwriting, isn't it?'

'Almost illiterate.'

'Oh, no – just peculiar. So spiky. Now where's that key?
Outside the porch, she says.'

May now found the key without difficulty and opened the
front door. A wave of warm air came to meet them.

'So much for your damp house,' said May.

'It'd be damp if it didn't have central heating.'

'Well, it does have central heating. George told me the
old ladies had it put in because they suffered so much with
rheumatism – one of them was crippled with it. This is a good
hall. Looks as if it's just been decorated.'

The panelling had been painted white. Doors stood open on
either side. May, going through one of them gasped.

'My goodness, this wallpaper might be new!'

It was a deep pink, with a raised design in ruby red.

'You couldn't keep this furniture,' said June. 'Or the curtains
and carpet.'

'I certainly shall. Everything goes with the wallpaper. I shall
get to like it all, just as I've got to like *art nouveau*.'

'I haven't and never shall – this or *art nouveau*. Though I'll
admit the wallpaper's handsome.'

'That's big of you.'

8

'If gloomy.'

'Of course it's gloomy on a dark morning. Now let's find the drawing room.'

It was on the other side of the hall. Here the wallpaper was a deep green against a yellowish background. The furniture included a cabinet packed with ornaments.

June, peering in on them, said, 'Don't tell me you like these.'

'I *shall*, when I know more about them. I must read up about William Morris.'

'I wonder if there's a William Morris kitchen.'

But the kitchen was reasonably modern except for the long, scrubbed table and pine dresser which even June had to admire.

'How I shall enjoy cooking in here!' said May. 'All sorts of wonderful things in great earthenware casseroles.'

'They'll feel embarrassed in that William Morris dining room.'

May, pushing open a door, said, 'They won't be eaten in that William Morris dining room. This is the room we shall virtually live in.'

It was long, with a large open fireplace and heavy white-washed beams. Three windows, one of them a French window, looked out on to a lawn beyond which was a grove of small, bushy trees. At the far end of the room there was an unusually large bow window with a window seat. May, moving quickly to it, said, 'Look! That must be the Hall.'

There was an uninterrupted view of it, across a neglected park dotted with ancient oaks, many of them obviously near the end of their lives.

'Palladian,' said May.

'Those pillars must make the inside dark.'

'George says it's going to rack and ruin – the whole estate is. And nothing can be done until the old man dies and the girl inherits, by which time it'll be too late for anything to be done.'

'Jolly prospect for the girl. And what a life for her, shut up in that tomb with an old man.'

'George gathered from the family solicitors that she's devoted to him. And I should think she's trying to prop up her inheritance. Well, perhaps we can make things a bit more cheerful for her.' May sat down on the window seat. 'June...'

There was a sudden note of appeal in May's voice which her sister instantly recognised. She sat down beside May and said, 'Yes, darling?'

'You do like *this* room, surely? It's light and cheerful even on this gloomy day.'

'Well, it's certainly the better for not being cluttered up with old-fashioned furniture.'

'I can do something marvellous in here, once I get a line on it. June, darling, please stop being against the house.'

'I don't give a damn about the house, one way or another. What I'm against is your leaving London. I simply can't imagine life without you there.'

'We'll be just one hour from Liverpool Street and twenty minutes' drive from the station.'

'You're forgetting how long it'll take me to reach Liverpool Street. Anyway, I can't keep dashing down here. And I can't telephone whenever I feel like it.'

'You can telephone ten times a day if you like, and reverse the charges.'

'Of course I can't. And why, why, why do you want to leave London? Neither you nor George are country-lovers.'

May, after heaving a heavy sigh, said, 'All right. You'd better have the truth. I simply can't stand having my nose rubbed in

10

George's goings-on any longer. Oh, I know they don't matter. I really do believe they're perfectly innocent.'

'Of course they are,' said June, who believed no such thing.

'But I can't go on…well, watching them. At best, the change of commuting down here may keep his mind off women for a bit. At worst, I shan't see what he's up to. I will *not* let myself be a nagging wife.'

'You know he really adores you,' said June, thankful she could mean it as well as say it.

May sighed again. 'I suppose I do – though sometimes…You'd think he could at least be a little more discreet when he knows how it upsets me to see him paying attention to other women. Oh, well, there it is. I'm sorry I've told you, really. I made a vow years ago that I wouldn't talk about it any more, even to you.'

'It's ages since you did. I took it that things were better.' In actual fact, she had merely taken it that May thought they were. 'Anyway, surely it doesn't matter, talking to *me*?'

'It's disloyal. You wouldn't talk to me if you had the same trouble with Robert – than which few things are less likely.'

'Oh, I don't know,' said June, who was quite sure she did know. Then she mentally touched wood. Perhaps it was unwise to feel a hundred per cent sure of any husband. 'Let's look at the rest of the house. And I'll try to be on your side about it.'

They went up the white-painted staircase and found six good bedrooms, some of them with fitted wash-basins, some smaller rooms and a pleasant if old-fashioned bathroom. May, counting rooms, said, 'I shall have masses of spare rooms, even when Corinna's down here and Dickon's home for his holidays. You can all come to stay. And the attics may be usable.'

She ran up the narrow stairs and called back, 'Excellent attics. Come on up. You get a good view from here. There's a

11

little garden hidden in those bushy trees at the back – with a sundial.'

June went up and dutifully admired the hidden garden.

'I wonder how you get to it,' said May. 'I can't see a path.'

'Probably the trees have grown together over the path.'

'What *are* those trees?'

'Difficult to tell when they've no leaves on.'

'I must read up about country things,' said May. 'But at least I can spot trees like oaks and elms even when they're bare. Oh, there's a house – over there, on the edge of the park. You can just see the side of it. That'll be the staff cottage.'

'Looks more like a barn. They don't paint cottages black.'

'They do sometimes – anyway, they tar them or something. It must be a cottage, it's got chimneys. We'll go and find it.'

Down in the hall May remembered they hadn't seen the room she had thought looked like an orangery. 'The one with tall windows.'

They found it at the end of a passage. It was very large and high, with a modern fireplace, many bookshelves, and a parquet floor. There were four of the tall windows that faced the front garden. In the back wall, a door stood open on to a tiled bathroom.

May said, 'Oh, this must be the room that was built as a bed-sitting-room for the crippled sister. George had tea here, not long before both sisters died – within a few weeks of each other. George said they were very gay and still quite pretty, though they were well over eighty.'

'I wonder what we shall be like if we live to be eighty.'

'You'll be a shade too plump and I shall be match-stick thin – except that I shall start overeating when I'm seventy. I can't bear brittle-looking old age. Of course you'll wear better than I shall. Beauty always wears better than mere prettiness.'

'Beauty? Me?' said June, genuinely astonished.

'You've always been... sort of on the edge of beauty. George was saying that, or something very like it, that last time you and Robert came to dinner. And to be brutally frank, he also said that you don't make the best of yourself. Well, God knows I've told you that, often enough. You need the hint of red in your hair bringing out – I'd look a real faded blonde if I didn't have a brightening rinse. And you should dress more revealingly. You bundle yourself up so. Incidentally, that coat's had it. Why aren't you wearing the one I treated you to?'

'I didn't want to get it wet.'

'Oh, tut!...Well, we don't really need this room but I may get a line on it. And the extra bathroom will be a boon. Now we'll find the staff cottage. Imagine still calling it that! Oh, and I must write a message for Sarah Strange.'

There was a pad and pencil on the mantel in the hall.

'Nice, a fireplace in the hall,' said May. 'We must have a fire in it when you all come down at Christmas.' She wrote on the pad, 'I love the house. My husband and I will come down on Saturday afternoon and then we can discuss everything. Looking forward to meeting you, May Clare.'

'That'll put the rent up,' said June.

'It's fixed already – and very reasonable.'

They went out, replaced the key on its nail, skirted the conservatory, which was completely empty (May again praised its potentialities) and made their way to the back of the house. Here they eventually found a tunnel-like path through the overgrown bushy trees which seemed likely to lead to the cottage they had seen. But soon other paths branched off and it was difficult to keep a sense of direction. June, after a minute or so, said, 'Do you know, I believe these trees are lilacs?'

13

'What, all of them? There couldn't be so much lilac.'

'Well, they all look the same and they're very like the old lilac tree in our back garden. Yes, I'm sure they're lilacs.'

'If so, Mother will go mad with delight. You know what a thing she has about lilac. She must come down when it's in bloom.'

'If she's back. I gather she's having a whale of a time.'

Their much-loved, long-widowed mother, who lived a colourful life on a large annuity, was completing a trip round the world by a prolonged stay with friends in America.

May said, 'She's supposed to be home by April. I wonder if we're walking in a circle. It's like being in a maze.'

'Nice idea, a lilac maze.'

'And we haven't struck the little garden. Oh, thank goodness, there's daylight ahead.'

They came out on to an overgrown lawn and at once saw the staff cottage. Black it was, tarred weather-boarding, but it was anything but gloomy. All its window-frames, the delicate barge-boarding of its two small gables, and its elegant iron-work porch were newly painted white. The whole effect was skittish.

'It's like something in a nursery rhyme,' said June.

'I wonder if it's a Regency *cottage orné*. No, those little pointed windows look Victorian Gothic.'

'So does the glass. How wonderful that it's still intact.'

The narrow white glazing bars divided the casement windows into a pattern of small octagons, and in each gable there was a circular window suggesting a sunflower.

May, getting the key from under the mat, said, 'I suppose the rooms will be tiny.'

The hall and the staircase were certainly narrow but there were two fair-sized sitting rooms, and the kitchen, which ran across the full width of the cottage, was large. Upstairs there were two

14

good bedrooms, two smaller ones, and a fairly primitive bathroom. A ladder-like staircase led to a loft lit by the two sunflower windows and a dormer window looking towards the Hall. The whole cottage was newly distempered white.

May said, as they came downstairs, 'What a waste that we don't need this.'

'Would you be allowed to let it?'

'I shouldn't think so and anyway I shouldn't care to. I suppose we could lend it, but we've no friends I fancy having so close. Oh, my God! Yes, of course!' The light in May's eyes suggested a soul's awakening. '*You* must come and live here. Oh, how marvellous!'

'You're raving mad,' said June. 'It's out of the question.'

'But it's absolutely ideal. Robert told me only last week how *he* wished he was moving to the country.'

'I dare say. But what about his work?'

'How often does he go to Fleet Street?'

'Oh, several times a week.' It wasn't true. He seldom went more than once, to deliver work and collect more books to review. And he was longing to take a year off from reviewing to write one of his novels (those novels which were so highly praised by important critics, but earned only a few hundred pounds). But coming here remained out of the question.

'Well, he can go up with George, either by car or train.'

'Railway fares are expensive. And what about Hugh? He couldn't come down here every night. He works later than George.'

'He could go to our flat, with Corinna. She wants to stay there until she finishes at her Drama School.'

'What, the two of them all on their own in the flat?'

'Certainly. And if they want to pop into bed together, why not? Then they might get over wanting to marry.'

15

'They won't get over it,' said June. 'They've been in love since they were children. And I think it's cruel of you to be so against them. Lots of cousins marry.'

'They're *double* cousins.'

The sisters had married brothers.

'Anyway, they will marry, whatever you say, just as soon as Hugh's in a position to, which ought to be fairly soon.'

'I know,' said May, gloomily. 'George is delighted with him.'

Hugh, June's twenty-year-old son, worked with his uncle in the City.

'Anyway, that doesn't affect the fact that we can't come and live down here. What about Baggy? There's no room big enough for his huge furniture.'

Baggy, the sisters' father-in-law (his nickname, originating in some now barely remembered family joke, was used even by his grandchildren) had lived with June and Robert ever since the death of his wife, ten years earlier – or rather, they had lived with him, in his large Edwardian house in the outer suburbs.

Only for a moment was May stumped. Then she said triumphantly, 'Baggy can live with us. He can have that big room with the tall windows – it'll make an ideal bed-sitting-room. He'll love having his own bathroom, surely?'

And I'd love his having it, thought June. Baggy, the kindest and least burdensome of old men, always avoided the bathroom during rush hours, but once he got into it he stayed an unconscionable time. And it would be very, very pleasant to be on her own with Robert in this exquisite little house – and Hugh and Prudence too, of course, whenever they could come. And Prue would so love the country in her holidays. All the same, it was still out of the question. She said firmly, 'Darling, it's most terribly kind of you, both to offer the house and suggest taking Baggy. But we just can't afford to live here.'

It had no effect whatever. May merely pointed out the cheapness of living in this tiny house – 'There'll be no rent or rates, George will take care of all that. And the move needn't cost you a penny – all your stuff can come down here with ours. And just think! Once you find you like it here you can sell your house.'

'It's still morally Baggy's. He only made it over to us to save on death duties. And he may not want to sell it.'

'Well, you can sell it *eventually*. And it'll bring in enough capital to earn quite a decent income – George will see to that. And then Robert can drop reviewing and stick to his novels.'

Which was what he wanted to do more than anything in the world, thought June. Everything was against her. With relief she said, 'Listen, there's our taxi hooting. And we've got to find our way back through that maze.'

But they were able to skirt the lilac trees by walking through the park and then get into the front garden by a small side gate. May, looking at the Dower House, said, 'Fascinating to think that'll soon be our home. And you'll be in that darling cottage.'

'That's enough!' said June with sudden fierceness. 'If you say one word more about it I won't even consider it.' Then she realised she had made a concession.

May pounced on it. 'But you *will* consider it? And quickly, because the instant I tell George he'll be on the phone to Robert.'

'You're not to tell George until I say you may. And if I go on thinking it's impossible, you're not to tell him at all. Please, May! Please promise.'

May did some quick thinking. What could account for opposition to a scheme that would benefit not only June but her whole family? And June had always disliked living in Baggy's ugly, inconvenient house, which she'd had to run with a minimum of help.

June, even more urgently, said again, 'Please, May!'

May, still puzzled, said, 'All right, I promise. No one's going to bully you into living near me if you don't want to.'

'You know it isn't that.'

May did know – which made it all the more puzzling. And then, as they crunched across the gravel drive to the taxi, she thought, 'I've got it!' Those unsuitable shoes, that shapeless coat with its worn fur collar – and that wispy headscarf! June, barely forty, her junior by two years, was letting herself get a mental middle-aged spread. She was terrified of change, couldn't assimilate a new idea. But she would, given time.

May smiled lovingly. '*Of course* it isn't that. You just need a breather – I'm an idiot to have rushed at you so. You just think it over quietly.'

'Oh, bless you,' said June fervently.

But she couldn't start thinking in the taxi. May asked to be driven around the countryside and June couldn't stop wondering if she would soon be living in it. Driving from the station she had felt inimical because it was going to rob her of May. But now, the villages, inns, churches and ancient houses charmed her and it was a joy even to look at distance… But still the idea of coming here was out of the question.

At the station at last, May and the taxi driver parted on beaming good terms, assuring each other they would meet again soon.

'Might get tea on the train,' said May, as they waited on the windy platform.

'Not me. I just want to sit quietly and think.'

'Well, good for you. Tell you what, we'll travel separately. Then you can think till you bust. Actually, I've some thinking to do myself. I want to get a line on that long room off the kitchen.'

June, relaxing in a corner seat – May, of course, had taken First Class tickets – said to herself: 'Now! Assemble your facts.'

But they had assembled themselves, at lightning speed, when May had offered the cottage. Robert had always longed to live in the country. Baggy would welcome the chance to live with George, firstborn and favourite son (not that Baggy hadn't always been wonderfully kind to Robert). Hugh, Prudence… their mother was sure of their delight. As for herself, it was the sharpness of her own delight that had scared her. Surely it was a danger signal? But what reason could she give for refusing? And could she now bear to refuse?

Come on, now, face it calmly, as she'd faced it for twenty-one years – longer, really, because she'd known about it even before her marriage. And never, in all her countless meetings with George, had she given herself away. And what the hell was there to give away? She didn't *love* George, as she loved Robert. There were times when she didn't even *like* George, those times when his goings-on made May unhappy. All she'd ever felt was a dizzying physical attraction, which harmed no one, not even herself. Indeed, she derived great pleasure from it; when a meeting with George was ahead she felt years younger. And would seeing him oftener (probably almost every day; what bliss!) really be dangerous? Perhaps just the reverse; she might get used to George. She couldn't imagine that, couldn't even wish it. But it might happen.

There was movement in the compartment as the man nearest the door rose to open it. May stood there with a cup of tea – which, being May, she had not slopped into the saucer. She handed it to June, smilingly thanked the man who coped with the door, and went.

'Oh, my darling, May,' thought June, stirring her tea. 'Rather than hurt you, rather than hurt Robert, I'd cheerfully die.' She didn't mention George, it never having occurred to her that he was hurtable. 'But I'm not going to hurt *anyone*. What I feel about George is just my private bit of fun. It's really only…' She had a flash of illumination. 'It's what Mother used to feel about Rudolph Valentino. She told me she could sit in a cinema positively dazed by him, even when she was newly married. Well, George is just my Valentino.'

Everything would be all right. She relaxed and drank her sweet, strong, nasty tea with considerable pleasure while she thought of the black and white cottage on the edge of the lilac grove, and George living just on the other side of the lilac.

When they reached Liverpool Street station May was outside in the corridor, waiting. Even before the train stopped, June said, 'It's all right. Of course we'll come if you're sure you want us – and George does.'

'George will be as delighted as I am. Oh, what fun it's going to be. I've got a marvellous line on that long room. I shall make it a sort of extension of the kitchen, with a huge scrubbed table. Oh, tell Baggy I'll give him lots of steak and kidney puddings.'

It was Baggy's favourite dish. Robert, unfortunately, disliked it.

June said, 'Ask George not to telephone until after dinner. Give me time to talk to Robert and Baggy. Of course, they may object.'

'You know jolly well they won't,' said May.

2

Robert had never owned a car and had only a hazy knowledge of routes out of London; but he did have a sense of direction. So it was not very long before he said to George, 'Surely we're not heading for Surrey?'

'No, indeed,' said George.

'But you said last night on the telephone that you had a client in Guildford. Guildford *is* in Surrey, surely?'

'Yes, indeed. And I do have a client there, a charming old man who'd have been delighted to give us lunch. And I knew you'd enjoy the outing. But we don't happen to be going on that particular outing. Not today.'

'Oh, well,' said Robert, unperturbed. Any outing with George was a pleasure. 'Where *are* we going, then?'

'To the Dower House,' said George without any change of expression.

'But you're out of your mind. It's tomorrow we're going to the Dower House – with the girls.'

'Exactly. And today we're going without the girls, to make sure the place really is fit to live in. That's all the more essential now we've persuaded you all to transplant yourselves.'

'But I thought you'd already had a surveyor.'

'Certainly. I got one in before I even discussed the house with May. It's in remarkably good condition. The old ladies had money of their own and they took care of the place. But… Oh, I want one final calm look, before it's too late. Things won't be calm tomorrow, with the girls around.'

'They'll be terribly disappointed if you change your mind now,' said Robert, adding mentally, 'And so shall I.'

'Well, it's ninety per cent certain I shan't change my mind. I found the place, I've had my eye on it for years. I made enquiries as soon as I decently could after the last Miss Strange died. Relax, Robert. You, certainly, should be glad to consider things calmly. You haven't even seen this cottage that's being wished on you. And neither have I. Couldn't find it when I came down with the surveyor and didn't think it mattered. Now, according to May, it's a jewel. I wonder if it's got any drains.'

'June noticed hot and cold water taps – and electric light.'

'Oh, everything will probably be all right. But I do have to be a little cautious as I shall be taking the place on a repairing lease. Not that I'm kicking about that. The Stranges can't afford any more repairs. That's why the rent's so reasonable.'

'I wish you'd let us pay a share of the rent.'

'Nonsense. If you don't live in the cottage it'll just stand empty. Oh, do cheer up, Robert.' George, waiting at traffic lights, cast a quick look at his brother. 'You're looking depressingly grim.'

'Sorry. It's just that…well, what am I to say to June about today? I can't hide where we've been from her.'

'I've got that all worked out. If I'm satisfied – as I expect to be – I shall own up to May. And then we'll all go down tomorrow with tape measures and whatnot and no worries.'

'But suppose you're *not* satisfied.'

'Then I shan't say one word about today. And we'll come down tomorrow and tactfully edge in objections – and also give the girls a chance to convert us.'

'But I couldn't pretend to June that I'd spent the day in Surrey.'

'Of course you could. I'd coach you on exactly how you *would* have spent the day in Surrey.'

'Definitely no, George. I never lie to June.'

'Oh, my God,' said George impatiently. Then the traffic lights changed. A few moments later he shot a swift smile at Robert and said, 'Sorry. To me a lie that's well-intentioned is merely tact. But of course I'm a devious character. Anyway, when we get back I'll come in and see June and confess how I kidnapped you. I'll explain everything. She'll understand.'

'But then she'll have to lie to May, won't she?'

'No,' said George with humorous resignation. 'I'll own up to June, own up to May. I'll own up in the Personal Column of *The Times* if you like. Now stop looking like the Rock of Gibraltar and let's enjoy our day. I shall like the house and you'll like the cottage. Everything in the garden will be lovely. I don't seem to remember there *was* much in the garden, except grass.'

'Might do a bit of gardening.'

'I shall enjoy watching you. Damn, it's raining.'

'Probably only a shower.'

But the rain was soon so heavy that the windscreen wipers could barely cope with it. George concentrated on driving.

Robert, cheerful now except for a slight fear that the chance of living in the country might yet be whisked away, meditated on his dear brother's character. No doubt George was devious – though the word seemed unsuitable for his open-hearted nature – but he was also kind, generous, affectionate, good humoured (if occasionally irascible) and, above all, happy. It was a theory of Robert's that happy people were basically good – and it was a theory that often led him to self-condemnation. For he wasn't particularly happy, the main reason for this at present being that he was tired of writing about other men's books. Now there seemed a chance that he could concentrate on writing his own; anyway, June thought this could be managed. She and Baggy had already gone into a huddle about it.

'The rain's set in,' said George gloomily.

'Still, it's pleasant to see the country.' They were now emerging from the suburbs.

'It's taken us nearly an hour to get little over halfway. Can't see myself doing this drive very often.'

'Anyway, you're going to use the train, aren't you?'

'I shall get damn sick of all the hearty commuters. Well, I shall be one myself.'

'You're never hearty, George.'

'Certainly not at the moment. Am I mad, condemning myself – and you – to five years in water-logged country?'

'You're not condemning anyone to anything. You're keeping the flat for the present and Baggy doesn't want to sell our house yet. At the worst, you could just use the Dower House for weekends.'

'I haven't taken the damn place yet,' said George, and then felt guilty. He had raised Robert's hopes, May was dead set on the move, and it really was time they took their turn with dear old Baggy. Still, it would be no joke if one uprooted two families and then found it had been a mistake.

Robert fell silent and tried to steel himself against disappointment. Even in London, he had much to be thankful for. He lived rent free, with considerable financial aid from Baggy (which Baggy planned to continue after the move as George would not hear of his father paying for his keep – if only there *was* a move!) And he had June.

If there was one thing in the world that inflated Robert's ego it was to dwell on the fact that he had June while George only had May. Nice woman, May, but Robert would never have married her, if George had opted for June and she'd fallen for him. Once, on their honeymoon, he'd discussed this possibility with her and she'd said, 'As if I'd ever have looked at George with you around! You're so much handsomer.'

Robert was far from conceited but he did know this was true. He had classical features and a head of quite spectacular fair hair. George's features were pleasantly nondescript and his brown hair couldn't have been less spectacular. But Robert also knew that George could almost always outshine him, without effort and even when he tried not to. So he'd said to June, 'What about George's charm?' She'd said she'd never even noticed it.

Soothing thoughts, and Robert took extra pleasure in thinking them here in George's expensive car. George had so many worldly goods and George now had the power to blight Robert's hope of a blissful country life. But George didn't have June.

Blighting seemed more than ever likely when they drove through the village nearest the Dower House. George spoke of his dislike of ye olde English inns.

'But this one's genuine ye olde, isn't it?' said Robert, who thought the inn, the church and even a far from genuine ye olde antique shop pretty attractive. 'Look at those beams.'

'No doubt the brewers stripped them. I sometimes think beams, like bones, should remain decently covered.'

If only it would stop raining! George, though basically euphoric, was also mercurial. Robert was well aware that his brother's last-minute caution was genuine and even sensible – but the rain simply wasn't fair. It would bias George's judgement.

In the lane to the Dower House the overgrown hedges brushed against the car.

'Probably scratching the paint to bits,' said George.

'They seem to be very young, gentle twigs,' said Robert, enchanted to feel so close to the coming spring.

The white gate was open. George drove on to the gravel, then pulled up and said disconsolately, 'I can't believe it's the same house.'

'Did you never before see it in the rain?'

'Never. I came once in the spring and then on a marvellous autumn day. And the last time – when I came with the surveyor – there'd been a fall of snow and the whole place looked like a Christmas card. Well, thank God it's still not too late.'

They drove to the front door. George, who had studied Sarah Strange's letter, knew where to find the key – and got wet in the minute he took to find it. Why couldn't they keep the blasted key *inside* the porch?

He had barely unlocked the door before a clear, hard, female voice called loudly, 'Hi, there!' He started, turned and saw a tall figure, dressed in an ancient Burberry, rubber boots and a particularly hideous waterproof hat, coming across the lawn. 'Vicar's wife or something, probably thinks we're trespassing,' he whispered to Robert and considered going to meet the approaching female; then merely called 'Good morning.' No point in getting wet.

The woman, who had a stride like a man's, reached them in seconds and said loudly, 'Don't come near me. I'm dripping. Just let me strip.'

She flung off the waterproof hat and began taking off the Burberry. George frankly gaped. Minus the hat she was possibly the most beautiful girl he had ever seen. Then he hastily helped her with the Burberry. He didn't say anything because she gave him no chance. She continued non-stop.

'I'm Sarah Strange. We met the first time you came to see my great-aunts but you won't remember. Anyway, I hope you don't. I was a mountainous girl of fourteen. For years I was afraid I had elephantiasis.'

'Well, you haven't got it now,' said George. She was slim, even in a pullover and two cardigans. He put the Burberry down on one of the porch seats and introduced Robert who, while admiring the girl's beauty, was feeling slightly deafened by her voice.

Sarah, leading the way into the hall, said, 'I'm just back from London. Did Mrs Clare come down yesterday? Oh, yes, here's a message.' She read what May had written, then turned to George. 'It says that she and you will be coming tomorrow.'

'So we shall,' said George. 'But my brother and I happened to be in the locality today so we thought we'd drop in.'

'I bet you wanted to look round on your own, and I don't blame you. Just let me stoke the heating – if it's still in – and then I'll point out all the snags. Oh, will you be using the cottage?'

Robert nervously wondered if this hard-voiced young woman would kick at having two families when only one rent was being paid. But when George outlined the plan for the cottage she merely said, 'Oh, good. That little house needs living in. It's a pet.'

They were now in the kitchen where, refusing offers of help, she was soon emptying hods of coke into a stove. 'The thing's fairly antiquated,' she told them. 'Of course you could go a bust and change to oil-fired central heating.'

'Good idea,' said George.

Robert felt cheered. George's mental mercury was rising – Sarah Strange had counteracted the rain. She proceeded to point out various defects in the kitchen but was assured by George that he would take care of them. Finally she said there were a few things upstairs she ought to warn him about.

Robert said, 'I'd rather like to look at the cottage just on my own. The rain seems to be letting up a bit.'

'Anyway, take my Burberry,' said Sarah. 'It'll cover most of you. Actually, it's my grandfather's. I'll show you the way.'

She accompanied Robert to the front door, helped him into the Burberry, and pointed out the small gate leading from the garden into the park surrounding the Hall. 'Go straight on along the edge of the lilac grove.'

'Then it *is* lilac?' said Robert. 'My wife hoped it was.'

'My great-aunts had a mania for it. They settled here when they were quite young and planted and planted, letting it run wild. There's every conceivable shade of mauve. When poor old Aunt Katie was too crippled to walk I used to push her round under it in her bath chair.'

George, at the door of the drawing room, now reclaimed Sarah's attention. 'Ah, this must be one of the wallpapers my wife was so impressed by.'

There would be no backing out now, Robert decided. Blithely he sped on his way.

Once in the park he saw the Hall. June had said it was gloomy. To Robert it was also fascinating, stimulating to the imagination. Could one write a present-day Gothic romance – or rather, an *anti*-romance? Nothing he ever wrote was romantic. But today he *felt* romantic. Could one so treat romance that it was no longer a word to be despised, as it was nowadays? Could one fumigate the sentimentality out of romance? One might, if the romance included no love story – and he never did write love stories. Or did the word 'romance' imply a love story and, if so, had it always and *need* it?

But before he had answered his own questions he had come to the cottage, stopped thinking of himself as a writer, and been overcome by a desire to paint. The little black-and-white house, flanked by stiff poplars, was *asking* to be painted. And he'd painted rather well while still at school. Might try again, might be a Sunday painter.

The key! He'd forgotten to ask for it. Then he remembered June saying it had been under the mat. He found it, entered, instantly knew the cottage was perfect; then raced through it wondering if there was any room he could grab as a workroom.

Perhaps the smallest bedroom, if they did without a spare room. But that bedroom was over the kitchen, there would be noise. Then he found the loft and claimed it. The perfect workroom and with a wonderful view of the Hall. *Of course* he would write about the Hall, and the book he would write about it would not only be his usual critical success; it would also appeal to a vast public. One didn't hanker to be a bestseller for the sake of the money (what nonsense; of course one did) but one did long to reach the minds of the many, as most of the really great novelists had done. What was the secret? Intensity of feeling, surely…

His feelings became so intense that he lost count of time and only came back to earth when some church clock chimed the half-hour. *What* half-hour? He hastily looked at his watch and found it was twelve-thirty. He must have been here the best part of an hour. God knew what defects that hard-voiced, unnecessarily honest girl might have pointed out. Some might be serious.

He gave one last loving look around, praying it might not be a farewell look, then hurried back to the Dower House.

Before he reached the gate from the park he caught a glimpse of George and Sarah sitting on the window seat of a wide bow window. Seen thus, without being heard, Sarah certainly gave no impression of hardness. Indeed, there was something madonna-like about the pure oval of her face, her wide apart eyes and serene brow – except that Robert couldn't for the moment think of any very dark madonna. Sarah's hair, with its pronounced widow's peak, was almost black. She wore it scragged back into a bun.

Unfortunately her voice, which he heard as soon as he entered the hall, was even harder than he had remembered, positively metallic. But at least it enabled him to locate the room she and George were sitting in.

She greeted Robert with, 'Well, did you hate it?'

'No one could hate it,' said Robert fervently.

'I ought to have warned you there's no central heating there and the bath's cracked. Of course you noticed.'

Robert, who had noticed neither the absence of central heating nor the presence of the crack, assured her that open fires would be enough for such little rooms. And George said he would provide a new bath.

Sarah, with a gentle smile, said in her harshest tones, 'The things you plan to do! We ought to pay you to live here.' She then looked at her watch and said she must dash. 'Grandfather doesn't like me to be late for meals. I'm sorry I can't ask you to lunch but he doesn't *quite* know about you yet. Anyway, our food's always awful.'

'I suppose he *will* sign the lease?' said George.

'Yes, he's promised. But he seems to have an idea that some old ladies – like his sisters – are coming here and I thought I'd let him go on thinking it until the lease is signed. He's not round the bend, you know; it's just that sometimes he's a bit… sort of withdrawn. Well, he's had a lot to withdraw from, what with family deaths, and *no* money, and the Hall liable to fall on top of us. If you hear a terrific crash that'll be what it is. Now I really must rush. See you and Mrs Clare and' – she smiled at Robert – 'your Mrs Clare, tomorrow. Oh, it's raining again. Could I have my Burberry?'

Robert helped her into it. She gave them both a last smile and hurried out.

George, watching her from the window as she strode across the park, said, 'What a very beautiful girl.'

'Pity about her voice,' said Robert.

'What's wrong with her voice? Sounded all right to me.'

30

Robert stared, then felt uneasy. If George really hadn't noticed that voice… He looked his brother in the eye and said, 'How old would you say she was?'

'Twenty. She happened to mention it.'

'Same age as Corinna.'

George looked defensive. 'I *am* aware of my daughter's age. Was that remark supposed to mean something?'

'Yes,' said Robert firmly. 'For God's sake don't start anything here, George – right under May's nose.'

'You're crazy. Just because I was reasonably pleasant to the girl…' He broke off and surprisingly added, 'All right, Robert. Thanks for the warning. Dalliance with Sarah is out.'

Robert believed him. It wasn't always easy to tell when George was lying but Robert could usually tell when George was speaking the truth; a confusing distinction but Robert knew what he meant by it. He said heartily, 'Thank you, George.'

As for George, the mention of May had reminded him of his main reason for living in the country. Goings-on were *not* to be under May's nose. It simply wouldn't be fair. A pity, rather, because he *had* been attracted – and he'd known several girls of twenty who hadn't been put off by a little age gap of twenty-five years. But fair was fair.

'Now we'll chase some lunch,' he told Robert cheerfully.

'You wouldn't like to see the cottage?'

'It can wait till tomorrow when the girls are here.'

'You're sure about taking the place now?'

George looked surprised. 'Of course. I told you I was ninety per cent certain. It's an excellent proposition, even if that nice, honest girl did point out some defects.'

Ah, but that nice honest girl's beauty had discounted the defects – and the rain. Robert felt deeply grateful to Sarah

Strange. Might put her into his Gothic anti-romance – her voice was certainly anti-romantic.

He took a quick look round in case George had left a cigarette burning. It would be a pity (and quite a bit Gothic) if the house burned down overnight. Then he followed his brother out through the driving rain to the shelter of the car.

3

Baggy was alone in his bedroom.

The removal van had gone. Robert and June, after seeing it off, had gone too, he to the *Onlooker* offices, she to Liverpool Street Station. May and June, going by train, would get to the Dower House before the van. Baggy was to lunch with George in the City and then, in the late afternoon, George would drive him and Robert to the country. Everything had been carefully planned by that arch-planner, May. Baggy was fond of May but not quite as fond as he was of June, whereas he was fond of Robert but not quite as fond as he was of George. Well, in the country he would gain George without losing Robert and June. And May was a superb cook.

He looked round the denuded room. The bed still remained, May having persuaded him to let her supply one more suitable for a bed-sitting-room. A really comfortable one, she had assured him. It was no use pretending the bed he had slept on for nearly fifty years was comfortable. It had, in fact, three sags, the middle one made by him during the years since his wife's death. Still, he was fond of that bed, which had been the latest thing when he and Mabel chose it: reddish mahogany inlaid with yellow satinwood.

Well, it could remain here quite safely, and probably for a considerable time. For Baggy, until his retirement an astute house agent, considered this a bad time to sell the house. 'Just think of it as money in the bank for you,' he'd told Robert. 'And later on it'll be *more* money.' Robert had of course agreed with the utmost vagueness – hopeless to discuss business with Robert. George had undertaken to keep his finger on the pulse of the property market.

Not that Baggy couldn't do that himself. Often he wished that he hadn't retired – and at sixty-five, much too early. But it had seemed unavoidable. For nearly a year after Mabel's death he hadn't been normal. It wasn't simply her death that had shattered him; it was also the manner of it. He'd come round after a week of coma without the slightest memory of the accident – though they assured him he must have seen the out-of-control truck that had hit them, for he had braked, swerved, done all the right things. All he recalled was sitting in the car beside his wife discussing the holiday they were setting out on; he distinctly remembered asking her if she was getting too much draught from his window. And he was suddenly asked to believe that she was dead, cremated, her ashes scattered. Instructions for that were in her will, as they were in his; but somehow it made her death harder to take in for a long, long time.

But of course he had accepted it eventually and, he supposed, got over it. Still, leaving this house… He pulled his thoughts up. It was people, not places, that counted and he was singularly lucky: two sons, two daughters-in-law, four grandchildren, and he was on excellent terms with all of them. You be thankful, he told himself, that you're not a lonely old man.

He made sure the windows were closed and latched, then gave one last look at the bed. Damn it, he wished he'd insisted on taking it. May and her bed-sitting-room ideas! Well, his huge wardrobe and dressing table would put paid to those and quite right too. A bedroom was a bedroom, even if you sat in it.

He'd better take a look over the whole house. June was none too reliable about latching windows. He went up to the top floor: excellent rooms, they could be converted into a flat. He assessed the potential rent. Then he went down and paid a last visit to the bathroom. He'd always liked it, a good square room and you could warm it up by opening the cupboard which housed the hot tank. The dressing table had been left behind – June said there would not be room for it. Automatically he opened the drawer to get his comb but June had packed it with all his other bathroom belongings. Better buy a pocket comb on his way to the Underground. With hair as thick as his, he needed one. Even thicker than Robert's, it was, and had once been even fairer. It had gone white early, a nice clean white. He glanced in the dressing-table mirror. Odd to think it had reflected his face for nearly fifty years. He couldn't remember how he had looked as a young man, couldn't go back further than, say, his early forties when he'd looked much as Robert did now. Though he'd never been handsome, as Robert was, and always much heavier.

Strange that he should be so unlike George, when he felt so much closer to George than to Robert. George was like his mother, the same eyes and that wonderful smile.

The thought of meeting George for lunch caused him to survey the rest of the house briskly. Hugh's room, Prue's room, the big room used by Robert and June... but they were all big rooms in his good, solid house. Downstairs the sitting rooms were still fairly full of furniture, his furniture. He'd offered it to June but she'd said it would be too big. She'd taken all the stuff she and Robert had first set up house with, small, inexpensive things; they'd had only a tiny house. Baggy liked to think how much more comfortable they'd been since coming to live with him.

Well, that was that. He closed the front door and tested that it was closed. He felt slightly uneasy about leaving the house all on its own but it was fully insured and the police had been notified.

A pity it looked like rain. June had so hoped to have a fine day for the move.

May, scurrying into the Dower House porch, said, 'Have we ever come down here when it wasn't raining?'

'It wasn't that first day,' said June.

'The sun wasn't shining. Still, if we've liked the place on dreary days it's a good test.' She unlocked the front door and said happily, 'Almost *too* warm, isn't it?'

The taxi driver followed them in, carrying two suitcases of food. Sarah Strange had undertaken to get in bread and dairy products but May was taking no chances on such things as meat, and had come prepared to feed her family, and June's, until she could get the hang of local shopping. It was the same taxi driver who had first brought them to the house and he said this was a good omen. May, as she overpaid him, heartily agreed. 'Though why it should be, I can't think,' she remarked to June, as he went.

They unpacked the food in the kitchen and Long Room (now its official name) and then awaited the removal van. May's 'line' on the Long Room had come off handsomely. She had happened to mention to Sarah that she wanted a long, scrubbed pine table, whereupon Sarah had offered one from a disused kitchen at the Hall. Smuggled in to see this, May had also collected a dozen kitchen chairs, a low dresser to use as a carving table, and four red leather armchairs from an Edwardian smoke-room unsmoked in for a good forty years. (Sarah had shown May this room and others but allowed no glimpse of old Mr Strange.) Thus equipped May had only had to buy curtains (handwoven, beige and white) and some heavy rush matting, and might have found such economy thwarting had she not gone to town on new furniture for all the bedrooms – which, as she pointed out, was necessary as she could not denude the flat.

All the new furniture had already been delivered so the bed-rooms, as well as the Long Room, were in good order. The removal van would mainly be bringing June's belongings – and, of course, Baggy's mammoth bedroom suite.

The van did not arrive until May was cutting sandwiches for lunch. She fed the removal men before breaking the news to them that all the furniture for the cottage would have to be carried there, as there was no road and the van could not be driven across the waterlogged grass of the park. The rain had stopped, but there was every indication that it would shortly start again, so there was a rush to do the job quickly. Luckily Sarah arrived and worked quite as hard as the men, and May and June carried what they could.

It was gruelling work but it was finished eventually, just as the rain began again. May then went back to the Dower House with the men and Sarah stayed to help June get straight.

June did not particularly want to get straight. She would have preferred to sit down and do a little quiet gloating – about the bliss of leaving Baggy's house and coming to this jewel, about Robert's happiness at moving to the country, about the joy of being so close to May. All this plus the glory of the fact that she would be seeing George at dinner. However, she acquiesced in Sarah's determination to get the beds made up and put the kitchen in some kind of working order. They then went back to the Dower House.

May, having tipped the men nobly, was just seeing them off.

'And now I must telephone George,' she said. 'I want to be sure he makes an early start. There'll be a lot of City traffic to drive through.'

But George, when she eventually got him, had decided against driving – 'Not in all this rain.'

'It's not too bad here,' said May. 'It actually stopped for a while, and it's *thinner* now.'

'It isn't here. It's very, very thick and looks determined. We'll come down on the 6.36 and eat on the train. That'll save you cooking dinner.'

'But I've got steaks.'

'Steaks will keep,' said George firmly.

Well, they would. And if she didn't have to cook a full meal she could unpack her clothes and all George's things. Also she was determined, from now on, never to nag George about what time he got home or what meals he missed. So she agreed cheerfully, and assured George the move had gone splendidly. Then she rang off and said brightly, 'Tea now, and I could eat an egg. I could eat two eggs, possibly three. Sarah, stay and eat three eggs with us.'

'I didn't know anyone ever ate three eggs,' said Sarah, 'but I could certainly eat *some*. I can't tell you what lunch was like. Well, our poor old cook's nearly eighty.'

'I could teach you to cook,' said May.

'But if I did the cooking, our poor old dear couldn't do the housework I do. And anyway, she'd be terribly upset if I cooked.'

As far as May knew, the only other help at the Hall was an elderly man who combined the offices of butler, valet and male nurse. She had a great desire to *cope* with Sarah – ask about her circumstances, advise her, help her. But Sarah, in spite of her frightful old clothes, her friendliness, and her habit of deferring to May and June, retained a touch of aristocratic aloofness. 'Or am I being class-conscious?' May asked herself, starting to get tea. 'I only know I'd as soon offer advice to royalty.'

Sarah, after her eggy tea – never before had she handled an electric toaster – said she must go, in time to have sherry with her grandfather. The rain had now definitely stopped and there was a hint of watery late-afternoon sunshine beyond the Hall. May, gazing at it through the bow window, said, 'I never realised this window faces west. Then the others must face south.'

She opened the French window, to let Sarah out, and let in a gust of cool, damp air.

'Let's go for a walk,' said June.

'Heavens, no. Everything's sopping wet.' May hastily closed the window behind Sarah. 'And I've lots to do. Come and see what you think of Baggy's room. That awful wardrobe and dressing table have wrecked everything.'

'They won't look as bad to me as they do to you. I've seen them every day for ten years.'

But they looked worse than June had expected. Baggy's Edwardian house had been their spiritual home. This austere room wasn't. But at least she could praise the curtains. 'They must have cost you a fortune – for those enormous windows.'

'Yes, they're good ones, but I'd have liked something more modern. George didn't think I could risk it. I wanted to get some good rugs but when Baggy heard about the parquet he said he didn't want it covered.'

'He sets a lot of store by parquet. That's the old house agent coming out.'

'Let's make the divan up. I've got the blankets and linen out. I wonder how soon I can find some domestic help.'

'Sarah says there isn't any,' said June.

'There will be. It's just a matter of hunting efficiently and paying enough.'

May's efficiency and ability to pay enough had really staggered June during the month since the move had been decided on. Builders, plumbers, house furnishers… all had been invincibly driven to work at enormous speed – and at enormous cost. Even the expenditure on the cottage must, June knew, have been considerable. May had insisted on supplying new curtains and new carpets, not to mention the bath and all sorts of improvements June would never have thought of making. For May's generosity kept pace with her extravagance. Actually,

June never thought of May as extravagant. There was a shrewd-ness about her expenditure which made the word unsuitable. But money certainly poured out. And if June protested May invariably said, 'George can afford it.'

Darling May… and darling George… and of course darling Robert. June, when Baggy's room was in readiness, said, 'What time will the boys be back?'

To May and June, their husbands were still 'the boys', just as to George and Robert their wives were still 'the girls'.

'Let's see…' May worked it out. The hour's journey from London, then the taxi drive… 'They should be here by eight. We'll unpack our clothes and then have baths. Is your immersion heater on?'

'I shouldn't think so.'

'Well, you can have a bath here. And we'll dress up a bit. I only hope they don't miss the train.'

Owing to Baggy's opinion that any train journey was a serious undertaking, he and George arrived at Liverpool Street Station before they were allowed on their departure platform. They had to stand in a patiently waiting queue.

'Ridiculous, when the train's actually in,' said George.

'They probably have to tidy it up,' said Baggy pacifically. He'd had a wonderfully pleasant afternoon sitting in George's office, marvelling at George's business capacity and feeling that he, Baggy, was basically responsible for George's success. As a very young man George had said he fancied some business which was connected with money and Baggy had given him an introduction to an old friend who was an investment consultant. George had made himself invaluable and, on his employer's retirement, taken over the business with extreme success. This was mainly because he combined flair with caution and had a talent for both stimulating and reassuring his clients. It was Baggy's opinion that George would end up as a millionaire. George said this was laughable… but did not consider it inconceivable.

Robert, who had never wanted to do anything but write, arrived now holding a copy of the *Onlooker* – a most distinguished paper, Baggy considered, and he always read Robert's book reviews with pride, but he never had any desire to read the books Robert reviewed. But Baggy wasn't much of a reader nowadays. He had been once, oh yes, he had been, when Mabel was alive. They'd often read aloud to each other. But books weren't what they used to be.

Robert had not before made the journey by train and at first found the crowd confusing. But once he had got into the right queue, some yards behind George and Baggy, he surveyed the scene with great pleasure. So many lives, so much to stir the imagination! Now that he was leaving London he wondered why he had never wanted to write about it. But the country would be even better. That gloomy Hall, home of the Stranges, was beckoning. Ideas had been crowding his mind.

The queue moved. Robert caused a delay by not having his ticket ready. George, waiting for him inside the gates, said, 'Sometimes I think you give a performance of the absent-minded literary man.'

'I don't. I'm afraid it comes naturally,' said Robert, who was always trying to give a performance of the non-absent-minded, non-literary man.

Baggy said anxiously, 'We must hurry or we shan't get seats.'

But there was plenty of room in the diner and still quite a long wait before the train started. George decided he would in future arrive two minutes before the train was due to start – though

41

of course he would come by an earlier train and have dinner at home. He did not favour meals on trains.

But he was glad to see how much his father enjoyed this one. Baggy had soup, steak and kidney pie with vegetables overflowing on to the tablecloth, and apple pie with ice cream – the latter a mixture new to him. Robert had bacon and eggs, his favourite meal. George, himself, had a chop and rather wished he hadn't.

Still, he found the journey pleasant. Baggy and Robert were so obviously happy (what dull lives they must lead if dinner on a train with a bottle of wine was such a novelty; well, things would be better for them from now on). He also enjoyed watching some of his fellow-diners. There were two very pretty girls, with an almost equally pretty mother, just across the gangway. Probably one often saw the same people when commuting. And perhaps this attractive trio would get off when he did. But they did not – and just as well, he reflected as he helped Baggy down on to the platform. Interest in local femininity was out.

Once in the taxi, Baggy had a sudden attack of nerves. Suppose he hated his new home? He had refused to inspect it, feeling that having welcomed the idea of living with George he didn't want to be put off. Perhaps it would turn out to be a mistake. But if so, he must hide it from George and May. And in the country one could always go for long walks. He peered out at the twilit countryside. Yes, he'd go for long, long walks and get his weight down, as his doctor was always advising him to.

Robert was concentrating on seeing the Hall. There was a place where you could catch a glimpse of it in the distance – but you had to watch out for it. Yes, there it was and behind it one last flush of afterglow, most dramatic, 'Look, look quickly,' he implored George and Baggy. But by the time they looked, trees had cut off the view.

42

George was feeling slightly tired. He'd found it irritating to have Baggy at his elbow all afternoon and since then he'd had to play the host – not that one ought to grumble at that. And the girls would be pretty exhausted and need bucking up. He mentally shook himself – and was rewarded by sudden exhilaration as the taxi drew up at the Dower House and the front door was flung open revealing the lighted hall. May was in a blue dinner-dress, June in dark red – bless them, they'd dressed up to celebrate. With any luck, May would have chilled some champagne. He wished Hugh and Corinna were already here – well, they'd be down for the weekend.

Having hurriedly paid the taxi he dashed in to kiss May and June, then turned to Baggy. 'Welcome home, Father.'

As a rule, Baggy liked to be called by his nickname, but tonight he found the word 'Father' valuable. And how like George to have thought of using it.

But George had not thought about it at all; his use of the word had been purely instinctive – as his words and his acts so very often were when he did the absolutely right thing.

4

Corinna, returning from a late class at her Drama School, expected that Hugh would be outside the flat waiting to be let in. She was relieved to find he wasn't. With luck she could now get time to change her clothes, which she greatly disliked.

She was wearing a sloppy tweed coat, a black sweater, a plaid mini-skirt, thick black tights and heavy shoes. Her own tastes were for the pretty clothes that suited her prettiness but whenever she wore these her fellow-students greeted her with cries of 'Dainty Doris' and 'Corinna's going a maying'. All the really talented girls at the school dressed hideously and sloppily and seemed to do it without effort. She had to work hard at it.

The flat looked slightly denuded but her bedroom was intact. She hastily put on a short, fluttery nightgown and negligée; never before had she had the chance to wear these for Hugh. It flashed through her mind that he might not think the outfit respectable, but it was a sight more respectable than some of her day clothes. There were layers and layers of nylon net between herself and the outer world. And this was the kind of thing that suited her.

Sometimes she wondered if her eternal battle to be with-it was worthwhile. Only today Sir Henry Tremayne, who sometimes amused himself by taking classes at her school, had said to her, 'Dear child, you are invincibly a sweet, old-fashioned girl who will make a devoted wife and mother, but I more and more doubt if you will ever make an actress.' And she did so desperately want to make an actress; she'd grown keener and keener, ever since she'd begun training.

Sir Harry (he liked to be called that) when talking to her after the class, had said that her work might benefit by a fuller experience of life and hinted that he'd be willing to supply it. Of course he'd only been joking – he was old enough to be her father, older than her father, actually, just a few years. (But Sir Harry looked younger and he really was a marvellous actor.) Still, there might be something in what he said. And there were several of her fellow students who were more than willing to provide her with experience – and *they* weren't joking. Their offers had been expressed far more crudely than Sir Harry's. (And she wasn't quite sure he had been joking.)

Not one word of this did she intend to tell Hugh. It would be like asking him to do something about it. And she was sure he wouldn't want to, at present. Nor did she want him to… really. Only if there ever came a time when she felt something had to be done, then it obviously had to be done by Hugh. Anything else was unthinkable.

The doorbell rang. She delayed only long enough to run a comb through her short, fair hair, trying to soften its rigid cut. Hugh still pined for the days when it had reached halfway down her back.

When she opened the door to him he said, 'Darling, how sweet you look!'

Then they kissed, as they had kissed at every meeting of their lives. Even as babes in arms (born in the same week) they had been held out to each other.

Hugh then said, 'Now let me look at you properly. Oh, you're not going to a party, are you?'

'In a nightgown?'

'*Is* it a nightgown? It's not like the kind my mother wears.'

'Surely you've seen them on television?'

'I suppose so,' said Hugh vaguely. 'But I didn't realise women actually slept in such things.'

'Well, it's a negligée, too, of course. I just thought you'd like it better than any of my dresses.'

'I do – I like it madly. Am I sleeping in Dickon's room?'

'Yes, just dump your case in and then we'll have dinner. We've been left a kind of casserole thing, to warm up. I'll put it in the oven.'

Hugh, having deposited his suitcase, looked round his cousin's bedroom with interest, not having been in it for some time. It struck him as very luxurious for a schoolboy's bedroom; when he sat down on the bed it seemed to him almost funnily soft. But the decorations reflected an austere personality. The only picture, quite a good abstract, was positively bleak. It was signed 'Dickon'. Hugh would have greatly disliked to own such a name but his young cousin thrived on it. Any attempt to shorten either Dickon or Corinna had always been heavily frowned on by their mother.

Corinna came in and sat watching Hugh unpack. He asked if Dickon was pleased about the move to the country.

'Well, he doesn't *mind*,' said Corinna, 'which is the nearest he gets to being pleased, these days. Which reminds me, I had a postcard from him this morning saying he'd ring up tonight to find out if he and Prue can sleep here tomorrow and Saturday. Brian's bringing up a party to the National Theatre.'

Brian was the headmaster of the co-educational school at which Hugh and Corinna had been, and Dickon and Prudence now were. George was paying Prudence's fees, as he had once paid Hugh's.

'Well, that'll be all right, won't it? As we're going to the country.'

'I did mean to wait until Saturday morning – Sir Harry's taking an evening class tomorrow. But we can go by a late train.

47

Brian's letting Prue and Dickon spend the whole weekend here. There's a lot they want to do.'

'*We* used to come up for that kind of jaunt.'

'I know. I wonder if they're getting dependent on each other, as we did. If poor Mother has them to worry about as well as us, she'll go out of her mind. She's terrified that she'll end up with two-headed grandchildren. I suppose there is nothing in her ideas?'

Hugh said equably, 'Darling, we've talked this out again and again. Of course there's *something*. But our families on both sides are so very sane and healthy; I can't see any harm in duplicating that. Nobody's deaf or dumb or demented.'

'Great-aunt Mildred's quite a bit demented.'

'She's not. She's just maddening without the excuse of being mad. I think she's the one person in the world that I dislike.'

'You've never forgiven her for calling you "Little St Hugh".'

'Well, who would?' And the damn name had stuck. He never did anything halfway decent without someone digging it up. 'Anyway, she's sane enough and outstandingly healthy, looks years younger than she is, just as darling Fran does.'

'Fran' was their shared maternal grandmother, Frances Graham, always called 'Fran'. Hugh, in extreme youth, had confused 'Gran' with 'Fran' and a very ungrandmotherly woman had preferred to be 'Fran' to all her grandchildren.

'Fran's all for our getting married,' said Corinna. 'But she favoured an experimental period.'

'One gathers she had an experimental youth.'

They had never even discussed the possibility of an experiment. Always, always they had been determined to *marry*. But they'd been in no particular hurry about it. Hugh needed to consolidate his position in his uncle's business and was pretty sure he could

– in fact George, never niggardly with praise, had already made that clear. And Dickon had made it clear that he wouldn't be joining his father. (To Dickon, the City was a dirty word.) Hugh hoped to end up as his uncle's partner.

Corinna said, 'Anyway, nobody can stop us marrying once we're twenty-one.'

Hugh looked at her quickly. They would be twenty-one in less than a year. Had she then decided she wanted an early marriage? He was relieved when she went on, 'Not that we'll get married so soon, will we?'

'No, indeed,' said Hugh heartily. 'I need to make more money and you want to have a bash at the stage.'

'Oh, that! Sometimes I wonder if I shall even get started. No one ever gives me a word of praise. It all goes to the girls with huge noses and hacked hair.'

'Well, your hair's quite a bit hacked, love. Not that you don't look very pretty.'

'I don't want to look pretty. Sir Harry told me that I'm invincibly an ingénue – and nowadays there aren't any ingénue parts. I think I'll dye my hair black.'

'If you do, I'll divorce you before we marry.'

He had finished unpacking and was setting out a few possessions on the dressing table. She came and stood beside him, looking at herself in the glass, and then at him. 'Our children will certainly be blonds,' she said. 'Or if there's anything in Mother's theories, they'll have snow-white hair.'

'Very attractive,' said Hugh. 'Let's have supper.'

'It won't be hot yet. But we can have a drink – unless Mother's taken it all down to the country.'

They found some sherry and drank it while Corinna laid the kitchen table and ground coffee beans.

'Why not Nescafé?' said Hugh. 'Saves so much trouble.'

'Mother says all instant coffee tastes of Bovril. Nonsense, really. I'll ask Mrs Whatsit to get us some.'

'Isn't it time you stopped calling her Mrs Whatsit – after all these years? One day you'll do it to her face.'

'Oh, we do – didn't you know? She likes it. That's because Father did it once by accident and then made a joke of it. She adores him. Like so many women, one rather fears.' Corinna's tone had become worldly-wise.

Hugh made no comment. He couldn't, with honesty, refute the implied criticism of his uncle and had too much grateful affection for him to endorse it.

The telephone rang.

'That'll be Dickon,' said Corinna, answering the call at the kitchen extension. But she found herself talking to her mother, who sounded extremely cheerful.

'Darling, are you all right? Has Hugh come?'

'Yes, of course I'm all right, and he has. We're just going to have supper.'

'Put some sherry in that casserole – Mrs Whatsit always forgets. Oh, I wish you were both here. Everything's marvellous. We're all celebrating with champagne.'

'Lucky you.' Corinna intended to sound politely envious.

'Well, you must celebrate too. I've left plenty of wine for you. – What, George?... Your father says you're not to get tight.'

'We won't,' Corinna assured her mother.

'No, of course you won't. It was a joke, darling.'

Corinna then listened while her mother described the move in full, sent messages to Mrs Whatsit and the Hall Porter at the flats, and ascertained what train Corinna and Hugh would be coming by next day. Considerable laughter could be heard on the telephone and May several times said, 'What did you say, darling?' when Corinna hadn't said a word. May finally ended the conversation by saying, 'Love to Hugh. And mind you have a good time.'

Corinna, hanging up, said, 'Mother seems to have gone terribly young. And she was using her talking-to-America voice like when she talked to Fran last week. Fran told her not to shout.'

'When's Fran coming back?'

'Not till May.' Corinna got the casserole from the oven and dutifully put some sherry in it, then said, 'Do you want to bother with wine?'

'Might as well. Though I believe I like the idea of wine better than the wine itself.'

Corinna, not wishing to put him off, refrained from saying it didn't mean a thing to her, either way. It was one of the occasions when she was reminded of how much more luxurious her upbringing had been than his had. As children they had called their respective families the Clares and the Poor Clares – but had had the tact to keep this from their parents.

They settled down to supper at last and greatly enjoyed it. Corinna, over their second glass of wine, said, 'It *is* fun that I can have you here at the flat. It's almost as if we were married, isn't it?'

She had mentioned marriage again and now he felt sure she wasn't speaking casually. She was looking at him intently. Was it that she already knew she'd no chance as an actress and therefore wanted an early marriage? If so, of course he would agree – he couldn't conceivably deny her anything he was able to give her. He looked at her with love and said, 'Darling, are you sure you wouldn't like to be married soon? It could be managed. Uncle George could persuade Aunt May – or we could elope to Gretna Green.'

She laughed delightedly. 'Would Mother come chasing after us? No; I'm sure we're wise to wait quite a while before we marry. But if you should ever find the waiting difficult…'

She gave him a blue-eyed, questioning stare which he found disturbing. Never before had she even hinted… and it was now more than a hint surely, more like an invitation. And that nightgown… Good God, he'd been bloody simple, imagining it was early *marriage* she wanted. And he mustn't, he simply mustn't humiliate her.

He said, untruthfully, 'Darling Corinna, of course I find it hard to wait. I thought you wanted us to – and I thought you were right. But if you ever change your mind, we needn't wait – not even another minute.'

She was instantly happy, now she knew he was willing.

'Well, at least let's have coffee first,' she said gaily, springing up to clear away the plates. Then she added seriously, 'I was only thinking of *you*, darling, truly.'

'Then you want things to go on as they are?'

She brought the percolator and some peppermint creams to the table. 'I do, if you do.'

'And I do, if you do.'

'But if we change our minds – either of us – it's all right?'

'Fully understood.' He now thought he had misinterpreted her look of invitation – and the nightgown. Anyway, all he could actually see was the negligée.

'But let's try to go on being idealists – if that's what we are.'

'Most people these days would call us freaks,' said Hugh. 'Anyway, good luck to us.'

Happy though he was that she required neither early marriage nor instant seduction, he was a little sad that they had merely talked round the subject, not discussed it frankly. People who loved each other as they did ought to be able to share their thoughts fully. He hadn't fully shared his with her and he doubted if she'd fully shared hers with him. Why not? Embarrassment, fear of hurting each other…Well, at least she was looking happy.

As indeed she was, having made sure of his availability. She hadn't dared count on it because, much as he disliked being called Little St Hugh, he always had been very good. Darling Hugh, to put his feelings for her before his principles. And she didn't really want him to seduce her. It was just that if Sir Harry and her fellow students kept putting ideas into her head, one never quite knew… and sometimes one did get a bit worked up. Well, she wasn't worked up now. She was happy and peaceful, as she always was with darling Hugh.

They drank their coffee and ate expensive peppermint creams, radiating love and cherishing inner secrecy. Soon the telephone rang.

Corinna said, '*This'll* be Dickon.'

Dickon was telephoning from his headmaster's study which could be borrowed in the evenings by pupils who wished to telephone their families. Prudence, perched on the desk, was amusing herself by switching the desk light off and on. When it was off, she could see, through the wide picture-window, the moon rising over Buckinghamshire countryside. When she switched on, the room became cosily intimate. There was a smell of pipe smoke, tweed, and pine soap which Prudence found pleasant. At ten years old she had been in love with Brian Foster. Now, a mature fifteen, she sniffed his room nostalgically.

Dickon, having been assured by Corinna that he and Prue could have the flat for the next night, said, 'Though if you'd rather not clear out we could all doss down together. You and Prue could share the parents' bed and Hugh could have your room.'

Corinna said, 'Thanks, but I'm not wild to share a double bed, even with Prue.'

Prue, her ear now close to the telephone, interpolated loudly, 'Me, neither. Nasty things, double beds.'

'The parents have got new twin beds at the Dower House,' said Corinna.

'Marriage breaking up, no doubt,' said Dickon. 'We must beg them not to make us children of a broken home.'

'Ha, ha,' said Corinna satirically. 'I wonder why so many boys get facetious when they turn fifteen.'

'Quite true,' said Dickon. 'I have a sort of nervous itch to be funny. But I'm on to it.'

'Good for you. Any exciting school news?'

'Well, exciting for some. We're having a tiny sex-wave.'

'Oh, dear. Does Brian know?'

'Yes, indeed. He's torn between notifying parents and doling out contraceptives. Actually, there have only been two cases but it may be catching.'

'I never heard of anything like that in our time. Just a minute... Hugh says neither did he.'

'Well, you wouldn't, either of you. To the pure, all things are pure.'

'Who are you calling pure?' said Corinna indignantly.

'You, love – and Hugh. Ever so, both of you. Well, shall we catch a glimpse of you tomorrow?'

'I doubt it,' said Corinna. 'I'll leave the key with the Hall Porter. Hope you enjoy the National Theatre.'

'I shall enjoy it more when you're its leading lady.'

'Facetious again,' said Corinna coldly. 'Well, goodbye.'

Dickon, hanging up, said, 'She sounded peeved by my last remark.'

'I don't wonder. She thought you were making fun of her.'

'I suppose I was, really. Well, we both know she can't act.'

'We don't *know* anything of the sort. The fact that she wants to so much may mean something.'

'Only that she got taken to a good many theatres when she was young and impressionable.'

'So did you and you don't want to act.'

'Ah, but I'm not impressionable,' said Dickon. 'Actually, I wouldn't mind doing something on television, documentaries or the like. I'd try if I had Hugh's looks.'

Dickon resembled his father, without as yet enough personality to make an ordinary face interesting.

'I wouldn't want to act even if I turned into a raving beauty.'

'Which one doubts if you will,' said Dickon judicially. 'But you won't be too bad when you've slimmed down a bit. I don't actually dislike red hair. We'd better go. Brian, in his new, suspicious mood will think we're up to something.'

'Not us, surely. He's always saying we're like brother and sister.'

'He said that about Hugh and Corinna – lulling Mother into a state of false security. Whereas even before they left here they were mooning around looking like star-crossed lovers.'

'Why star-crossed?'

'Because they were so good and so beautiful. You know it's pretty ironic that Mother chose a co-educational school for us four to stop us falling in love with each other. She told me that.'

'Well, it's a sound idea on the whole,' said Prudence. 'You can't count Hugh and Corinna, because they've loved each other from birth. Oh, I know there are flukes like our mini-sex wave but, for the average child, co-education's wildly unromantic. I haven't felt a spasm of attraction for anyone since my first term, and then it was for Brian.'

'Good God, how repulsive,' said Dickon. 'Well, let's get back to your ex-heart-throb.'

Prudence switched the desk light off and took one last nostalgic sniff at the room. Then they rejoined their Headmaster, who was presiding over a debate on 'We can preserve law and order while preserving the complete liberty of the individual'. Dickon intended to speak against the motion. Prudence intended to consider Brian carefully, in case any spark lingered in the ashes. She didn't feel hopeful.

5

Whenever June looked back on their early days in the country she remembered sunshine, vividly green grass, budding trees, wonderful meals and much laughter – even when things went wrong, they went wrong amusingly. All this, in retrospect, was jumbled together in a vague blur of happiness; she found she could not recall very many actual days, they merged into each other. But there was one day – or rather, night – which she could recapture in detail and often did, thinking of it as a trend-setter for the weeks that followed.

That particular night was their first. She would always remember George and Robert and Baggy coming out of the spring evening into the white panelled hall of the Dower House. George had kissed her and admired her dress, and Robert – not always so tactful – had admired May's. Then they had all escorted Baggy to see his bed-sitting-room which he had said was very impressive; after which, having taken the cushion-piled divan for a sofa, he had asked where the bed was. May had whipped off the divan cover to show him, and George had bounced on the divan to demonstrate its softness, and then they had left Baggy to have a wash in his very own bathroom, and trooped off to the Long Room.

George had called for champagne which, of course, May had ready. (She'd said to June, 'He's sure to want to celebrate – and whether he does or not, *I* do.') And they had toasted each other and their new homes, and George and Robert had been given a full account of the whole day. Then there had been a telephone call to Hugh and Corinna, followed by conversation about what those two might be up to, the general impression being that they wouldn't be up to anything, in spite of May's half-hopes

57

to the contrary – 'Well, there's a *chance* that it might stop them marrying.' June said she was shocked by May's attitude and they all discussed present-day permissiveness. June said she was as permissive as anyone about other people's children but not about her own – 'or perhaps it's just that I feel it's awful to talk about it, somehow it's an invasion of their privacy'. She was then given more champagne by George who said, 'I bet the four of us would have been permissive all right, if there had been anything to stop us getting married as soon as we wanted to.' But it turned out that George was alone in thinking this.

After that, someone had remembered that Baggy was all alone and George went to get him. He drank very little of his champagne and June told May that cocoa was his evening drink. Cocoa was one of the things May had *not* brought with her, but she had some cooking chocolate and was able not only to make Baggy a cup of it but also supply him with a Thermosful to see him through the night. She also cut *foie gras* sandwiches for everyone. June disapproved of these because of the poor tortured geese but, for once, swallowed her scruples along with the *foie gras*.

May chivvied them all to bed fairly soon because George would have to catch an early morning train; he had booked the taxi that had brought them from the station. Torches were found – trust May to have a special torch drawer, already equipped – and then George and May insisted on escorting Robert and June through the lilac grove; May had by now learned her way about this. In the torchlight, the grassy paths were brilliantly green, here and there sprinkled with lingering snowdrops. And out on the little lawn in front of the cottage, the daffodil shoots were already thick.

'How marvellous everything's going to be,' said May.

'How marvellous everything is now,' said June.

George told Robert he ought to carry June over the threshold of the cottage.

'What nonsense,' said June, 'I weigh a ton.'

'Let's see,' said George, and himself carried her into the little hall.

Much laughter, much kissing goodnight. May kissed June, George kissed June, Robert kissed May – to June's relief; Robert, unlike George, was not a natural kisser and, though fond of May, did not always pay her as much attention as June felt he should. But tonight he behaved with so much warmth that she almost expected him to kiss George.

Robert hadn't wished to go over the cottage that night – 'We should start shifting furniture around' – so they'd gone straight upstairs; from the landing window they'd seen flashes of light where May and George were making their way back through the lilac grove. June was glad that the beds were made up and turned down invitingly, and she had put out Robert's pyjamas and dressing gown.

He said, 'How good of you to find time to unpack for me.'

'I'm afraid I didn't have time to unpack *all* our clothes.'

'Plenty of time for that tomorrow. Plenty of time for everything.'

'Bliss, sheer bliss. Oh, Robert!' In sudden exuberance she flung herself on him.

He was welcoming, if slightly astonished. 'Are you sure you're not too tired?'

'Oh, I wasn't really making overtures. But I can't say I *am* tired.'

'I can't imagine ever being tired again.'

Somehow the fact that they were all on their own in this tiny house and the tiny house was all on its own in the countryside – not cheek by jowl with neighbouring houses (and no Baggy in the next room) – seemed to June both romantic and sexually exciting – 'It's like being on our honeymoon.'

'It's not, thank God,' said Robert, and reminded her of various ludicrous aspects of their honeymoon including the uncomfortable hotel bed and the drunk gentleman who had thumped on their door, at the most tactless of moments, wanting to know *why* this room wasn't his. They exchanged memories while they undressed and learned their way round the bathroom – June said, 'There ought to be a law that the hot taps are always on the same side.' (Not that, as yet, the hot water came out hot; but Robert surprised himself by finding out how to put on the heater.) Then, with the light out, they stood at the window to take a last look at the night.

'No moon,' said June, with slight complaint.

'There was one but it's clouded over. Anyway, a moon would really be too much.'

In the early days of marriage June, after reading that some women, while being made love to by their husbands, thought of some other man, had – while responding enthusiastically to Robert's love-making – allowed herself to think of George. The experiment had not been a success. She had ended by feeling she was insulting both Robert and George and, for once in her life, had had no fun whatever. She was, on the whole, pleased about this because it proved to her that she loved Robert in every way and nothing she felt for George menaced Robert's happiness. She was just a wonderfully lucky woman who could find complete satisfaction in her marriage plus a little extra satisfaction (known to nobody but herself) outside it. *Nothing* to worry about.

And that first night at the cottage, lying awake after Robert was asleep, but not lying awake through any lack of satisfaction, she allowed herself the extra satisfaction of recalling her feelings when George had carried her over the threshold of the cottage. 'Mrs Have-it-both-ways,' she told herself. 'Well, lucky old me.'

The next morning the sun shone and the honeymoon period for both households was well and truly underway. June and Robert slept until May thumped on the front door and shouted an invitation to breakfast with her. She had already been up for well over an hour, given George breakfast and seen him off in a taxi, taken Baggy breakfast in bed – 'Though he insisted on getting out of bed to eat it' – and made her plans for the day. Foremost of these was the discovery of some domestic help.

And by lunchtime, after an almost house-to-house enquiry in the village, she had unearthed a thin, wiry Mrs Matson who never had but thought she might. And it was to turn out that Mrs Matson was really three helps, not one. On the slightest provocation her aged mother-in-law and fifteen-year-old daughter would come up and lend a hand. Only one Matson was officially employed. The others were merely rewarded by free meals. But the official Mrs Matson's wages were (unofficially) larger when Mrs Matson, senior, say, cleaned the silver or Miss Matson, say, did a bit of weeding. It was all probably illegal but it worked splendidly.

May also unearthed, only a few days later, an excellent carpenter who put up two magnificent cupboards on a landing – 'Such bliss to be able to hang up all one's summer dresses in winter and all one's winter dresses in summer, instead of putting them away in cardboard boxes – and however much tissue paper one uses the creases never really come out until the clothes are cleaned, and one had them cleaned before they were put away.' June's summer and winter clothes shared a wardrobe with Robert's suits and only got cleaned when they were dirty, but she admired May's summer and winter cupboards and assisted with the painting of wild roses on one and snowdrops on the other. May then decided that these looked 'amateur' and painted them out – 'After all, I can remember which cupboard is which.'

June eventually came to the conclusion that May was invincible as regards laying hands on any kind of help she might conceivably need – 'If you wanted to have the Crown Jewels repaired you'd find someone to do it.'

'Well, Tom tells me there *is* a particularly good little working jeweller, two villages away. I did think I might have one or two things reset.'

Tom was the taxi driver who had first brought them to the Dower House. May came to use him much as if he were her chauffeur and his taxi her private car. 'Well, it's cheaper than buying an extra car – and I'd have to learn to drive it. And Tom's so helpful.'

June was roped in for all May's outings and always given a share of May's discoveries. (Mrs Matson, *mère et fille*, spent a good bit of time cleaning at the cottage, and the carpenter put up shelves wherever the cottage could find room for them.) The sisters were always happy in each other's company. 'Really,' May pointed out after a few weeks, 'we've spent more time together than in all the years since we've been married. Oh, June darling, it *is* working out, isn't it? And the boys like it.'

The boys undoubtedly did. Robert, now, even enjoyed his critical work and his one day a week in London. And he would have started his novel at once had he not been put off by too much help from May. She persuaded Sarah Strange to show him over part of the Hall and he even had a brief meeting with Sarah's grandfather who, if vague, was civil. Unfortunately Robert found both the old man and his house disillusioning. They weren't Gothic, they were decayed Edwardian, quite unlike the Hall's Palladian exterior and Robert's mental picture of crumbling glories within. He must return to the Hall of his imagination. It would come back in time. Meanwhile, he would relax and enjoy the swiftly unfolding spring.

What George enjoyed as much as anything – to his surprise – was getting up early; well, not the actual getting up, but being up, being given breakfast by May, driving himself to the station through the fresh early morning, then the hour's journey on the train when he almost always had a First Class carriage to himself and could put in uninterrupted work on the day ahead. The return journey was as convivial as the journey to town was solitary. The train was usually full and he was soon on chatting terms with any number of cheerful men commuting to their country homes. George liked men *en masse* – but not women; women needed to be known individually. Not that, for the present, he felt any need to know any women in any way, apart from May and June.

He found his evenings delightful. May always gave him an admirable dinner, and if, as occasionally, she had some job to finish afterwards, he would stroll over to see Robert and June. There was nearly always something he wanted to discuss and often some present he wanted to take. George particularly liked bringing presents home for the two households; food, books, gramophone records, absurd puzzles. Baggy would spend hours over the puzzles.

The dear old man was generally believed to be both comfortable and happy – and so he was, he frequently told himself, once he'd got used (well, more or less) to his room. (Never would he forget that first night. When he closed his heavy curtains – you had to pull complicated strings – he felt claustrophobic, but with the curtains unclosed he seemed to be sleeping in the front garden; *not* normal to sleep in a ground-floor room. He'd been thankful for May's Thermos of hot chocolate. He had that every night and it was an improvement on just one cup of cocoa; not that he lay awake much now he'd got quite to like his squashy bed.)

He felt sure his daily walks in the country air were healthy – if none too safe: no pavements, and cars came so quickly and rarely sounded their horns; also he could have done with more houses. On London walks he had found it interesting to notice when house property changed hands and to investigate, when possible, what price had been paid. But what really counted now was the pleasure of seeing George every evening. And May's cooking was splendid – though he wasn't nowadays particularly interested in food; old age, no doubt. Probably old age, too, accounted for his aversion to his bathroom. Baths had become a duty rather than a pleasure. Well, wisest to take each day as it came along – which, anyway, one had to.

Hugh and Corinna, on their first weekend, approved of everything but with less exuberance than their parents could have wished. Hugh realised that a little more excitement would be welcome and gave Corinna the hint. 'We must churn it up a bit – and tell Prue and Dickon to, when they come at Easter.'

'I doubt if they'll oblige,' said Corinna. 'Were we as superior as they are, when we were their age?'

'I fear we're still pretty superior, from our youthful parents' point of view. Let's show some bright-eyed enthusiasm.'

On their second weekend Hugh and Corinna were there when the Vicar called. May, at first, had feared an influx of callers but Sarah Strange had reassured her. 'There's no one in the village who's likely to call except the Vicar – and he's a very harmless old bachelor.'

Harmless or not, May decided he must be made to understand that none of them were churchgoers. She had just broken this news to him – after a compensating good tea – when Hugh, feeling sorry for the deflated old gentleman, said he would come to church on Easter Sunday. May was not pleased.

'It's the thin edge of the wedge,' she protested to Hugh, after the Vicar had gone.

'But darling Aunt May, he didn't do any wedging. I offered.'

'Very, very unwise – and when I'd extricated us all so tactfully. And I did say he could count on us to subscribe, and send things to bazaars and jumble sales and whatnot.'

Corinna said, 'I must say I was surprised at you, Hugh. It was almost hypocritical, seeing how you feel about religion. Your disapproval is – well, positively religious.'

'It won't harm us to expose ourselves to it just for once, in a nice old country church.'

'Us? You can count me out.'

He looked at her in surprise. 'Are you really cross?'

She was and she wondered why; then knew. She felt she couldn't bear it if Hugh got any gooder. Then she noticed his anxious eyes and relented. Church wouldn't affect him, one way or the other. And she liked him for being kind to the old Vicar. 'No, of course I'm not cross,' she assured him. 'And I'd better come with you – to make sure you don't get roped in to teach at Sunday School or something frightful. We'll get Sarah to take us with her.'

Sarah, more than willing to be friends with every member of both families, showed particular eagerness to be friends with Hugh and Corinna. They decided she was starved for youthful company and were particularly nice to her; though a couple of times, when they saw her striding across the park towards the Dower House, they slipped out and went for a walk on their own. That is, they began to walk on their own but Sarah seemed to know by instinct where they had gone and came after them. The second time she did this it occurred to Hugh that she was like a dog able to follow one's trail. He remarked on this to Corinna, after they had separated from Sarah, adding, 'Bonnie used to do that, remember? It was a good thing she had to go to the country, really.'

'She didn't have to go. You sent her.'

'It was the right thing to do.'

Corinna opened her mouth to speak, then stopped herself. She had been going to point out to Hugh that he could now again have a dog. But why mention it? Why not get the dog for him as a surprise – and at last make up for his sacrifice of Bonnie?

She had been small and white and of no known breed but extremely pretty and well-behaved. Hugh had bought her from the Battersea Dogs' Home with money received on his tenth birthday. Shortly after this, Corinna had come to spend a Saturday with him, and the two children had been allowed to go to the pictures on their own. They had shut Bonnie up in the back garden (this had been soon after the move into Baggy's house) but she somehow got out and caught up with them just as they reached a busy crossing. Hugh said he must take her home. Corinna said that would make them late for the pictures. She gave Bonnie a brisk slap and said, 'Go home on your own, bad dog.'

Bonnie, when acquired by Hugh, had been a cowed little dog and she had only recently become un-cowed. The slap cowed her again but left her with enough strength to dash out into the traffic. Hugh dashed after her. Corinna feared he would be run over and when he returned, carrying his dog, Corinna slapped her again saying, 'Bad, bad Bonnie. It's all your fault.' Hugh pushed Corinna away and she fell backwards into the road, actually knocking a cyclist over.

Neither Corinna nor the cyclist were much hurt, but that very afternoon Hugh gave Bonnie to the people next door, who were on the point of moving farther out of London. Corinna, and his whole family, begged him not to but it was no use. He kept telling himself that he might have killed Corinna, that the bicycle might have been a car. And he was agonised by the rage he had felt when he pushed her. He wanted to punish himself for that, and he did.

Bonnie simply started a new life and certainly a safer one as she was nowhere near any traffic. After a few months Hugh and Corinna went on a Green Line bus to visit her and saw that, though she remembered Hugh, she was now devoted to her new owners. Corinna had at once stopped harrowing herself about Bonnie but, even now, she could feel harrowed about what Hugh must have felt when he was ten years old.

Having got the idea of giving him a dog she at once made sure that neither her mother nor her aunt had anything against it, and then decided to consult Sarah. The only dogs at the Hall were four aged spaniels (quite, as far as Corinna was concerned, indistinguishable from each other) but Sarah had spoken of going to local dog-shows and would probably know how a dog who looked something like Bonnie could be obtained. So the next day, having made sure that Hugh was busy gardening, she intercepted Sarah as she walked to church.

Sarah was most anxious to help and, after hearing the story of Bonnie, quite saw that the new dog ought to resemble her. But as she was of no known breed, this presented difficulties.

'Surely there must be a breed that's near to her,' said Corinna. 'She was *so* pretty – a bit like a smooth fox-terrier but with a long tail. And she was snow white all over.'

'White,' said Sarah thoughtfully. 'How about a bull-terrier. I know someone who breeds them.'

'Oh, not a bull-terrier. I've always thought they were very peculiar dogs.'

'So they are. But nice-peculiar. How about a white boxer?'

'I don't like their pushed-in faces. And they're so chunky. Bonnie was so very slim and graceful, with lovely floppy ears. She was a bit like a very small Dalmatian but without spots. Do they all have spots?'

'They certainly do,' said Sarah. 'But some of them have fewer spots than others. The woman I know who breeds bull-terriers breeds Dalmatians too. I'll skip church and take you there now. We can catch a bus in the village if we run for it.'

They ran, Sarah out-stripping Corinna who only caught the bus because it waited for her. Having recovered her breath she said, 'But Sarah, a Dalmatian won't really be like Bonnie.'

Sarah said patiently, 'Bonnie was a mongrel, Corinna. Mongrels aren't quite like any breed.'

'That really ought to make them valuable,' said Corinna.

The kennels were two villages away. Corinna expected them to be clean, white and well-kept, suitable for pure-bred dogs. In actual fact there wasn't a lick of white paint to be seen and she formed the impression that the various ramshackle sheds might collapse in anything like a gale. A number of wild-seeming dogs were milling round in a field which was more mud than grass. They barked furiously on sight of Sarah and Corinna and continued to bark while Sarah talked, or rather, shouted to their owner who came out of an adjacent cottage. She was an elderly square-shaped lady in mud-spattered tweeds. Corinna, deafened by both the barking and the shouting, said she wasn't really sure she wanted a dog. This made no impression so she said it again at the full force of her lungs, adding, 'Anyway, I need a *gentle* dog.'

The tweedy lady looked delighted. 'Then I've just the right dog for you. She's indoors because she's too sensitive to play with these rough beasts. Come on in.'

The cottage looked little less ramshackle than the kennels but the sitting room was pleasantly furnished and there was a good fire. In front of this lay a very small Dalmatian who instantly sprang up and dashed behind a sofa. The tweedy lady hoicked her out saying, 'This is Penny; possibly the most exquisite Dalamatian I've ever bred. Indeed, she's quite unique. Stand up, Penny.'

Supported by her owner, Penny just managed to stand, then collapsed and rolled over on her back, registering abject terror.

'Oh, Bonnie used to do that when Hugh first had her,' said Corinna, stooping to soothe Penny – who whimpered piteously and then summoned up the strength to dash behind the sofa again.

The dogs outside, who had quietened down, now barked louder than ever.

'Someone else has arrived. Excuse me a moment,' said Penny's owner.

Sarah closed the door after her and said hurriedly, 'Now, listen, while you've the chance. Quite probably, this dog *is* unique. She's got perfect dark eyes, dark nose, straight tail. She's beautifully made and her spots look like being superb. But she's undersized – at eight months old she's no bigger than most five-months-old pups and already she's losing her puppy fat. Of course she'll go on growing for quite a while yet, but not enough for the show ring.'.

'Who cares? She's the same size as Bonnie and very pretty. And she's not happy here.'

'Oh, that's just her nervous temperament. I assure you the old girl's been pampering her – I'm surprised she's willing to let her go. There is just a chance that she'll grow big enough to make a champion.'

'She needs loving for her own sake, not just because she might be a champion. Here, Penny darling –' Corinna, crawling behind the sofa, managed to get hold of Penny who, suddenly

69

succumbing allowed herself to be carried like a baby. I'll have her. How much will she cost?'

'I should think around ten guineas. More than enough for a little freak but nothing like enough for a potential champion.'

Penny's owner then returned and said that she couldn't, after all, bring herself to part with the dog. But she finally agreed to accept ten guineas for her, provided she could eventually offer a mate for Penny and have the pick of the litter.

'Not that I want her to have puppies,' said Corinna. 'Surely she's too nervous?'

'Best thing in the world for her,' said the tweedy lady, heartily. 'But not at her first heat, which will be in a couple of months or so. You'll have to be very careful of her then.'

'I'll explain all that,' said Sarah. 'We'll take Penny now and Corinna will send a cheque and you can send the pedigree. We'd better have a taxi.'

While the taxi was being telephoned for Corinna said, 'I didn't want her till Easter, when Hugh'll have four days to be with her.'

'Well, I'll keep her at the Hall till then,' said Sarah. 'We must take her now in case the old girl changes her mind again.'

The taxi came and Penny was borne off in triumph – to be car-sick all the way home. Fortunately the driver was sympathetic and gave them a large newspaper. Sarah tipped him handsomely when they reached the Hall.

'Don't let me forget to settle up for this and for the bus fares,' said Corinna, who had come out without money. 'Oh, poor little Penny.'

'She'll be all right now she's on solid ground,' said Sarah. 'Wonder what her house-training's like? Not that it matters while she's here. I'll bring her over on Good Friday, on my way to church. Got to fly now or I shall be late for grandfather's lunch.'

Corinna, hurrying home across the park, reflected on the fact that ten guineas would make a sizeable hole in her quarter's allowance. Should she ask her father to pay, or at least, help? No, this must be entirely *her* present to Hugh. How he would adore Penny! Everybody would, including Prue and Dickon who would soon be home. She felt a warm glow at the thought of bestowing so much pleasure. Roll on, Happy Easter!

6

Corinna would have preferred to call for Penny the very first thing on the morning of Good Friday but, like the rest of her family, she had a strong feeling that the Hall must never be encroached on. So she waited, watching at her bedroom window, until she saw Sarah and Penny setting out. Then she hurried out and met them halfway.

Sarah, by then carrying Penny, said, 'She's not used to being on the leash yet. And she's not fond of walking. Lots of young dogs aren't. They enjoy playing but don't care for solid exercise.'

'Perhaps their legs get tired – and hers are such little legs.' Corinna gently took a floppy paw. Penny gave the impression that she would like to take her paw away but really hadn't the strength.

'I'm afraid she's still very nervous,' said Sarah. 'But sometimes she's quite skittish and she wasn't frightened of the spaniels who were all very fatherly to her. And she's already house-trained except that if you pet her it's apt to turn on her waterworks. Of course you mustn't scold her for that because it's sheer emotion – happens with lots of bitches and they grow out of it. Still, it's best not to pet her when she's on a carpet, and be careful of your lawns; bitches make brown patches on them. It's ammonia or something – burns the grass. Hello, there's Hugh.'

He was coming to meet them. Corinna would have liked to be alone with him when she sprang the surprise of Penny on him but could hardly ask Sarah to make herself scarce. Sarah, however, said she must go or she would be late for church.

'We'll be coming with you on Sunday,' said Corinna.

'Wish you were coming today – for my sake, not yours; Good Friday's rather a gloomy service.' She handed Penny over, waved to the approaching Hugh, and sped on her way.

Hugh, on reaching Corinna, said, 'Hello, has Sarah got a new dog?'

'No, *you* have,' said Corinna. 'She's Penny, a replacement for Bonnie, at last – with my love.' She held the little dog out to him.

His first reaction was one of dismay, instantly followed by fear that he might have shown it. He smiled broadly and said, 'Darling, how marvellous!'

'Take her,' said Corinna, finding it difficult to hold the now wriggling Penny.

'Let's put her down. Here, give me her leash. She might bolt.'

But Penny, once on the ground, merely rolled on to her back. Hugh knelt and scratched her stomach, trying to get his feelings sorted out. He had been dismayed largely because he would have preferred to choose a dog for himself, and he would certainly have chosen another lost dog. But one could not dislike this appealing pink stomach where dark spots were showing through the sparse hairs. And it was adorable of Corinna to give him a dog. Never must she know he wasn't pleased. And damn it, he *was* pleased, of course he was. His eyes met Corinna's as she, too, knelt beside Penny, and he no longer had anything to hide. Corinna was an angel, Penny was enchanting – anyway her stomach was. He gently turned her over and managed to keep her on her feet long enough to examine her.

'She's a *bit* like Bonnie, isn't she?' said Corinna, anxiously. 'Except for the spots. And she's perfect except for being rather small. She's really – well, a *miniature* Dalmatian.'

'Splendid,' said Hugh heartily. 'All dogs should be available in miniature sizes.'

'Anyway, she may grow a lot – and even if she doesn't, she might become the mother of champions. I've bought a book on Dalmatians for you but only had time to skim through it.'

'Let's go back and study it.'

On the leash, Penny either sat down and refused to budge, or pulled in the opposite direction. Let off the leash, she started for the Hall and was caught with some difficulty.

'Perhaps she's missing the spaniels,' said Corinna. 'You'll have to carry her, like Sarah did.'

'Just as well she's a miniature.'

At the cottage, June, Robert and Prue welcomed Penny and then they all went with her to the Dower House where again she was warmly received – too warmly for her self-control.

'Sarah warned me about that,' said Corinna, 'but she'll grow out of it. And it's only on the rush mat.'

'I don't approve of fussiness in country houses,' said May. 'But just keep her out of the front rooms. Those carpets are valuable. Oh, dear, it's happened again. I must buy lots and lots of towels to mop up after her. And of course she must have toys.' May's eyes brightened at the thought of something to shop for.

'Let's play with her outside,' said Prue.

'And let's not *all* play with her,' said Dickon. 'There are too many huge creatures towering over her.'

The four younger Clares escorted Penny through the French window. Corinna decided to forget Sarah's warning about the lethal effect female dogs had on grass. One really could not protect all the grass in the countryside.

'I hope Hugh won't get too fond of that dog,' said Robert. 'He suffered such agonies when he sent Bonnie away.'

'So did Corinna,' said May. 'I've often thought that was when this trouble between them started.'

'I wouldn't exactly call it trouble,' said George.

May sighed. 'Oh, well…! What's everyone going to do? Why don't you all go out? It's a shame to waste this sunshine. What a marvellous spring! I can't remember one wet day since we came.'

'*I* can,' said Baggy. 'There have been ten.'

'Funny how they've vanished from my mind,' said May. I do remember how it rained the day we moved in but somehow that belonged to London weather.'

George said there had been plenty of rain in London but it had cleared up when he got home in the evening.

'No,' said Baggy firmly. 'There have been days when it rained from when I got up until I went to bed.'

Robert said, 'Remembrance of weather is so subjective; the weather becomes part of what one was feeling when one experienced it. In a way, we've *invented* our truly magnificent spring.'

June felt a pang of concern for Baggy. He could hardly have been sharing the general bliss if he'd noticed the rainy days enough to count them. She also felt a pang of guilt, because she was so much enjoying not sharing a house with him. Robert and she could now eat just what they liked and eat it just when they liked; they particularly liked it on trays by the fire when there was something worth watching on television. They enjoyed weekend meals at the Dower House but they were fairly firm about staying in their own tiny home on weekday evenings – though they were always delighted when George joined them. He invariably said that May was 'busy making jam'. May had long ago decided that she could buy better jam than she could make but for George the phrase covered any activity of May's which caused him to be left on his own.

It occurred to June now that when May was 'making jam' and George was at the cottage, Baggy must be having a lonely evening. But May had recently told her that he seemed to want to retire to his own room after dinner.

'Well, I must get on with lunch,' said May, and declined June's offer of help. 'There are three Matsons in the kitchen positively fighting each other for jobs. I must say they get a bit underfoot but I can't turn that old mother or that skinny daughter away before they've had their meal. Oh, do go out-of-doors, all of you.'

But only Baggy went. George, Robert and June sat around in the Long Room, fully contented to do so, though they lamented that there were no Sunday papers on Good Friday.

Out on the lawn the younger Clares lolled in the glorified deck chairs recently acquired by May. Penny, finally exhausted by too much attention, went to sleep between Hugh's legs with her head on his stomach. He felt both honoured and cramped.

Dickon said, 'On the whole, I am favourably impressed by this place.'

'Me, too,' said Prudence.

But they refused to carry out Hugh's suggestion that they should churn up a little vocal enthusiasm. Dickon said, 'One must not patronise one's parents. If I *hated* everything perhaps I'd pretend a little – it would only be kind. But as I consider they've made a good choice I can afford to be natural.'

'Anyway, they'd see through it if we went all lyrical,' said Prue. 'And they must know we're pleased as we haven't criticised anything. Not that we should have any effect on them. They're pretty well drugged with satisfaction.'

'Drugged's not the right word,' said Dickon. 'Our parents are looking at life through the clear eyes of youth.'

Corinna got her book on Dalmatians and read it aloud (practising her diction) and, by the time May came out to see what Penny would take for lunch, Hugh had definite views about diet for young Dalmatians. 'Plenty of meat and milk and not too much starch. You really mustn't overfeed her, Aunt May.' He dislodged the sleeping Penny, complained of pins and needles in places he didn't know one could have them, and went with his aunt to choose suitable food. May passing through the Long Room, again implored everyone to get out into the sunshine. 'You can't just sog here all day.'

But they could. Apart from a short tour of the garden to admire daffodils and almond blossom, and the time spent on admirable meals, Good Friday was mainly spent in sogging, around a log fire that was an insult to both the sunshine and the central heating. But on Saturday a walk and a drive were undertaken – there was surprisingly little traffic if the main roads were avoided – and Prue and Dickon explored the village. Hugh and Corinna had done this long ago and simply concentrated on Penny who fluctuated between somnolence, playfulness and sudden attacks of abject terror.

'I think she must be more nervous than most puppies,' said Hugh. 'Not that she's really a puppy at eight months old.'

'She's young for her age as well as small for it,' said Corinna, and wondered if dogs, like humans, could suffer from arrested development – not that she mentioned this far from cheering idea.

On Sunday Hugh much regretted that he had said he would go to church and no longer wished Corinna to go with him – 'One of us must stay with Penny.' Corinna was more than willing but pointed out that they would both have to leave her on Tuesday morning.

Hugh said he realised this only too well but every day would make a difference and Prue was going to take special care of Penny.

'And we'll ask Sarah to look in every day,' said Corinna. 'Do explain to her why I'm not coming with you today; she's expecting me. And you'd better hurry. She'll be waiting for you outside the church.'

On his way to the village Hugh failed to remember ever before going to a church service – unless weddings counted. At school religion had been taught on the same lines as history, with no particular religion favoured. One was, of course, free to believe in anything one liked but, on the whole, the intellectual climate had been anti-religion and he and Corinna, having no religious background, had soon decided it simply didn't matter. Hugh felt one should be reasonably good for the sake of being reasonably good, and not for the sake of religion. Corinna felt that if anyone could be as good as Hugh without the prompting of religion, then religion was unnecessary.

But, approaching the very beautiful old church, Hugh asked himself if he wanted such churches to be pulled down, fall into decay, or merely exist as memorials of a dead cult. He found he did not. He wanted other people to keep them alive – which could only be done if other people believed in what he did not believe in and, in fact, disapproved of. Difficult, very. Anyway, he'd suspend disapproval for this morning. If one accepted hospitality one must not sneer at one's host.

Sarah, waiting in the porch, said there was time for a walk round the churchyard. She wanted to hear how Penny was settling down. 'And once we go into the church we shall have to whisper.'

Hugh found it hard to believe that Sarah *could* whisper. She was now, possibly to compete with the church bells, talking very loudly and in her most metallic voice. Like the rest of his family he found her voice hard on the ear but he had discovered that one could get used to it – much as one got used to the noise of traffic.

Sarah, after being given an almost hour by hour report on Penny, said, 'It's a pity you didn't bring her to church. My grandmother always brought her pug.'

'Good gracious! Didn't the Vicar mind?'

'Oh, not at all. He said lots of dogs came to church in the eighteenth century and there was a man to stop them barking and fighting. The pug never barked, just snuffled a bit – and lots of people snuffle in church. There was plenty of room for her basket as we have one of the old box pews – next to the pulpit, so it's always noticed when I'm late. We'd better go in.'

Hugh had never even heard of a box pew. He found that this one resembled a small, square room, with a seat running all round it, a miniature fireplace and wooden walls nearly five foot high. There would have been complete privacy had not the pew been exposed to anyone standing in the pulpit and looking down.

'Do you ever have a fire in the fireplace?' Hugh whispered.

'My grandmother tried it one icy winter but the smoke nearly asphyxiated us – and the Vicar. So we settled for hot-water bottles and foot muffs. The church has a bit of central heating now; not much, but the idea helps.'

'Prod me when I have to kneel or stand or anything.'

'Well, it's the done thing to kneel when you first come into a church. Don't if you don't want to but excuse me for a minute.'

She knelt and he knelt too. The nearest to a prayer he could get was 'Good will to everyone' – to which he found himself mentally adding 'Especially Corinna and Penny.' Really! Shades of Christopher Robin! Sarah got up from her knees and he did too. The service began.

His main impression was of extreme restlessness. Stand up, sit down, kneel, get up again, find the hymns, sing, murmur – there was never a peaceful moment. He had rather looked forward to sitting back and looking at this ancient building while thinking of all who had worshipped here in the past, but if one spared a moment for private thought one got behind with the service. He soon began to look forward to the sermon when – presumably – one could take a rest.

He quite liked the hymns, especially as Sarah's voice was tuneful – astounding, seeing that even her murmured responses were metallic. His own responses were merely a blurred noise. Corinna had once told him that stage crowds often say 'Rhubarb, rhubarb'. He tried this and found it worked well, though Sarah did give him one surprised glance.

As he had expected, the sermon came as a relief, especially when he discovered that the Vicar looked across the pew, towards the congregation, so one could let one's eyes stray to the various monuments, hatchments and wall plaques, most of them connected with the Strange family. He was glad there was no stained glass except for some small, pale sections, which he guessed to be very old, let into the large clear windows. His eyes finally rested on the altar brasses where the brilliance of the cross had such a mesmeric effect that a gentle nudge from Sarah was needed to make him realise that the sermon was over.

He felt a distinct sense of shock when he learned that Sarah was going to Communion. 'Wait for me, will you?' she whispered, 'unless you'll come along, too, and somehow I don't think you will.'

'No, thank you,' said Hugh, who considered Communion a sort of symbolic cannibalism. How *could* people? He watched the rite with something approaching horror.

During the walk home he asked what, exactly, it had meant to her. She said, 'Well, nothing much, really. But the Vicar would be hurt if I didn't take it sometimes. He confirmed me.'

'But surely it's the heart of the Christian religion,' said Hugh. 'Either one ought to believe in it utterly or have nothing to do with it. To me, it's just terribly *nasty*. I'm sorry. I shouldn't have said that.'

'Why not?' said Sarah equably. 'As a matter of fact my grand-mother felt the same.'

'She didn't like the idea of it?'

'Oh, she didn't mind the *idea*. She just minded drinking out of the same cup as other people. Anyway, she wasn't at all religious, really, though she thought religion was all right for what I'm afraid she called the lower orders.'

'Does your grandfather ever come to church?'

'No, indeed. *He* thinks religion is only all right for women.'

'I wonder what will happen to it,' said Hugh. 'It seems to have very little relevance to the modern world. Still, I'm glad if it's a help to you.'

'A help? Religion?' Sarah spoke as if the very idea was astonishing. 'I go to church because it's expected of me – besides, it's a bit of a change. But it doesn't *help*. I don't see how it could.'

'Well, neither do I,' said Hugh. 'But some people are able to lean on it.'

'I find one jolly well has to lean on oneself.'

Her tone was perfectly cheerful – perhaps she found her life less dreary than he imagined it to be. Wondering if she had resources he didn't know of he asked if she read much. She said yes, she was fond of reading and often read aloud to her grandfather – 'We've masses of old novels that were fashionable when he was young; some of them aren't bad. And of course there's Wodehouse; he's jolly good. And some of our really old books are splendid; I suppose they're classics, really. I like books about the eighteenth century that were written in the eighteenth century, if you know what I mean.'

He said he did and was surprised to learn that she enjoyed Fielding and Smollett and Richardson – with whom his own acquaintance was a trifle sketchy. She added, 'But of course I love *new* books when I can get hold of them. Your aunt's lent me a lot. It must be lovely to *buy* books.'

'Aunt May's a great one for the latest bestsellers.'

'They're terribly inviting, aren't they? So shining and nice to touch. I don't always like what's inside them but I love having the chance of them. You can't think what a difference it's made to me since you all arrived.'

'Come and have lunch,' said Hugh impulsively. 'I know Aunt May would be delighted.'

'If only I could! But I must lunch with grandfather. Do you mind if we hurry a bit?'

It took him all his time to keep up with her. Her legs, he reckoned, were quite as long as his – though he thought he was a fraction taller than she was.

They parted at the Dower House gate, Sarah heading for the Hall and Hugh heading for Corinna and Penny, who were on the lawn outside the Long Room.

Corinna said gladly, 'Oh, Hugh, she's been splendid – and not one accident. Oh, dear! Well, it's a compliment to you, really.'

June and George came out of the lilac grove. June said, 'We're trying to hurry the lilac. It simply must be out when your grand-mother gets here. She's just telephoned from Paris to say she'll be home the week after next.'

'Oh, marvellous,' said Hugh. It seemed unfair that he should have a delightful grandmother years younger than her age when Sarah was stuck with an antique grandfather quite possibly round the bend.

May came to the French window and said, 'Get ready for lunch, everyone. George, you'll have to carve the ducks.'

Hugh wished Sarah could have had a share of them.

7

Fran Graham was expected on the last day of her younger grandchildren's Easter holiday. She had planned to arrive for lunch but, soon after breakfast, she telephoned to say she couldn't come until the evening. She found she had to spend the day with her sister, Mildred.

May said, 'Oh darling! That means you'll see hardly anything of Dickon and Prue. Why must you be with Aunt Mildred?'

'I'm afraid it's a bad case of hurt feelings. I haven't seen her since I got back. And you still haven't invited her. I think you'll have to.'

'No, Mother. We're all *enjoying* ourselves. Oh, well, later on, perhaps. Can you get here for dinner?'

'No, I'm sure I can't. She really wants me to spend the night at her ghastly boarding house. Why, why, why does she have to live there? It isn't as if she's poor. I shall be lucky if I can tear myself away in time to get dinner on the train.'

'You can get it on the 6.36 but...'

'I know. I've already looked the trains up.'

'But, darling, we'd be so glad to have dinner late for you.'

'No,' said Fran, in a tone which her daughters always accepted as final. 'I'm not tying myself to any train and I don't want to be met. You just expect me when you see me. And Prue and Dickon can stay up till the small hours and talk to me. Goodbye now.'

Dickon, as his mother replaced the receiver, said, 'I take it that old Mildew's playing up.'

'You really mustn't call your great-aunt "Mildew". One day you'll do it to her face.'

'Serve her right. You can't deny the name suits her.'

'I shouldn't dream of denying it,' said May. 'If we do have her down here I expect she'll blight the crops. Darling, go to the cottage – how much longer must they wait for a telephone? – and let them know about your grandmother, but make sure *they* all come up for both meals. I've got such masses of food. And if you see any lilac that's actually out, bring some in for Fran's room.'

Dickon, strolling through the lilac grove, decided the lilac in bud was too young to survive if cut. And anyway, he didn't want to bother. He wanted to go for a walk with Prue.

He collected her, after telling of Fran's postponed arrival.

'Such a pity,' said Prue, as they started out. 'I was looking forward to having the afternoon with her. What a bore Mildew is.'

'I wonder if something frightful happened to her in her youth – sort of blighted her and turned *her* into a blight.'

'More likely something ought to have happened and didn't. I asked Fran about that once and she was quite a bit snubbing.'

'She's often protective about Mildred,' said Dickon. 'Can you imagine them as girls together?'

'There's a photograph of them. Fran's got an Eton crop and a short slinky dress – most sophisticated. Mildred's all frilly and coy.'

'She still is. Well, if they have her here, let's hope it's while we're at school. Are you glad to be going back?'

'Extremely glad,' said Prue without hesitation.

'Me, too. That's odd, considering we both of us like our families. And no one could say they were bossy or possessive.'

'Less than ever, down here. They seem completely occupied with their own affairs.'

'I must say their interests seem a trifle narrow,' said Dickon. 'Mother cooks, Father eats what Mother cooks. Your father only *thinks* about writing his novel. What's your mother's particular line, I wonder?'

'I don't think she's ever had one. But I do notice she seems specially happy here. Perhaps it's the relief of not having Baggy in the house.'

'Was he a nuisance? I don't seem to notice him much.'

'I did. Oh, I'm fond of Baggy but I did sometimes wish he didn't have to be with us every evening.'

'Now he usually goes to his own room.'

'I wonder if he feels he ought?' said Prue thoughtfully. 'Oh, gosh, I suddenly feel guilty. I haven't done a thing about Baggy, all these holidays. I used to make an effort to be kind to him – well, talk to him, anyway.'

'We could ask him to come for a walk with us this afternoon. But I think he takes a nap after lunch. Let's go along to his room with him after dinner. I've barely been inside it.'

'Me, neither. Yes, let's do that. Shall we go into the woods?'

'Not yet. I like them better higher up.'

They skirted the Hall, on their way to the wooded slope beyond it. Dickon, after a glance towards the Palladian portico, said, 'What do you make of Sarah Strange?'

'Practically nothing,' said Prue. 'Oh, I don't dislike her; I just don't get her. To me, she's a beautiful blankness.'

'I agree she's not quite us. But she doesn't strike me as altogether unintelligent. Hugh and Corinna get on with her.'

'Well, Hugh gets on with everyone. And Corinna's more used to Society girls than we are.'

'Is Sarah a Society girl?' said Dickon. 'If so, she's a Society girl without any Society, poor brute.'

'I dare say. But that doesn't stop her from being what she is. It's a question of… well, social status. And don't tell me that sort of thing's out of date. Of course it is. But it still exists.'

'Does Sarah make you feel inferior?'

'Quite the reverse, I'm afraid,' said Prue. They turned into the wood and walked in single file until they reached a clearing, on the crown of the hill, where they sat on the grass. From here they could look down on the roofs of the Hall, the Dower House and the cottage.

'Father ought to see this view of the Hall,' said Prue. 'It might get him started on his Gothic novel. Rooftops are highly romantic.'

'Not that rooftop. It appears to be a rubbish dump. Look at the iron bedsteads. And good God, there are *seven* enamel potties.'

'Potties? What a coy word.'

'Well, they were still called that when I last met one,' said Dickon. 'Who would put them on a roof?'

'Servants – too lazy to carry them downstairs. I suppose they just chucked them out of the attics.'

'Why bother? The attics can't be needed now. They've only got some old woman and a man who looks after Sarah's grandfather.'

'That junk's probably been there since the house was teeming with servants. Your potties may be valuable antiques. The cottage looks nice from here. You wouldn't think a black house could look so cheerful.'

'It's all the white paint,' said Dickon. 'I rather fear the word for it is "cute". There's a lot of yellow moss on the Dower House roof. I suppose that's all right?'

'I expect old tiles can stand a lot of moss. It's lichen, really. Looks lovely. Is your mother ever going to tackle the conservatory?'

'She still hasn't struck the right wicker furniture. Well, we'd better go back for the mammoth lunch that was planned for Fran. Your father and mother are just setting out.'

'Accompanied by Penny,' said Prudence. 'Oh, look, she's lying flat on her stomach waiting to be carried. I always thought puppies were lively.'

'She *is* lively – as long as she's not expected to walk. Come on. Mother may have something that'll spoil.'

Prue said, as they made their way down, 'I never realised, until these holidays, just how marvellous Aunt May's cooking is. I used to think she put on a special show whenever we Poor Clares came to a meal. But I know that the food's at the same level all the time. I'm not sure I approve.'

'Because of starving babies in India?'

'Oh, not that – because the food wouldn't go to the starving babies if we didn't eat it. But taking a great interest in food is so *elderly*.'

'I see what you mean. Still, I'm looking forward to my lunch.'

'And don't think I'm not,' said Prue. 'We're late, let's hurry.'

They were distinctly aggrieved when they found that the first course had been cancelled. It was to have been asparagus, fabulously early.

'I must save it for Mother tomorrow,' said May.

'While we're on our way back to frugality,' said Dickon.

May looked worried. 'You always say they feed you well at school.'

'So they do, darling. But not on early asparagus.'

May relented. 'All right. I'll telephone for some more.'

After lunch Robert set off to see the chamber pots on the roof of the Hall, Baggy went to his room, and May told June her latest plans for the conservatory – 'Though I still don't feel sure I've got the right line on it.' Prue said she must do her packing and Dickon said he would keep her company. His mother always did his packing. Prue considered her mother a very scatty packer and invariably declined her offer of help.

Dickon, on their way through the lilac grove to the cottage, said, 'Rather a pity we shan't see the lilac at its best. I suppose Hugh and Corinna will be wandering here hand in hand.'

'I doubt if they get as far as even holding hands. Yet one never for a moment doubts that they love each other. There's a... a sort of *aura* of love about them.'

Dickon said, after consideration, 'I can't make up my mind if an aura of love is pure woman's magazine or a good description.'

'Probably a bit of both.'

They continued to talk while Prue packed, but about school personalities, not about their families; it was as if the packing provided a halfway house to school. Indeed, by the time they returned to the Dower House the Easter holiday was virtually over for them and they were on their way back.

Still, they remembered their intention of being kind to their grandfather, and after dinner Dickon said, 'May we come along for a last chat, Baggy?' He half hoped that the phrase would leave Baggy with the impression that there had been earlier chats.

After a momentary hesitation due to sheer surprise Baggy said, 'By all means,' and led the way.

'What a fine room this is,' said Prue, following her grandfather in. 'It would make a good studio.'

It would indeed, thought Dickon, as it had four north windows. By contrast with the sunset-flooded Long Room it was depressing. He would have expected his mother to give Baggy a sunny room – but women weren't too bright about aspects. Best not draw attention to it, anyway.

'How lovely the daffodils must have looked,' said Prue, gazing out at the front lawn. At the moment they were looking anything but lovely as the faded heads and yellowing leaves were being left to die back. 'You ought to have some flowers in here, Baggy. Tulips or something.'

'So your Aunt May says. But I've never cared to have flowers in my bedroom. Your grandmother always said they must be put out at night.'

'Like the cat,' said Dickon and then regretted it. This cursed facetiousness!

'We never put our cat out at night,' said Baggy. 'Your grand-mother didn't hold with it. Of course you don't remember her.'

'Indeed I do,' said Dickon. 'And I remember the cat, too. It was a very fine cat.' He added hastily, though he barely remembered his paternal grandmother, 'And grandmother was a dear old lady.'

Baggy never thought of his wife as an old lady. Of course she'd have been one by now. It would be interesting to move her on in his mind, try to see her as she'd be if she'd lived. He would think about it on his walk tomorrow. That wasn't the kind of thing he let himself think of at night; too apt to keep one awake.

Prue said, 'You should have television in here.'

'No need,' said Baggy. 'I can watch it in the Long Room if I want to. Not much of interest these days.'

'You used to be so fond of it,' said Prue, remembering many evenings when she had watched it with him – and the sound had had to be up louder than she could have wished.

'Seems to have gone off. Your aunt and uncle seldom watch it and I can't say I blame them.'

Prue thought, he'd like it all right if he watched *with* someone. Perhaps she ought to give her father and mother a hint. But they did deserve a rest from Baggy, after years of insisting he should have his favourite programmes, most of which her father detested. She said brightly, 'You've your own bathroom now, haven't you? What luxury! I don't think I've seen it.'

Baggy opened the bathroom door.

'Oh, what a lovely bathroom,' said Prue. 'Dickon, come and look at the nice white tiles. And so tidy! Very different from our old bathroom, Baggy.'

'Still, that was a good bathroom,' said Baggy defensively, feeling a wave of nostalgia for his nightly soak in it. He had always refrained from taking a morning bath, leaving the coast clear for the rest of the family. But after ten o'clock in the evening he felt he could take his time as all the bedrooms were fitted with wash-basins. Unfortunately they were not also fitted with loos, as Prue happened to be remembering. How often had she sat in her bed-room wondering how long, oh Lord, Baggy would go on soaking.

'Oh, I remember that bathroom,' said Dickon. 'It was like a junk shop, what with all Prue's old bath toys.'

'I suppose Mother threw those out before she moved,' said Prue, without regret.

Baggy had regretted them and still did. Indeed, he had a sudden wild idea that a couple of plastic ducks might do something for this hygienic, repellent bathroom. Woolworth's, perhaps? Absurd, of course. He must be in his second childhood.

Prue continued, 'Anyway, it must be marvellous to be able to have a bath any time one wants to. I'd probably have three a day.'

Baggy, nowadays, took a brisk morning bath purely for the sake of cleanliness. He had only once tried a bath at night, when the white tiles under the brilliant strip-lighting had made him feel more in cold storage than in warm water.

He led the way back to his bed-sitting-room and invited them to sit down, wondering what to say next. He was surprised that he should find it difficult to talk to his grandchildren, especially Prue, who had lived in the same house with him for so many years.

Dickon, in a mature tone, said, 'Well, I take it that the move to the country is paying good dividends.'

'Yes, it seems to be giving pleasure,' said Baggy.

'I expect you're enjoying Aunt May's cooking,' said Prue.

'Yes, excellent, excellent.' But Baggy sometimes thought it a mistake to have such good food at *every* meal; it eliminated the possibility of occasional treats. He added now, with both politeness and truth. 'Your mother used to do some very tasty little suppers.'

'Oh, she still does those. Nice things on toast.'

Baggy and Prue enumerated these until they couldn't think of any more. Dickon racked his brains for some topic that would really interest his grandfather, then realised he wouldn't find one. The trouble was that the old man had drawn into himself. Why, exactly? He was obviously more comfortable than he had ever been with the Poor Clares. (And the Poor Clares, Dickon was glad to think, were more comfortable than they had ever been before. He often felt disturbed because his own family was richer than Prue's.) Oh, no doubt all that was wrong with Baggy was just increasing old age.

The light was fading. Prue said, 'Shall I put the lights on and draw the curtains for you, Baggy?'

'Yes, I suppose it's time.' He always hung on to the daylight as long as he could. 'But you'd better let me draw the curtains. You have to pull strings.'

He went to a window, then said, 'Hello, here's a taxi. Some girl appears to be arriving.'

Dickon, joining him, said, 'That's no girl. That's my grandmother.'

'Fran does have a girlish figure,' said Prue, then raced after Dickon who was already on his way to the front door.

Baggy followed, more sedately. By the time he reached the door they were getting Fran's cases out of the taxi and she was paying the driver. Baggy stood watching, wondering if it was right for any woman of Fran Graham's age to look so young – or, anyway, to dress so youthfully. Looked quite nice, though. Fran was always so well turned out. His wife had admired her – but been a bit dubious about her. What was the word Mabel had used? Was it 'fast'? You never heard that word now. Anyway, Mabel had accused herself of uncharitableness; after all, they didn't know anything and Fran had always been so pleasant to them. Still, he'd never felt quite at ease with her. He said to him-self now, 'She comes from a different world.' Then he stepped forward to greet her.

Fran said, 'Baggy, darling! How lovely to see you.' She embraced him warmly which embarrassed him, but he was pleased when she added, 'You've got to help me – they're trying to put my rent up. I've brought my lease to show you.'

Once she was in the hall the rest of the family were soon milling round Fran. She was escorted to the Long Room and discouraged from pouncing on the sleeping Penny. June said, 'If she wakes she'll be the end of all conversation. And she needs her sleep if she's to grow. You can play with her tomorrow, Mother.' May unearthed the fact that Fran had had no dinner. 'But any-thing will do. A sandwich or just a piece of cake.' May decreed soup and cold chicken.

'And champagne, of course,' said George, making for the refrigerator.

Fran did not protest. She knew it would be useless; also she liked champagne.

May, on her way to the kitchen, called to June. 'Show Mother the lilac grove before it's quite dark.'

'I'll see that tomorrow,' said Fran firmly. 'Now I want to con-sult Prue and Dickon about something, before we plunge into George's champagne. Can they show me my room?'

Her grandchildren, carrying her cases, escorted her upstairs.

'Mother put you at the back of the house,' said Dickon, 'so that you could see the lilac grove.'

Really, that lilac grove! Her daughters had mentioned it in every letter since the move to the country. But she said enthusiastically, 'Oh, lovely! Well, this *is* a charming room. What a pretty chintz! And a chaise-longue. I love a chaise-longue in a bedroom.'

'Mother got it at a country house sale,' said Dickon. 'Did you really want to consult us or were you just making grandmotherly noises?'

'I *never* make grandmotherly noises. I want to ask you about my skirt length. On your honour, both of you. Is it too short?'

Prue said at once, 'Not a bit. You look a dream. That lovely tweed!'

'Now don't be perfunctory, darling. This is a case where it isn't kind to be kind, if you know what I mean. I did think this skirt was all right but your Aunt Mildred has rather shattered me. She says it's not decent at my age.'

'She would,' said Prue. 'Seeing that she wears full skirts down to her ankles.'

'Well, she's the picturesque type, isn't she? But I must admit she had me worried. Dickon? And I'll respect you for life if you tell me she's right.'

'Swish about a bit.'

'It's too tight to swish but I'll waggle my hips.'

'They're too slim to waggle,' said Prue enviously.

Dickon, after a full minute's consideration, said, 'It's all right, Fran, truly – because you have such superb legs. They must be among the great legs of this century.'

'But what about my knees? It's knees that give one's age away.'

'Well, you're only showing glimpses of them. Hold your skirt up a bit. Ah, now I see what you mean. Look, Prue, they've gone the smallest bit knobbly.'

'I'd swap mine for them any day. I'm terribly ashamed of my fat legs.'

'But it's a lovely soft youthful fatness,' said Fran, 'and you'll slim down at any minute. I do know my knees are better than most mature knees but still…'

Dickon interrupted her. 'You're absolutely all right – but not one eighth of an inch higher, Fran darling. I've a theory that women get kind of drunk about skirt lengths and go higher and higher.'

'Well, I'll promise not to. Thank you, Dickon. I shall regard your opinions as the last word on the subject.'

'Shall I unpack for you?' said Prue.

'No, we mustn't keep your uncle's champagne waiting. Oh, I've some presents for you. Remind me, before we go to bed.' When would that be? She'd had something of a day and the turned-down bed was inviting. 'How pretty that spotted muslin canopy is – not that it's really spotted muslin nowadays – all nylon or something. You wouldn't believe the materials that have vanished since my childhood.'

'There's Father calling,' said Dickon.

Fran enjoyed her supper and hearing about the delights of living at the Dower House and cottage, but she declined being shown anything. 'Not until tomorrow. I shall be fresher then.'

'You're as fresh as a daisy now,' said George, plying her with more champagne.

'How about just a whiff of the lilac grove?' said May. 'It's rather fun by torchlight.'

'*Tomorrow.*' Blast that lilac grove. Of course she'd once had a thing about lilac but that now seemed to her light years ago.

'Tell us what you thought of America,' said Robert. He liked and admired his mother-in-law and felt sure a comment she had to make would be interesting.

'Oh, Robert, I'm so sick of all the travelling I've done that I don't even want to talk about it. But it'll ooze out by degrees. How's the novel? June's letters made it sound most exciting.'

'Still germinating,' said Robert, suddenly wondering if he could put Fran in it. She still seemed so astonishingly young.

(Girlish? No, too sophisticated for that. Mildred was the elderly girl type – and highly embarrassing.) Could he have an old, old character whose youth was miraculously preserved, as if in amber? Not that Fran, in her early seventies, was all that old, but certainly older than she looked. Then she closed her eyes for a second and, without their liveliness, age had a temporary victory. He whispered to June, 'I wonder if your mother's tired.'

'Oh, she's never tired.'

And indeed, she was now chattering as gaily as ever, asking George if he enjoyed being a commuter. But when she learned how early he had to get up she at once said, 'And here I'm keeping you up! To bed with all of us.'

Robert was pleased with his perspicacity. She was tired all right. He countered George's 'Nonsense, the night's still young' with 'Well, *I'm* going to London tomorrow and if I don't get a full night's sleep I'm hopeless. Home, June and Prudence!'

Fran surreptitiously glanced at her watch. It was barely eleven; with any luck she'd get a full eight hours. She hurried her good-nights but remembered to make a date with Baggy, to discuss her lease – 'If there is anything to be done I must do it soon.'

Baggy agreed eagerly. Really, a very pleasant little woman and still quite pretty. You couldn't make out if her hair was fair or silvery. No doubt she did something to it.

For all her hurrying, it was well after midnight before Fran had unpacked and unearthed Dickon's present and one for him to give to Prue in the morning – 'And don't wake me up when you leave with your father. I'm a hag if I don't have my sleep out.'

'Goodnight, dearest hag,' said Dickon, embracing her. He considered her an ace of grandmothers.

She was in bed at last, under the nylon draped canopy. Really, that canopy! Positively bridal. Not that her own bridal bed had been anything like this. Brass, she remembered; highly unromantic. But one hadn't been a romantic bride. She put the bedside light out. God, she was tired. Mildred was enough to tire a rhinoceros. How soon must one break to May that Mildred simply had to be invited – and for a solid stay, while her ghastly boarding house was redecorated. Well, no need to think of that now. No need to think of anything else tonight. Nothing, absolutely nothing more could be demanded of one tonight.

But it could. She had left the window too wide open and that breeze, so delightful on her face now, could give her neuralgia by the morning or even a stiff neck. Get up, woman!

She closed the window all but a crack and made her way back to bed, bumping into the frilled dressing-table stool. May had gone to town over this bedroom. Dear May, dear June, dear all of them. A pity Prue and Dickon were going back to school but there were Hugh and Corinna to look forward to. And Mildred needn't come yet.

She composed herself to sleep... 'And love it was the best of them, But sleep worth all the rest of them'... how often she remembered those lines just before falling asleep, and she hadn't the faintest idea who wrote them or what they came from.

8

Fran, waking soon after six-thirty, realised that the stirring of the household had awakened her. She heard doors open and close, bath water running, Dickon's voice – instantly hushed by his mother's 'Quiet, darling, we shall disturb Fran.' Well, they *had* disturbed Fran and Fran must expect it every morning unless she could acquire the knack of sleeping through noises occasioned by George's early morning start. Did he really need to get up at six-thirty? Yes, she supposed so, in order to bath, shave, breakfast, drive to the station, spend an hour on the train, and be in his office, say, by nine-thirty. Well, well, poor George – and poor May. But she'd never seen them looking happier.

She stretched, then relaxed. It looked like a sunny day – or was it just that the background of the curtains was yellow? Her eyes followed the delicate pattern of green leaves on them. Of course she wouldn't be able to sleep again…

She slept until her small travelling alarm clock went off at 8.45. May had undertaken to bring breakfast at nine o'clock and Fran never liked even her daughters to see her before she had given her appearance some little help. She was back in bed in a decorative bedjacket before May arrived with the tray.

'How pretty you look,' said May. 'I knew those bed draperies would suit you. I do hope we didn't disturb you.'

'Indeed you did and it was heaven being me and not you. I've put in nearly a couple of hours more sleep. They say you need less sleep as you grow older but I seem to need more. How can you bear to get up so early?'

'Oh, we're used to it now and we can sleep late at the weekends – though even then, we get up fairly early. This move to the country's done all I hoped it would, Mother. George's goings-on were due to the fact that he was bored. Not that they ever amounted to anything, of course.'

'Indeed, no,' said Fran heartily. If May wanted to cover up, then cover up May should.

The heartiness had been a shade histrionic. May shot her mother a dubious look, then said, 'Well, anyway, he hasn't spent a night in London since we moved down here.'

Fran's memory travelled backwards around half a century. Surely 'goings-on' weren't necessarily a night-time occupation? But George might be too busy for afternoon dalliance.

May continued, 'Of course the great thing is that I've stopped nagging and wanting him to stay in every night. I even shunt him off to Robert and June sometimes. He loves having them always available. Oh, everything's worked out splendidly.'

Fran, wading into bacon and eggs with considerable pleasure, said, 'You mustn't give me a breakfast like this every morning. I shall put on pounds.'

'Nonsense, darling, you never do – and neither do I, thank God. June ought to watch herself. Still, it suits her to look fairly opulent – if that's the word I mean.'

'It sounds right for her now. She's certainly looking her best. I dare say it's a relief not to have Baggy. Is he a cope?'

'Not in the least,' said May, with brisk pride. 'I make sure he has everything he needs but I don't fuss about him the way June did. And I'm sure he prefers my way because he co-operates so splendidly – makes full use of his room, comes punctually to meals and then clears out from under one's feet. And he amuses himself, goes for his walk every morning at ten-thirty.' A bell rang below. 'That'll be the asparagus – it was coming up in a taxi. Excuse me, Mother dear.'

Fran had a mental picture of a taxi-borne stick of asparagus imperiously ringing the doorbell. Well, she must get up, and hurry her bath, if her talk with Baggy wasn't to make him late for his walk. Old people didn't like their regular habits interfered with – at which thought, she sighed. She never linked herself with 'old people' but her dislike of hurrying her bath was distinctly elderly. She also disliked sharing a bathroom – so much to-ing and fro-ing of her sponge bag.

But it was a nice, large, sunny bathroom – with a fireplace in it! Once, in her very earliest childhood, she had seen a fire alight in a bathroom, snow against the window pane… pleasant memory.

She found Baggy waiting for her in the hall. He said, rather tentatively, 'Perhaps you'd come into my room? The bed *is* made.'

'Oh, I'm longing to see that room. May's letters have made it sound superb.'

'Well, there's a fine floor.'

Fran eyed the sea of parquet warily; so easy to slip on. 'Yes, this really is magnificent.'

'May wanted me to have rugs but I said not.'

'Quite right.' Rugs on parquet were more slippery than parquet – and nothing short of close-carpeting would help this room much. And one would need to cram the shelves with books. Nothing was more furnishing than books and more un-furnishing than empty bookshelves. As for Baggy's truly terrible furniture! But she was able to say truthfully, 'What a wonderful roomy wardrobe.'

'That's an old friend.'

'And there's your bathroom.'

Baggy regretted the door had been left open. The least said about that bathroom the better.

By contrast with the sunny bathroom upstairs this one struck Fran as positively polar. She said involuntarily, 'Needs a bit of cheering up, Baggy. Coloured towels would help.'

'May offered me some but I thought they'd be too fancy for a man. It *is* a chilly bathroom.' Then he felt guilty. Mustn't criticise when so much had been done for him. Even to his grandchildren he hadn't actually said anything against the bathroom. Still, he went on, 'Those tiles have a cold smell. Sounds silly, but they have.'

Fran sniffed the tiles. 'I think the trouble is that they just have an unsmell – the whole bathroom has. Bathrooms ought to smell of something nice, like bath salts.'

'Yes, I liked it when June used those. But a man couldn't.'

'Of course he could, though bath oil would be better. I'll get you some pine bath oil – good for rheumatism.'

'Are you much troubled with that?'

'Never,' said Fran firmly. 'I'm a bit stiff sometimes but I take no notice of it. Take notice of stiffness and it calls itself rheumatism. Get your mind off it and it goes away.'

'Mabel used to say that. She was a great believer in Coué.'

'Oh, Baggy, I haven't thought of Coué for ages. What was it one had to say – "Every day, in every way…"'

'"I'm getting better and better," Mabel used to say it every morning.'

'I shall try it tomorrow. How nice to be reminded of Coué.'

Baggy, pleased with himself, led her back to his room and settled her into his best armchair, then said, 'Well, let's have a look at that lease.'

He put his spectacles on and became very professional. She noticed that, though usually slow in his movements and reactions, he assimilated the lease in what seemed to her no time at all. Then he pronounced, 'They're within their rights. No doubt at all. Of course you might try bluffing a bit. Are all the flats full?'

'No, they're not. You see, they're old-fashioned, but mine happens to suit me. Got good cupboards. Most of the new flats are just empty boxes.'

'You could try a *doubtful* letter – say you'll have to look around. You've got a month before you need to decide. I'll draft something for you.'

'Oh, would you, Baggy? I really am paying enough for such a tiny place – you could put two of it in this room. Not that I mind the smallness. Less to look after.'

'And you travel a lot.' Baggy's tone implied respect for enterprise, though he wasn't sure he approved of elderly gadding.

'I'm through with it now. I want to put my feet up and take down my back hair, as my mother used to say. Funny how expressions linger on. I haven't had any back hair since I was a child.'

'Mabel had some. She used to use that expression. Well, we're none of us getting any younger.'

Fran was suddenly annoyed with herself. She had, through her desire to be pleasant to Baggy, been joining him in his obvious acceptance of old age. She said, with much energy, 'You're not to say that. Back to Coué.'

Baggy chuckled. 'Every day, in every way, I'm getting younger and younger?'

'That's going a bit far. But one can say that one doesn't feel older than one did yesterday. Perhaps it's best not to think about it at all.'

May came in with morning coffee for Baggy. 'You're to have yours with June, Mother, and you should go now or it'll spoil your appetite for lunch. I'll start you on your way.'

Fran found herself whisked to the Long Room and out through the French window. Ah, there was the lilac grove. She'd better go to town about it. 'But it's enormous, May. I never saw so much lilac.'

'And there's going to be every shade of mauve – it's not fully out yet. You could get to the cottage through it but you might get lost – I haven't time to take you. I'll show you how to skirt it.'

She led Fran into the park. 'There! You can see the cottage. That's the Hall, over there. Now I must get lunch started.'

Fran thought the Hall impressive but gloomy. Strolling along the edge of the lilac grove she turned her attention to it. Well, she could admire it even if she couldn't feel emotional about it. Actually, this wasn't the kind of lilac she'd ever been emotional about. Her kind had been white, not mauve, and had had long stems with all the leaves stripped off. Flower-shop lilac. But this lilac probably smelt the same. She pulled a spray towards her. It didn't smell as she'd expected it to – indeed, it mainly smelt like Baggy's tiles, cold. Well, it wasn't fully out yet.

Ah, here was the cottage. Some small, stiff tulips were growing against the black weather-boarding. Fran laughed delightedly as June came out to meet her. 'Darling, it's enchanting – like a Toulouse Lautrec can-can dancer, throwing up black skirts to show her frilly white drawers. Now I see why you had to have this exquisite black-and-white dog.' She stooped to pat Penny who had followed June from the cottage.

'Oh, she wasn't chosen deliberately. And I rather wish she was less exquisite – I mean, tougher; I'm so afraid something will happen to her. I also wish Corinna hadn't chosen a bitch; they're murder to lawns. Look at all the brown patches.'

'They'll recover – and come up much greener than the rest of the lawn. Dear Corinna! Are she and Hugh still wasting their heaven-sent opportunities at the flat?'

'Mother darling! You don't deserve idealistic grandchildren.'

'Well, I'm in favour of the young getting experience before they settle down.'

'Let's go in.' June was apt to feel shocked by her dearly loved mother's permissiveness – no, not shocked exactly; embarrassed. And she was thankful that Fran, though she would hint at the permissiveness of her own youth, never volunteered details. Robert could never understand June's feelings about this. He would have been fascinated to hear about Fran's goings-on in the twenties.

Penny was now looking up hopefully. 'The creature wants me to carry her,' said Fran, picking her up. 'How nice she feels! It's such ages since I let myself have a dog.'

'You hardly could, the way you dash about.' June steered her mother into the cottage. 'Of course you mustn't expect it to be as grand as the Dower House.'

'Your red stair carpet's pretty grand.'

'May gave us that. I love seeing it through the open front door. This is the sitting room.'

Fran took her time before pronouncing. 'It's a great success. How well all your small pieces have fitted in.'

'Yes, the scale's right but they're pretty cheap – they were all we could afford when we first married.'

'They don't look cheap. And I like your handwoven curtains. This room would be *too* pretty if you'd used chintz.'

'May gave us the curtains – she's been wildly generous. George too; he won't accept a penny of rent.'

'That must make things easier.'

Actually, it didn't, as they'd lived rent free in Baggy's house too. But the cottage cost less to run, largely because May paid for so many things: repairs, cleaning… and they had so many meals at the Dower House. 'Oh, everything's easier here,' said June happily. 'Come and see the kitchen while I get the coffee. And put that dog down. She's heavier than she looks.'

'But she loves being carried. She's gone all limp.'

Fran nursed Penny while drinking coffee and praising the kitchen, but relinquished her before going to see the upstairs rooms. Those red-carpeted stairs looked steep.

She found the bedrooms a little bare. Some of May's frilliness wouldn't have come amiss here. But June had never been a frilly girl and, very possibly, simplicity was best in these tiny rooms. Fran continued to praise everything.

'Are you equal to the stairs to Robert's study?' said June. 'I'm afraid they're really only a glorified ladder.'

Not particularly glorified, thought Fran, tackling them on all fours, but she was enthusiastic about the loft. 'I'm sure Robert does wonderful work here.'

'Well, he will. At present he's apt to work in the garden. He's still only thinking – apart from his reviewing.'

Fran, eyeing the piles of books on the floor, said, 'As he hasn't room for those on his shelves, couldn't he lend some to Baggy?'

'He offered to, but Baggy said there was no point in having books around that he didn't read.'

'They'd make his room look less bare. So would pictures.'

'He didn't bother to bring any. I must say the ones in his house were pretty frightful. Marcus Stone and Maude Goodman and the like.'

'Mabel's taste, probably. Poor Mabel – and poor Baggy.'

June looked worried. 'You don't think he's unhappy?'

Fran, remembering all the years June had coped with Baggy, said hastily, 'As far as I know he's blissful. Is that the creature whimpering? Isn't she allowed upstairs?'

'She won't face them – unless she's carried.'

'Let's take her for a walk. You can show me that lilac grove. May said I'd get lost in it.'

'So you easily could.'

They went down and Fran again picked up Penny, with considerable pleasure. Really, one had been dog-starved.

There was still the dining room to see and admire. Fran said, 'Again your early-married furniture has fitted in splendidly. I'm beginning to think of you as a couple of newlyweds.'

'I said, the night we moved in, that it was like being on our honeymoon.'

They went out into the sunshine. Fran, setting Penny down again, said, 'Will she follow?'

'Until she gets tired – which will be pretty soon. You'll soon learn to find your way about our lilac maze. I must show you the little hidden garden.'

Walking along the narrow, tunnel-like paths, Fran could see little except the twisted green trunks of the ancient lilacs and a network of branches overhead. Scarcely a head of lilac was visible from below. But once they reached the grassy central space around the sundial the lilac was all around them, some of it fully out.

'This really is lovely,' said Fran. 'And all the more so because one feels one's enclosed in a world of lilac.'

'May and I knew you'd love it – and so do we. Lilac's part of our childhood. Father used to bring you such masses and masses.'

Fran felt belatedly guilty. She must, then, have told the poor man it was her favourite flower – as indeed it had been but for a reason she wouldn't have liked him to know. She ought to have kept her fondness for it to herself. Still, she'd made him pretty happy, she believed – deservedly happy, good, kind man. And there was no point in feeling guilty towards a man who'd been dead all of thirty years.

June continued, 'I always feel this is somehow a *secret* garden, which makes it more fun. And it's completely sheltered from the wind. That garden seat's surprisingly comfortable. It's an old one. May had it painted white.'

Fran was admiring the graceful, intricate pattern of the iron-work when a gong boomed from the Dower House.

'May's installed that to call people in for meals,' said June. 'You can hear it as far off as the cottage. We needn't hurry, though. She gives us fifteen minutes' grace.'

They returned to the maze-like paths and came out into the sunshine. 'Well, this certainly is a delightful place,' said Fran. 'The house, the cottage, your miraculous sea of lilac. I don't wonder you're all so happy here.'

'I don't think I've ever been so happy,' said June. 'Mother, do you remember Rudolph Valentino?'

Fran stared. 'Now what in the world made you mention him?'

'I've no idea. His name just flashed into my mind.' June, feeling herself blushing, was thankful her mother had stooped to pat Penny, who had collapsed on the grass, indicating exhaustion.

'Isn't it extraordinary the way things do that? You've probably seen some photograph of him recently.'

June clutched at this. 'Yes. It was shown on television.'

'Wish I'd seen it – though I was disappointed when I saw a bit of one of his films not long ago. Such a smooth, blank face. A wonderful smile, though.'

'Funny I should suddenly mention him. I suppose I remembered that you admired him.' Really, one must be more careful. She'd mentioned Valentino simply because she was thinking of George, thinking of how much he had to do with her present happiness. But no harm had been done and it was a useful warning. Her darling mother was, as a rule, both observant and intuitive.

A pleasant smell of asparagus floated towards them. They went in to May's truly magnificent lunch.

9

Life at the Dower House, Fran discovered, could be at the same time full and leisurely. She talked, ate, walked, explored the locality in Tom's taxi and, when the sun shone, put in a good deal of time lying in the hammock now installed on the lawn outside the Long Room windows. 'The creature' usually lay on top of her; after a few disasters their joint hammock technique became masterly.

As her first weekend approached Fran became worried in case Penny showed too much devotion. Hugh might resent it. But Hugh had nothing to resent as Penny instantly transferred her allegiance. (Fran, though relieved, was also slightly piqued.) And Hugh was grateful for his grandmother's interest in his dog.

'You're doing her good, Fran,' he said. 'She's far less nervous.'

'And I really believe she's grown since we saw her on Monday,' said Corinna.

Fran, seeing Hugh and Corinna together, reconsidered her views about them. June had been right in considering them idealistic, and idealism obviously suited them. And though, in Fran's opinion, Corinna's goodness was merely that of a sweet, pretty, harmless girl, there was something positive about Hugh's goodness – he was good, as it were, from strength, not from weakness – rather the opposite to his father. Fran considered Robert's vagueness a sort of weakness; only in a famous writer would she have found it completely excusable. She thought him a distinguished writer but not an exciting one and she found his occasional novels difficult to read. Still, she was proud when they received such critical acclaim, she liked him, appreciated his many good points, and greatly admired his good looks. But he never attracted her as much as George did.

George, in Fran's opinion, was wildly attractive, all the more so because he was not noticeably good looking. She thought of his very ordinary brown hair and eyes, rather round head and face, childish nose (quite a good mouth, though) as simply a background waiting to be lit up by his charm. Indeed, the charm lit up more than George's personality; it lit up his surroundings. When he came home in the evening the atmosphere at the Dower House became that of a house where a party is due to start.

And he never missed an evening – or, for that matter, his train. Day after day he returned, apparently untired, to hand round evening papers and – as often as not – small presents, dispense drinks and have a pleasant conversation with Fran before they all settled down to one of May's dinners.

Fran was alarmed about the amount of food she was eating. Her first lunch had been asparagus, grilled sole, and strawberries; her first dinner, smoked salmon, roast chicken, and crème brulée. She had said, while tucking into the crème brulée, 'Darling May, a month of food like this and I shall have to slim for a year. Surely two courses would be more than enough?'

George said, 'It's no use, Fran. We all have to give in to May's ruling vice, which is vicarious gluttony. She loves seeing people eat.'

'You need a good dinner, George,' said May firmly. 'But you can refuse anything you don't want, Mother. I shan't mind.'

'It's a case of lead us not into temptation,' said Fran. 'Oh, well.' She accepted a second helping of crème brulée.

But after a couple of weeks, having put on a skirt that was suspiciously tight, she decided she must seriously watch her weight. And there were no bathroom scales. She mentioned this while having morning coffee in the Long Room, with May and Baggy.

'They got left behind in London,' said May. 'I'll buy some.'

'No, *I* will. I'll go shopping this afternoon. There are several things I want to get and I shall enjoy poking around that nice old town.'

May, who had already poked round their nearest town as much as she cared to, said she would be tied up that afternoon but she'd order a taxi for two-thirty. Baggy, then, in a very tentative tone, asked Fran if he might come with her. He added hastily, 'I only mean in the taxi. I won't bother you while you're shopping. It's just that I've some shopping to do myself.'

'But of course, Baggy,' said Fran heartily, having noticed his tentative tone. There was no doubt about it; Baggy was very often tentative and she was less and less sure he was happy. 'I shall love having you.' She had rather fancied an afternoon on her own but must certainly jump at this chance of giving him an outing.

'Time you started for your walk, Baggy,' said May briskly, as she carried the coffee-tray to the kitchen.

Baggy, when the door had closed behind her, said he would like Fran's advice on his shopping. 'But it's a secret from May for the moment,' he whispered.

Anything said in the Long Room was liable to be overheard in the kitchen. 'Then I'll come to your room,' said Fran.

She accompanied him and prepared to be very interested in his secret. She waited until he had settled her in his armchair and then said, 'Now, Baggy.'

'Remember that first lunch you had here when there was asparagus? May asked you if you'd had enough and you said you'd never in your life had enough asparagus.'

'Did I, Baggy?' said Fran, slightly bewildered.

'Of course May offered you more but you said what you meant was that, as asparagus was a first course, one always had to save some appetite for what was to follow – so one never, *really*, had enough asparagus.'

Fran laughed. 'Yes, I remember now. It's something I've often felt.'

'And you said it was much the same with strawberries because *they* come at the *end* of a meal when one hasn't enough appetite left to eat a lot. I was very much struck because that's how I feel and I'm sure lots of people do. So I thought… you see, I want to give everyone a treat.'

He then plunged into explaining that he had often given June and Robert treats – 'It was easy, then, because there were lots of expensive things they never had. But it's difficult with May and George as they have expensive things at almost every meal. And I do want to buy them something special for next Sunday, to make a celebration!

'It is somebody's birthday?' May's was over, June's not yet – how she'd once disliked those names her husband had fancied, but she'd long ago got fond of them. 'May' was so old-fashioned that it was positively distinguished. 'Perhaps it's yours, Baggy?'

'It's nobody's. It's in honour of me being still alive. You see, I made Rosehaven over to Robert to save him death duties but I had to live seven years or he'd still have had to pay them. I was a bit afraid Fate might bump me off just to spite me but now it looks as if I shall make my bet – that is, if I can hang on till Sunday.'

Rosehaven? Of course, it was his singularly ugly suburban house. She said, with feeling, 'How kind and sensible of you to make that plan. It's sad I shall have so little to leave. I've often wished my husband hadn't tied up so much in my annuity.'

'No doubt he wanted to make sure that you'd always be safe. Still, it'd have been a bad investment if you'd died young.'

'I'd never have done anything so wasteful,' said Fran. 'But about this celebration…'

'I'd like to give them all an asparagus feast for Sunday lunch – a real glut of asparagus, and then a glut of strawberries.'

'It's a marvellous idea.' Fran meant it. She couldn't imagine a more delightful meal. But would May settle for a lunch without a middle course?

'We shall need dozens and dozens of bundles. There'll be eight of us and May likes those women in the kitchen to have what we have. I'd say we'd need four dozen bundles.'

'Baggy, dear!'

'Yes, really. And baskets and baskets of strawberries.'

'I wonder if we can get them, Baggy. Strawberries must still be fairly scarce.'

'There's a good shop May patronises. They'll be able to order them – and enough asparagus.'

'You don't think we ought to discuss it with May?'

'If we did, it wouldn't be a surprise. Oh, I know it can't be a complete surprise because she'll have to cook the asparagus, but the surprise will be when we tell her it's ordered.'

'Of course it will,' said Fran heartily. She found his desire to give this treat extremely touching – and really rather clever and original. May must be made to see the cleverness and originality. 'That's settled, then. I won't say a word. Now oughtn't you to start your walk?'

But he said he would skip his walk and she realised he wanted to go on talking. She didn't mind, except that talking to him usually meant that one had to call the tune, start all the subjects, and it wasn't too easy to find ones that interested him. There was no more to be said about her flat as she'd not yet had an answer to the letter he'd drafted for her. However, she managed to keep the conversation going for an hour or so and then said she must dress for their outing. 'I'll change before lunch so that I shan't keep the taxi waiting.'

On her way upstairs she asked herself how she could make the afternoon pleasurable for the old man. They would have tea somewhere. And she'd wear clothes she thought he would like. She had a pale blue tweed suit. Most men liked pale blue and the older they got the more they liked it. She herself thought it insipid but not bad if mixed with other colours. She would wear a yellow sweater. Quite a good combination. And she'd do a little something to her hair and make-up.

Her trouble was rewarded at lunch when Baggy said how nice she looked. 'Mabel would have liked that shade of blue. She always admired the way you turned yourself out.'

'How nice of her,' said Fran warmly, trying to remember Mabel. All that came to mind was a bundlesome figure reminiscent of a small-size cottage loaf and a face like a pretty cauliflower.

May saw them off in the taxi, after arranging that Tom would pick them up in the market square for the return journey. 'And of course charge it to the account, Tom. Don't let them pay you a penny.' She closed the taxi door on them, glad of an afternoon to herself. She was now considering a quite new line on the conservatory.

Fran had been none too certain that the little town would be equal to Baggy's needs, but she found that the largest fruit and vegetable shop was considerably better than the one she dealt with in London. The manager did not flinch at the mention of four dozen bundles of asparagus and, though strawberries were still expensive, any amount could be obtained for a definite order. Everything would be delivered early on Saturday morning. The only surprise shown was when Baggy produced his cheque book. The Dower House credit would have been good for any amount.

'Well, that was all very satisfactory,' she said as they came out of the shop. 'And a truly princely present, Baggy. Now what ought we to do?' She looked around, slightly bewildered. This wasn't the sleepy little market town she had expected it to be. One was in some danger of being pushed off the pavements by the crowds. 'Will you come with me while I do my shopping?'

But Baggy stuck to his undertaking to let her shop on her own, and this wasn't only out of consideration for her. He planned to buy a new pair of country shoes and then study the windows and showcases of the town's three house agents. There would be photographs and particulars of properties for sale. Always interesting to note what prices were being asked. But he told Fran he hoped she would do him the honour of having tea with him.

'Oh, Baggy, I meant to ask *you*!'

'Well, I got in first,' said Baggy, looking pleased. 'Shall we say five o'clock? That looks like a good tea-shop.' It was a few doors along the street in a handsome Georgian house, its façade little changed. 'Now off you go. Women always take longer over their shopping than they expect to. Mabel always did.'

Fran, amused by this suddenly dominant Baggy, started off at a brisk pace but soon slackened it; one really could not walk fast through so many shoppers, most of whom were dawdling. They were also jostling – and the perambulators were the worst jostlers of all. Their pushers seemed to think they had an invincible right of way. Well, they probably deserved it; shopping while coping with a pram must be exhausting. What handsome vehicles most of them were, positively the Rolls Royces of pramdom. She extracted her instep from under a wheel and turned into a side street that looked worth exploring.

Here there were fewer and smaller shops and far fewer shoppers. This was more like the town she had expected. How delightful the houses were, some Tudor, some Georgian, some imposing, some quite humble – she came to a close of ancient cottages which were little better than slums but still beautiful in their decay, with geraniums in their none-too-clean lattice windows. Fascinating that they should still exist little more than a stone's throw from the busy High Street with its Woolworth's and supermarkets. She wasn't against progress. One mustn't expect little country towns to crumble uncomplainingly just to oblige one's sense of the picturesque, but it was pleasant to find survivals such as this. But the whole street, much of it well preserved, was a miracle of survival.

A clock with a deep, musical chime struck the half hour. How right that sound was for her surroundings, how it crystallised the moment – in a way, made time stand still. Strange that a chime denoting the passage of time should somehow annihilate time. She was pleased with the thought… But she must get back to the High Street and do her shopping before exploring the town further.

She walked springily, enjoying the afternoon sun and feeling extremely well. A little tune was running in her head. After lunch, while waiting for the news on television, she had seen a cartoon teaching children how to cross roads. There had been a song – 'Fanta, the elephant, going to school…' The *baby* elephant had to learn its kerb drill. 'Left, right, keep to the rule.' It was a catchy tune. She found herself prancing along to it, absurdly feeling that she was Fanta. But even a baby elephant must feel heavier than she did. She was herself as a child, at any moment she might take to skipping instead of walking. What nonsense…

Back in the High Street she wondered where to buy bath-room scales. A good chemist would have them – and she now remembered she'd said she'd give Baggy some bath oil. There was a large chemist on the other side of the street. She crossed without difficulty owing to a hold-up in the traffic – though eeling between the waiting cars was something of a feat; Fanta, the elephant, wouldn't have had the figure for it. Yes, there were some scales in the chemist's window. But before going in she'd just glance at the dress shop next door.

It called itself a Boutique – and with justification, Fran considered; it was her idea of what a Boutique ought to be. In the window were two light-weight suits, three summer dresses, some excellent cashmere sweaters, a couple of unusual belts and some original costume jewellery. One didn't often see such a mixture of pretty things assembled together. Fran had bought no new clothes since her return to England and one of these suits was just her style. She went in.

She bought the suit (leaf-green; she'd had something like it when she was a girl) and arranged for the necessary alteration (it had to be let out, not taken in as most ready-made clothes had to be for her; oh, those Dower House meals!) Then she investigated the costume jewellery and chose brooches for herself, May and June (large stones, barbarically set, wearable at any hour of the day – strange that if they'd been real stones one would only wear them for full-dress occasions; she hardly ever wore her few pieces of real jewellery). Finally, she bought a large, felt frog, green and yellow, very cleverly designed. It reminded her of a felt frog she'd owned in the twenties – though that frog had worn a top hat.

'It'll do for one of my granddaughters,' she said mendaciously, as the frog was put in a carrier bag printed with psychedelic flowers. (And very possibly Corinna and Prue would like it. Mascots were even more popular now than they had been in her youth; only nowadays they were said to be Freudian. Anyway, Corinna and Prue weren't going to get the chance to like this frog.)

She paid the bill by cheque (how trusting shopkeepers were) and said, 'Now I must fly – is that four o'clock striking?' But even as she said it she knew, with sudden guilt, that it must be five. And she still had the scales to buy. But she was only a few minutes' walk from the tea-shop. If she could get served with the scales quickly...

She hurried out of the Boutique and into the chemist's, bought the scales and Baggy's pine bath oil, also some green, pine-scented soap. Then she ran into a snag: the scales could not be delivered for several days, and she wanted them quickly; having to have that suit let out had been a horrible warning. She would take the scales with her.

There was no carrier bag strong enough to hold them and she wasn't going to wait while they were made into a parcel – already it was five-fifteen. She grabbed the bag containing the bath oil and the soap, the frog's psychedelic bag, the little bag of costume jewellery, and her handbag all in her right hand and then got her assistant to put the scales in the crook of her left arm and open the door for her. Now, hurry, hurry!

But nobody else seemed to be hurrying and no sooner had she managed to get beyond one slow mover than she found herself behind another. Besides, her feet now disliked hurrying or even walking at all. Damn it, she couldn't have aged suddenly! It then dawned on her that the scales were not only a ton weight on her arm but also on her feet, which were now being expected to carry a heavy woman. Really, she was *laden* – and the tea-shop was farther away than she'd realised.

She told herself to stop grizzling. 'You'll be there in a minute.' The scales were slipping. She paused to adjust them – and someone bumped into her. She then decided she'd have to change arms and stood in a doorway to do so. It meant putting everything down and picking everything up again. And she soon found that it was impossible to nurse the scales in her right arm (why? because one carried babies in one's left arm?) and she had to stop in another doorway and change everything over again. And the inexorable clock, which no longer held any charm for her, struck again; she was half an hour late. But at last, at last, it was blissfully there, the tea-shop. Now she only had to cross the road.

She stood on the kerb watching a steady stream of cars. (A woman standing beside her said resignedly, 'Factory going-home time.') She could see no pedestrian crossing. How *did* one get across? If there was a momentary break in the traffic on her side of the wide street, cars on the far side were sweeping past. She noted that hardy souls got as far as the middle of the street and then waited. She'd simply have to do the same… and very nerve-wracking she found it, standing there unauthorised by any island, expecting cars to crash into her behind. Really, this country High Street was more dangerous than Piccadilly Circus. At last! She could make it now if she was nippy. She started out – and instantly saw that an approaching truck was coming faster than she'd realised. She began to run, or rather, she intended to begin; what actually happened was that she found herself incapable of running. She simply *could not run* – it was like some nightmare in which one had leaden feet. Run, run! But she was still only walking, and the damn truck wasn't slowing down in the least… Somehow, somehow, she staggered to safety only a couple of seconds before the truck swept past. And then, for no reason at all, her legs gave way and she sank to the pavement, dropping everything she was carrying. The clanging scales sounded like a car smash.

Various people rushed to help her. There was a clamour of voices. Someone asked if she was hurt. *Was* she? Surely that couldn't be her, screaming? It was not. It was the frog inside its psychedelic bag; one of her elbows was on it. (She hadn't known it was a squeaker.) She raised her elbow and said, 'That wasn't me, it was my frog.' This only added to the confusion – someone said 'Her dog's been run over.' Fran gasped, 'Not dog, frog in bag,' then found herself helped to her feet. She distributed thanks and apologies, as her possessions were restored to her – 'Such a silly thing to do' – then saw Baggy coming towards her. Thankfully she accepted his assistance into the café.

'What happened?' said Baggy, having settled her at his window table. 'Did you slip or something?'

'It was my legs, they just gave way – because a truck was coming. Oh, Baggy, *I couldn't run*. It must have been because of the scales; they weigh a ton.' She sorted her purchases. 'What a miracle your bath oil didn't break!' She handed it to him, with the soap.

His thanks were interrupted by the arrival of a waitress.

'Tea and hot-buttered toast – with jam,' said Baggy, somehow implying that jam would be a strong pick-me-up. 'All right for you, Fran?'

Fran nodded gratefully and asked where the Ladies' Room was; as well as feeling sure her make-up needed repairs she wanted a few minutes on her own to recover herself. Her legs, as she mounted the stairs, were still shaky.

The Ladies' Room, on the half-landing, was deserted. She sat down at the little dressing table, closed her eyes, felt dizzy and instantly opened them; mustn't give in to dizziness. Briskly she coped with her appearance… that was better, no more dizziness. Now just forget the whole ludicrous incident.

Coming out of the Ladies' Room she faced a short flight of stairs at the top of which a door stood open on to a large empty front room which looked as if newly decorated. The pale green walls were the exact shade of the walls in a Bloomsbury bed-sitting-room she'd had as a girl. Would this be an extension of the tea-rooms? She doubted that for she now saw a roll of expensive-looking grey carpet and handsome window curtains. This must be a flat. At once curious, she mounted the few steps and looked in.

Afternoon sunlight was flooding in through the two tall windows, just as it had in her Bloomsbury room. How very like it this room was! Not that she'd had such an expensive carpet or curtains. Her floor had been covered with pale Chinese matting and the curtains had been printed linen, green and white.

She found herself conscious of an extraordinary sensation. She was back in that bed-sitting-room, she saw everything in its rightful place: the divan, her few pieces of furniture – picked up second-hand and painted by herself – the Lovat Fraser rhyme sheets drawing-pinned to the screen which hid what she called 'the kitchen'. This was more than remembering, she was *there*...

And now she saw the lilac, masses of it in her two Devon pitchers, three jugs she had borrowed from the crone in the basement – and, of all things, a bucket! Masses and masses of long-stemmed white lilac. And now she could smell it – and it didn't smell at all like the lilac at the Dower House now in full bloom. And in a flash, she knew why. What she was smelling in memory was the scent she had used in those old Bloomsbury days, a scent called *Le Temps de Lilas*. It was that scent which had caused him to *inundate* her with lilac – she had been almost hysterical with pleasure when he arrived positively weighed down with it all. He had put it down on the floor and they had sat amongst it, laughing and kissing. And later... That had been the first time, so long remembered, so long forgotten – and now suddenly *there*.

But only for a moment, perhaps only for a split second. Then she was back in her seventies, a respectable elderly lady whose legs would no longer run. And she would be very, very glad of a cup of tea.

10

In the taxi, on their way home, Baggy asked Fran if she would tell May about his projected treat. He rather feared May might try to overrule his wish to have nothing but asparagus and strawberries.

Fran was sure she could sell the idea to May. It might help to say that the French often had asparagus feasts – and they well might, for all Fran knew to the contrary. 'You leave it to me,' she told Baggy reassuringly.

He was happy to do so. His liking for her was increasing and he was more and more impressed by what he thought of as her *savoir faire* – the expression seemed to suit her. He had greatly enjoyed their tea together. She had seemed a little distressed when she returned from tidying up – no doubt she was still shaken by her fall. But she had quickly pulled herself together and been most amusing. They had looked out of the window at all the people hurrying home from work and had agreed that the shortness of the girls' skirts was perhaps a bit much – 'Though attractive, when the girls have good legs,' said Fran. 'It's funny how much sexier short skirts are than bikinis, if you know what I mean.'

He found that he did – he had seen bikinis on television. Feeling rather daring he said, 'Well, with bikinis you can see that a girl's decently covered – well, just. But with mini-skirts one's never quite sure there's anything under them.'

'Exactly,' Fran agreed, laughing. 'And I suppose that decency, like justice, must be *seen* to be done.'

He had thought that very good and had taken pleasure in having this sophisticated conversation with Fran – a conversation he would not have dreamt of having with either of his daughters-in-law. He couldn't even imagine having it with Mabel. But Mabel had been wrong in thinking Fran might be fast. That word would always have been too crude for her. '*Mondaine*' was the right word. He was pleased with '*mondaine*'. She was a real woman of the world.

They had gone on to discuss the behaviour of the modern young and Fran's tolerance had almost won him over. One of her theories was that drugs were often a substitute for religion – 'Some of these kids are seeking for something beyond materialism, though they may not know what they're up to. Perhaps we're to blame – I mean, most of us. We've let religion slide and not found any substitute to hand on. Not, of course, that one can be deliberately religious; that's sheer hypocrisy.' He had agreed and later he had agreed that, as one grew older, one got lazy about taking an interest in music and poetry. (He had never taken an interest in either but, while talking to Fran, he felt he might have, if he'd tried.)

One way and another he found the tea-time conversation most stimulating; indeed, he had enjoyed the whole afternoon and was sorry that it was over… though he was a little tired. He leaned back in the taxi and closed his eyes. It might be wise to lie down for half an hour or so before dinner.

While he was resting Fran told May and George about the asparagus feast, She chose a good moment, George having come home in the kind of spirits that lift everyone else's, and May always feeling at her best when about to serve a dinner she was proud of; and she really was extremely pleased that Baggy had taken so much trouble.

'And I think it's most original of him,' she said warmly. 'Probably nobody's had exactly that idea before.'

Fran instantly censored her idea of mentioning the French and substituted, 'It'd be the kind of meal that they'd like to put in Sunday supplements, with huge coloured photographs.'

'Not complicated enough,' said May. 'They doll everything up so.' She seldom took any notice of other people's recipes; when not cooking simple, basic dishes, she liked to do her own creating. 'Well, I think it's absolutely sweet of Baggy, don't you, George?'

George was almost moved to tears, not only by Baggy's generosity but also by the fact that the old man was celebrating having kept alive for seven years. 'What can we give *him*?' he asked May.

'Oh, I'd leave him on the giving end for once,' said Fran. Anyway, she was convinced Baggy had no material needs they didn't supply. What he lacked was their need of him and she wasn't going to put that burden on their consciences at the present pleasant moment. (And she doubted if it would ever do any good.) Then she added, 'But there is one small thing might please him. Have you any green towels for his bathroom?'

'Of course I have.' May also had pink, blue and yellow towels and some printed with large red roses. 'But he asked for white.'

'Still, I'd like to try some green ones – to match the bath oil and soap I bought him.'

'I'll find you some after dinner.'

Baggy came in and received a hero's welcome which obviously both pleased and embarrassed him. And he remained the centre of attention throughout dinner. But soon after he had drunk his coffee he went off to his room.

'Let me have those towels, May,' said Fran. 'I want to see how they look before he goes to bed.'

Carrying them to his room she advised herself to go carefully. He *had* said he thought coloured towels fancy. Mustn't force them on him. She tapped on his door, remembering her mother's precept: 'Never tap on a sitting room door. Always tap on a bed-room door.' In spite of May's efforts, Baggy's room was ninety per cent bedroom.

He called 'Come in.' And, on entering, she felt sure he was pleased to see her. Still, she enquired if she was disturbing him.

'Not doing anything,' said Baggy, who had been sitting in his armchair staring at nothing whatever.

'May and I thought you might like some bath towels to go with the bath oil.'

He looked at the towels with interest tinged by suspicion. '*Green* towels? Mabel was always worried about the green dye. Something to do with arsenic.'

'I absolutely guarantee there's no arsenic in these,' said Fran. 'And they'll make the bathroom more cheerful. Come and see what you think.'

She found the bath oil and soap already set out, the soap already in use. Quickly she made a display with the towels. May had – trust May – included a bath mat.

'Well, I must say…!' Baggy's pleasure was obvious, though he quickly added, 'Are they really all right for a man?'

'You'd be surprised, the things men use nowadays – aftershave lotions and toilet water and whatnot. Green towels are positively virile.' She whisked the white towels and bath mat into the dirty-linen basket. 'There! Transformation scene!'

Baggy began to chuckle, without explanation.

'What is it?' said Fran, a shade nervously.

'Perhaps I ought to have got my bath toys,' said Baggy, still chuckling.

'Your what?'

'I had a fancy for some the other day, when Prue and Dickon were in here. There used to be some bath toys at Rosehaven.'

She had a flash of intuition. That awful bathroom at Rosehaven, with its toothbrushes and mugs and all sorts of personal possessions – yes, she remembered the bath toys – for Baggy it had added up to companionship.

He had stifled his chuckles. 'Sorry, Fran. You must think I'm in my second childhood, talking about bath toys.'

'If you are, I am, too. I actually bought myself a toy today. I'll show you.'

She hurried upstairs, got her frog, and came back brandishing it gaily. 'Look, Baggy!'

'Well, that is a fine frog. I never saw anything quite like it.' She handed it to him and he examined it carefully. 'How beautifully it's made.'

She was instantly sure that he coveted it. With a faint pang of loss, she said, 'Will you accept it – as a nonsense present? Of course it isn't a bath toy. You couldn't float it.'

'I didn't actually *play* with the bath toys,' said Baggy, with a touch of hauteur. 'No, of course I can't accept it. You bought it for yourself!'

'I only meant to enjoy it until I used it as a present for someone. I really bought it because it's so well designed – funny and yet pretty.'

'I've liked frogs ever since I was a child,' said Baggy. 'Never see them down here, though I walk past several ponds. They say all the spraying has killed them.'

'We must think of this as the epitome of all frogs. It's really more a work of art than a toy.'

'So it is,' said Baggy respectfully. 'Well, thank you, Fran. It will remind me of our afternoon together. I did so enjoy it.'

'So did I – except for my ridiculous fall. By the way, I'm not going to mention that to the others.'

'Quite right. They fuss if one so much as trips.'

Fran, having suddenly thought of something she wanted to do, said, 'Now I expect you like to get to bed early. Do you read

127

in bed? I always look forward to that. I've a whole shelf of Agatha Christies – I can read them again and again. Funny how they can be both soothing and exciting at the same time.'

'Mabel used to like them. We sometimes read them aloud to each other in bed. Not sure I could get interested on my own.'

'I shall send you some – nice, light paperbacks, easy to hold.' But he probably wouldn't read them. He had to be *with* someone to enjoy himself. If only one could teach him the pleasures of independence! What a hope! Still, she'd try… later. She'd had enough of him for today.

'Goodnight, Baggy, dear,' she said briskly, and went off on a little private ploy.

She got her rubber boots from the hall cupboard. There was usually a heavy dew and, anyway, she couldn't accomplish her ploy in high heels (though low heels might be cheating a bit). Quietly, she went out through the front door. Now where could she count on not being observed? The front lawn was no good; Baggy's curtains were still undrawn against the late twilight. She made for the gate leading into the park.

Once through it, she said to herself, 'It's simply not true that you can no longer run. You were tired, heavily laden. It was a moment of panic. *Of course* you can run. Now off with you, full tilt!'

It wasn't very full tilt but it was… well, a kind of running. Anyway, it wasn't walking. And was it difficult! She seemed so heavy from the waist downwards. And how jarring it was!

She pulled up after a few yards. Well, one just had to accept it. How sneaky old age was, always springing surprises. She hadn't had the faintest idea that she was past running.

Perhaps she'd try again in a few minutes. She strolled on through the park and reached the edge of the lilac grove. A faint, sharp scent was wafted towards her. She felt slightly aggrieved because it wasn't as richly sweet as *Le Temps de Lilas* scent... She could see the little bottle she'd bought for herself, and the enormous bottle he had given her. His bottle had outlasted the affair; she'd kept just a little of the scent for years and years. She hadn't been surprised when the affair ended; the miracle was that it had ever begun. Such a well-known man, famous really. How much had that counted with her? Quite a lot. She'd worn the affair like a feather in her cap – which didn't make the ending any easier; one's vanity as well as one's feelings suffered. If he was still living he'd be, good God, nearly a hundred. She'd never moved him on beyond fifty – so she was now old enough to be his mother. Absurd thought...

Rather shattering, that experience in the flat over the tea-shop. Not her line, really; too like nostalgia, which she never encouraged. But if the past did still exist, somewhere... well, it did. And of course one would like to believe it did because, in a way, it implied some kind of everlasting life, which she hadn't believed in since she was a child.

It was almost dark now, she'd better go back. But first she'd practise running again... After a couple of minutes she slowed down – jarred and panting. Oh, what the hell! With luck – and care – she'd probably never need to run again.

Standing still to regain her breath she heard a bird singing very sweetly. A late blackbird, probably – but surely no black-bird sang quite as late as this, or quite so sweetly? 'I believe it's a nightingale,' she thought delightedly. Where was it? There was a little wood not far beyond the cottage, she remembered. Yes, the trill was coming from that direction.

She listened a moment longer, then hurried to the cottage; she could see its chimneys against the still faintly luminous sky. She must get confirmation that it was a nightingale; she'd never heard one before. And of course she wanted to share it, and take credit for it. She felt childishly proud to bring news of a nightingale.

The curtains at the cottage were undrawn and she could see that the tiny sitting room was lit only by the television screen, against which two heads were silhouetted. She felt guilty at breaking in on such peace but June and Robert wouldn't want to miss a nightingale. Ah, the programme had ended; the credit titles were coming up. She hurried through the open front door and into the sitting room.

The creature, from her basket, gave a very feminine bark. June and – it proved to be George – turned from the screen.

'Quick,' said Fran. 'There's a nightingale – if it is one. Where's Robert? He's sure to know.' Robert was knowledgeable about natural history.

June ran upstairs and appealed to Robert, who said he wasn't sure one could hear nightingales in May, but he'd look it up.

Fran said, 'Oh, heavens, while he's looking it up it'll go away.' She hurried out of the cottage, followed by June and George. 'Now listen!'

Dead silence from the nightingale.

'It *would* do that,' said Fran. 'Wait! There it is.'

'Oh, I shouldn't think that's a nightingale,' said June. 'Wouldn't a nightingale sing more sweetly?'

Fran said indignantly, 'I don't see how a bird *could* sing more sweetly. Do you expect it to whistle a tune?'

June laughed. 'I really believe I did. Perhaps it's because I've heard so many songs about nightingales. Yes, of course. That must be one. How lovely!'

Robert came out of the cottage with the information that nightingales could be heard between April 15th and June 15th. 'So we're fully entitled to one. Yes, that's a nightingale all right.'

The now fully accredited nightingale continued to sing non-stop.

'Let's see if we can track it,' said Fran.

Robert went in for torches. June called after him, 'Be sure you shut the front door when you come out.' She explained to Fran that Penny was very sensitive and restless. 'I've an idea she's coming into season.'

'Such a ridiculous expression,' said Fran. 'Sounds as if she's something to eat. *My* dogs, no doubt vulgarly, just came on heat.'

Robert returned with torches but said they must use them cautiously or they would scare the bird. 'And we can do without them if we keep to the park. It's level walking.' He led the way with Fran.

Soon there was no doubt that the singing came from the little wood.

'Let's not go any closer,' said Fran. 'Well, this is something I shall always remember.'

June, standing with her arm through George's, said, 'Me, too.'

A clock struck. The nightingale, as if resenting competition, stopped singing.

'That was the stable clock at the Hall,' said Robert.

George said, 'That place gives me the shivers. Look at it now, there's only one room lit up – if you can call it lit up. What a hell of a life for that girl.'

Fran pricked up her ears. She had met Sarah at tea one Saturday afternoon and been astonished by her beauty, and even more astonished that George showed so little interest in her. Had he been merely disguising his interest from May?

Robert said, 'We really ought to see more of her, June. She's so nice and I've stopped minding her voice.'

Fran's ears switched their interest to Robert. Then she accused herself of being ridiculous. If Robert ever showed even a flicker of real interest in any woman but June, that would be the day!

'Hugh and Corinna see quite a lot of her,' said June. 'Oh, there it is again.' The nightingale now surpassed itself. 'I wish May could hear it.'

'Where *is* May?' said Fran.

'Making jam,' said George.

The nightingale now rested again. The party headed for the cottage. It was quite dark now and Robert and George shone their torches ahead. A light breeze wafted the scent of the lilac towards them.

'Heavens, how lucky we are,' said June. 'Lilac and a nightingale! And there's a marvellous laburnum coming out near the cottage – and a may tree.'

'"The lilac, the laburnum and the may",' said Robert. 'I'm sure that's a quotation but I don't know who wrote it. Funny how one likes to quote. It seems to crystallise things.'

They were back at the cottage now. Robert's torch shone on a drift of cow parsley, left on the edge of the lawn.

'"Where the cow parsley skirts the hawthorn hedge",' said Fran. 'And I do know who wrote that: Rossetti, the most loved poet of my girlhood.' She sighed, partly because it was so long since any poetry had given her pleasure and partly because a marvellously romantic setting was being wasted. Robert walked with his mother-in-law, George walked with his sister-in-law – though even if Robert had walked with June and George with May, Fran wouldn't have considered it romantic. She never did consider marriage romantic; just, at best, reasonably comfortable, as her own marriage had been. She said now, 'We must send Hugh and Corinna to hear the nightingale.' Though she wasn't sure that even Hugh and Corinna measured up to her idea of romance. The truth was that, for her, romance needed a touch of the illicit. She rebuked herself for such a disreputable idea but really felt quite unrepentant.

'Come in,' said Robert, opening the cottage door.

'No, thanks, I'll get back now,' said Fran.

'Me, too,' said George. 'Goodnight, June, darling.'

The light from the hall was shining full on June's face. Fran stared incredulously. Surely there was no mistaking the look in June's eyes as George stooped to kiss her? Oh, God, that was one bit of illicit romance Fran didn't favour. Then she relaxed. June was now looking at Robert with exactly the same loving expression. It was simply that the dear girl had a loving nature.

'Tell May about the nightingale,' June called, as Fran and George made their way towards the lilac grove.

'We will, darling,' Fran called back. She must have been mad to think, even for a moment, that June would ever let herself fall in love with May's husband, ever do anything to hurt May.

George was saying, 'Funny how we used to think of this lilac grove as a maze. I could now find my way through it blindfold.'

'*I* couldn't,' said Fran, hanging on to his arm. Dear George, just the kind of man she would have fallen for in her youth. Was he really a reformed character? She doubted it. But long might May go on believing it.

They found May in the still empty, brightly lit conservatory, with an illustrated catalogue and a yard stick. She now favoured painted bamboo furniture – 'Might be better than wicker. Anyway, I've not seen any wicker I like. But I'm still not sure I've got the right line on this place.'

They left her to it.

11

On Thursday evening Corinna rang up to say that she didn't think she and Hugh would come down for the weekend – 'You see, we've got two seats for a first night – actually, Sir Harry gave them to me – and we rather fancied going out to supper afterwards, and I shan't fancy getting up early on Saturday morning. So we thought we'd just spend a quiet weekend in London.'

'But it's Baggy's feast on Sunday,' said May. 'Asparagus and strawberries.' She explained at some length, adding, 'Do make an effort, darling. I'm sure he'll be hurt if you and Hugh aren't here.'

'Hang on a minute… I'll ask Hugh.'

'Tell him Penny's coming into season, will you?'

'Oh, my goodness…' Corinna shortly returned to say, 'Hugh thinks we should come. Of course it *is* very sweet of old Baggy. And Mother, please listen: Will you ask Aunt June to be terrifically careful Penny doesn't get out?'

'I will, darling. Try to get here for Saturday lunch, will you? I'm having something nice.'

'All right,' said Corinna. Well, it would save cooking at the flat or going out for a meal.

May relayed the conversation to Fran, concluding, 'Sir Harry, as she calls him, seems to be rather taken with her. He used to upset her by saying she'd never be any good.'

'Is he making a pass at her – or whatever the latest expression for it is?' Fran, at Corinna's age would have been delighted to be made a pass at by a distinguished, middle-aged actor such as Henry Tremayne.

'Not that I know of. I'd wish him the best of luck – I would, Mother; anything to stop her marrying Hugh. It'll be just like brother and sister marrying. I suppose June *is* being careful not to let Penny out?'

'It's pretty tricky, seeing that they usually have the cottage door open. Why don't we have the creature here?'

'Of course! There's that little bedroom I haven't furnished yet. We'll bring her basket over.'

'And I'll undertake to exercise her and keep her amused,' said Fran, who was still dog-starved. 'I'll go and tell June now. She'll be greatly relieved.'

Penny was duly installed, to her satisfaction. Next to Hugh, Fran was her favourite person. It was Fran's belief that, with a little effort, she could make herself first favourite; but never, never would she make the effort.

On Saturday morning the arrival of the asparagus and the strawberries created something of a sensation. Even May, who always bought more than she needed, was staggered.

'Why on earth did you let Baggy order so much?' she asked Fran.

'Well, there are so many of us – and he said you'd want to feed three women in the kitchen.'

'Not on asparagus. They consider it a weed. I've got chops for them. I wonder if we could persuade Sarah to come?'

'And how about asking Mildred to come down a day early?' Fran had finally succeeded in getting Mildred invited to stay for a fortnight, having agreed to extend her own visit and act as chief brunt-bearer.

May shuddered. 'I'm not having Aunt Mildred one day before I need to.'

Baggy came into the Long Room, where his purchases had been set out for inspection. Fran and May received him with grateful enthusiasm.

'Truly magnificent,' said May, wondering how she could get so much asparagus ready to serve at the same time. Thank God the Matsons would stalk the strawberries. She hoped she'd ordered enough cream... With an effort she got her mind off tomorrow's feast and on to today's lunch.

Hugh and Corinna, on their arrival, were sent to see Baggy's present, now moved to the long slabs in the old larder.

'Frightening, isn't it?' said Hugh.

'Mother wants Sarah to help eat it. How shall we get hold of her? She may come over this afternoon but one can't count on it. She asked us not to telephone except in some emergency.'

Hugh, his eyes on the forty-eight bundles of asparagus, said, 'Well, if this isn't an emergency, I don't know what is.'

After lunch (modest, by May's standards, chicken and fruit; she had intended to make an exotic pudding but been delayed by the arrival of the feast) Hugh telephoned the Hall, with Corinna standing by. He was about to ring off in despair when Sarah answered. She said she hoped he hadn't been ringing long – 'Our telephone's shut away in a little room nowhere near anywhere. Grandfather doesn't think telephones should be on the loose. Is anything wrong?'

Hugh attempted to explain but made no headway. Sarah said, 'This is a terrible old telephone. Grandfather won't let the post-office take it away. Could you shout, please?'

Hugh shouted. Sarah, at last, heard the word 'asparagus' but formed the impression that he wanted some. 'Sorry,' she told him, 'our beds were exhausted years ago. Such a shame because I did so adore it.'

'Let *me* try,' said Corinna. She then proceeded to speak quite quietly but with careful far-forward enunciation and – miraculously, it seemed to Hugh – Sarah heard. At first she

137

said that coming to lunch was out of the question. Then she wavered. Finally she said, 'Oh, it would be marvellous. I'll see if I can arrange anything and then come over and let you know.'

'Don't bring any spaniels with you,' said Corinna. 'Penny's in season.'

'Oh, goodness! Do be careful with her. I'll be with you soon.'

Hugh said, as Corinna hung up, 'How excellent your voice production must be.'

'I think I've got control of it at last. Sir Harry took some of us to an empty theatre one morning and I could make myself heard right to the back of the gallery.'

Hugh wondered why she hadn't mentioned this triumph before – she often told him of her failures and of scathing comments Sir Harry had made on them. Perhaps she was going to be good. Hugh hoped so with all his heart. He had taken it for granted that she would eventually have to suffer disappointment. Perhaps he had been accepting her own, very humble, opinion of her work.

'Come and walk through the lilac,' he said.

'I keep expecting it to be over.'

'Oh, it'll last a couple of weeks yet unless the weather turns very hot – judging by the lilac bush we had in London.'

They strolled around the paths and the little hidden garden until they heard Sarah calling them and went to meet her.

'I've managed it,' she cried, triumphantly. 'The poor old darling couldn't bear me to miss a gorge of asparagus so he's going to have his lunch specially early. You mustn't think it's he who insists on my being there for meals. It's just that, if I'm not, I know he doesn't eat properly.'

'Do you actually have to feed him?' asked Corinna.

Sarah looked shocked. 'Goodness, no. But if he's on his own he doesn't concentrate. How marvellous your telephone voice is, Corinna. You seemed to be whispering right in my ear. And how ghastly you must think my voice is. I've only known how bad it is this last week. The Vicar's just got a tape-recorder and he let me hear myself on it. I was shattered – I sounded just like my grandmother. I always knew her voice was awful but I'd no idea mine was the same.'

Hugh told her she was exaggerating but Corinna simply said, 'You could cure yourself, Sarah.'

'You mean if I trained, the way you have,' said Sarah, looking wistful.

'Of course that would be ideal. But I think *I* could teach you.'

They had reached the lawn in front of the cottage, where there was some rustic garden furniture bought at a sale by May and painted white.

'Sit down and listen,' said Corinna. 'We had a Society girl in Sir Harry's class who spoke just like you do, and he said it was because she clenched her jaw. That does something terrible to your voice and to your enunciation. Sir Harry made this girl speak with her jaw absolutely slack and it made the most enormous difference – only she kept forgetting and then he'd yell at her, "Unclench, girl!" He says lots of Society women speak that way – and it's very catching; several of us started speaking with our teeth shut as tight as rat traps. Sir Harry was furious and said, if we didn't stop it and the girl didn't stop it, she'd have to go. After that, we were perpetually screaming at her – and at ourselves, "Unclench, unclench!" And she suddenly got cured and now has a particularly nice voice. Do you understand, Sarah? Now unclench, and speak with your jaw slack.'

After several false attempts Sarah managed a few words in a soft, breathy voice.

'Much better,' said Corinna, 'except that now you're hardly speaking at all. Don't be nervous. Talk at the top of your voice but keep your teeth unclenched. Do you know any poetry by heart?'

'No,' said Sarah, in her harshest tone.

'You've clenched again. Well, learn some, and practise it with your jaw absolutely dropped – it doesn't matter if you look like a village idiot. You work on it, hard, and I'll hear you next week.'

'I didn't know you could be such a bully, Corinna,' said Hugh. 'But I do see what she means, Sarah. Your voice does sound different when you unclench.'

'I shall never remember,' said Sarah, in her normal voice. She then remembered and repeated the words with a slack jaw and in a deep fruity voice.

'Sounds like Mrs Siddons asking "But will it wash?" said Corinna. 'You don't have to be sepulchral, just natural.'

The conversation continued, with Corinna frequently interjecting 'Unclench!' Hugh, impressed, was also a trifle bored. He went off to see Penny.

The door of the room allotted to her was open and she was not inside. Hugh raised the alarm. She was eventually discovered in Fran's room. They had both been enjoying an afternoon nap.

'I heard her whimpering,' said Fran apologetically. 'Actually, I've been having her in my room at night – she gets so lonely. But of course you'll want her with you, while you're here.'

Hugh, both jealous and grateful, said, 'No, that'd make her miss me more when I go on Monday. She'd better stay with you, Fran.' He added, with the light of battle in his eye, 'Have there been any dogs around the house yet?'

'Not yet. She's nowhere near at her height yet.'

'When did she start?'

'Your mother thinks, last Monday.'

Hugh, summoning up his recently acquired knowledge, said, 'Then I think the dangerous time will begin in the middle of next week. I'll ask Sarah. And please, Fran, do be very careful. Sarah says it would be terribly bad for her to be mated this first time.'

'It certainly would,' said Fran. 'She's nowhere near full grown.'

'I'm afraid she may be,' said Hugh gloomily.

'Well, she isn't. She's growing all the time. She's going to make an exquisite dog – aren't you, my creature?'

Hugh gave his grandmother a grateful smile, then put Penny on the leash and led her out.

Halfway through the lilac grove he could hear Sarah and Corinna talking. Again and again Corinna interrupted that conversation with a dictatorial 'Unclench!' Well, the elocution lesson must end now. He reached the cottage lawn and claimed Sarah's full attention for Penny.

Sarah, after discussion and scrutiny, said she thought Penny's dangerous period wouldn't be until the end of the coming week.

'Oh, good!' said Hugh. 'I shall be home again by then and can protect her.'

Sarah grinned. 'Dogs don't actually attack the house.'

'But I've read they've been known to gnaw their way through wood,' said Hugh.

'But not through brick walls. The Dower House is pretty solid.'

'Unclench,' said Corinna.

Hugh said, 'Darling, could Sarah be let off unclenching until we've finished talking about Penny?'

Corinna subsided. She was, anyway, finding both the conversation and the uninhibited examination of Penny a little embarrassing. No doubt she was being 'genteel' – as Sir Harry frequently accused her of being. But he hadn't accused her of it that day in the empty theatre. She had been alone with him there (the 'some of us' mentioned to Hugh had been an invention) and highly suspicious of his intentions. His behaviour had, however, been most professional and he had spent much of the time in the gallery, while she remained on the stage. But he had tested her voice production by making her say 'I love you' in various ways: gently, desperately, broken-heartedly, passionately, etc. He'd praised her for all these except 'passionately' and even then he'd added, 'Still, imagination did seem to be doing something to help out inexperience.' Then he'd taken her out to lunch and told her there was just a remote chance that she might be able to act. And he had said nothing whatever about assisting her to a fuller experience of life. Well, of course that was splendid.

She returned from thoughts of Sir Harry to find Hugh and Sarah now discussing the eventual mating of Penny which sounded even more embarrassing than the present arrangements for her non-mating. She said, It's teatime, in case either of you are interested. Anyway, Penny looks thirsty. And I'd just like to mention that you're clenching worse than ever, Sarah.'

'I'll practise on my own,' said Sarah. 'I swear I will. I'll start as soon as I get home.'

But when she arrived for the Asparagus Feast next day she was still clenching.

May afterwards declared that no meal she had ever provided had been so difficult to cope with as Baggy's asparagus. Saucepans had to be helped out by a fish kettle, a bread tin and an enamel bowl. Even so, she only cooked three dozen bunches. She felt sure that, if she cooked the lot, much would be left uneaten and Baggy would be disappointed. The feast *must* be a success for him – and she had certainly done her best to make sure it would be, having given instructions for family enthusiasm with the energy of a cheerleader.

And the meal certainly began well, with the massed asparagus (first instalment) looking magnificent in a mammoth punch bowl. Carrying out Baggy's wishes May had provided nothing else except melted butter and bread – long French loaves bought in Soho by George. (It was typical of him that he hadn't in the least minded travelling with them, inadequately wrapped and causing much amusement. Various commuting friends had hankered to duel with them.) And of course George had provided champagne. Baggy had raised no objection to that.

'Well, now,' said May, as she finally sat down at the table. 'This is all very exciting.'

It was as if a starting pistol had been fired. In a desire to please Baggy everyone began to eat quite extraordinarily fast, pausing only to praise and be grateful. The enthusiasm was perfectly genuine until the punch bowl had been replenished with a second instalment. Then the pace slackened and the compliments to Baggy become distinctly histrionic.

It was soon after this that Robert became so silent that June feared he was feeling ill. The truth was that he'd had the idea of putting an asparagus feast into his projected novel. He still intended this to appeal to a vast public – and a vast public, surely, liked to read about food being eaten? He could make something out of the crisp bread and golden butter, of the sunlight glittering on the champagne (it seemed to be getting very hot in the Long Room) but how could one lyrically describe a stick of asparagus? It hadn't really any beauty, and the piles of sucked stalks were rather disgusting, not to mention the melted butter running down people's chins. Perhaps he should make his asparagus feast revolting, which would be more in his line – only, this time, he didn't intend to write that kind of novel. Perhaps… but he suddenly knew he didn't want to think any more about asparagus for a long time, if ever. He came back into circulation, much to June's relief.

May also had become anxious, a fantastic idea having occurred to her. Was there some reason, quite apart from expense, why people usually ate only small quantities of asparagus at a sitting? She had read somewhere that if you ate pigeon every day for forty days you would die. Was there something like that about asparagus? And was champagne all right with it? Whisky wasn't all right with oysters. There was a third instalment keeping hot but she couldn't face it or let anyone else face it. She sprang up saying, 'Marvellous, marvellous, and we've finished the very last stick. Now for the strawberries.'

Strawberries had the great charm of not being asparagus. Robert decided *they* should go into his novel. The very words, 'strawberries and cream' had a fairy-tale charm. He saw them in startling contrast to the dark, gothic mass of his general idea. Yes, strawberries, certainly – perhaps wild ones, gathered at dawn by a heroine rather like Sarah but with a very different voice.

Not that Sarah's voice had been heard much during the meal. She had concentrated on eating. With the exception of Baggy, who had enjoyed watching everyone else eating but eaten little himself, she was the only person who retained her enthusiasm for asparagus. She said she could eat it every day for a year.

Well, she could eat it every day for a week, May decided. She should be persuaded to take the twelve still-uncooked bundles back to the Hall. No ugly head of asparagus should be raised again at the Dower House for a very long time.

Later in the afternoon Fran went to Baggy's room to tell him what a great success the feast had been. She found him sitting in his armchair doing nothing, except smiling gently.

She hoped he was basking.

'Oh, Baggy, everything was splendid,' she assured him.

'Truly, Fran? Did you all get *enough*?'

'We did indeed, and for the first time in our lives.'

But with asparagus, she reflected, as with several of life's especial pleasures, enough could be synonymous with too much.

12

At supper that evening (always 'supper' on Sundays, though otherwise indistinguishable from the usual 'dinner') Hugh remarked, 'Well, eat, drink and be merry – for tomorrow Aunt Mildred comes.'

Fran said, 'Now, listen, Hugh – in fact, listen everyone! It just isn't fair to expect the worst of Mildred and, what's more, it brings out the worst. What's so wrong with her, anyway? What does she do? She's a perfectly harmless old lady.'

'She's not and you know it,' said May. 'She rarely comes for so much as a meal without upsetting someone. How we're all going to stand her for a fortnight I simply don't know.'

Neither did Fran but she said firmly, 'Nonsense, darling. Anyway, let's all forget past irritations and do our best to be nice to her. Baggy, you'll help me, won't you?'

Mildred had only been invited to Rosehaven when June had felt it absolutely necessary, but Baggy knew her well enough to consider her annoying and what he would have described as 'very fancy'. Still, she was Fran's sister so there ought to be some good in her. Every day he became more devoted to Fran. 'Of course I'll be nice to her,' he said kindly.

'Sweet of you, Baggy.' Not that Mildred cared much for elderly men; she often said she felt an affinity with the young. Remembering this, Fran appealed to Hugh again, 'I wonder if you realise how fond of you she is.'

'I don't and I'd rather not,' said Hugh, then added a trifle impatiently, 'Oh, don't worry, Fran. I shall only be seeing her at the weekends. I expect I can keep the peace – if only she'll lay off calling me "Little St Hugh" and telling me my true vocation is the church.'

'It's meant as a compliment. She admires you enormously.' This was untrue. Mildred had recently said to Fran, 'Naturally I'm fond of Hugh but you must admit he's a bit goody-goody. So's his father. Of course they're both handsome but give me George every time.' If only George would be nice to Mildred, how Mildred would blossom. Fran, turning to him, said, 'Well, I know I can count on you, George. Even to Mildred you're always the perfect host.'

George had been wondering if, during the next fortnight, he could find it necessary to spend quite a few nights in London. But he might be a nuisance to Hugh and Corinna at the flat. Also, May might suspect he was up to something. (God knew he wasn't; astonishing how little temptation he'd had to face recently.) And he was still very much enjoying life at the Dower House. He felt capable of taking Mildred in his stride and he would come home every night positively exuding bonhomie.

'Tell me something she likes,' he said to Fran. 'Something I can bring home as a treat.'

'Liqueur chocolates – anyway, she used to.' Mildred was apt to be faithless to the things she liked, when someone took the trouble to buy them for her. But she'd like anything George gave her.

Robert said, 'June and I were discussing her last night, more or less burnishing our armour. It's absurd to pretend that she does anything really awful – well, not often. It's just that she's a past-mistress at the art of deflation. Almost everything she says takes the stuffing out of one, if only a little. And the effect's cumulative. I wonder *why* she does it.'

Fran could have told him but she wasn't going to. It would be handing over another stick to beat Mildred with. But unfortunately he was already on the track himself.

148

'I suppose,' he said thoughtfully, 'she practises deflation of others in order to *in*flate her own ego. Quite interesting, psychologically.'

Yes, of course that was it, Fran was sure; she was equally sure that Mildred didn't know what she was up to and was quite unconscious that her ego hadn't got all it needed. Indeed, she often infuriated Fran by her intense self-satisfaction. Still, there must be some basic lack, and Fran now saw a chance of enlisting sympathy for her sister. She said, 'Well, starved egos can be pretty tragic. Don't grudge her a little extra ego-food.'

'You're breaking my heart, Mother,' said May. 'We shall have to make a rule to ask each other, "Anyone fed Aunt Mildred's starving ego today?"'

Fran laughed, but ruefully. She suspected that feeding Mildred's ego might become a family joke.

June said, 'Let's hope that some of our general happiness rubs off on her. And it ought to help that she's coming at such a perfect time of the year. Lilac, laburnum, hawthorn, chestnut candles – and some of the fruit blossom's still out. In a way, I wish they didn't all come together; I'd like to spread them out over the whole summer. And there's the nightingale too. We must take Aunt Mildred to hear that.'

'She'll addle its eggs,' said May.

Fran looked at her curiously. It was unusual to see such a grim expression on her pretty, delicate features. Her dislike of Mildred was far more intense than anyone else's and Fran had never understood why. She had once asked May point blank and been put off with a noncommittal answer. Fran sighed. It was obviously impossible to enlist May's sympathy. Still, she was in her way, as good a hostess as George was a host.

'We'll go and hear that nightingale tonight,' Hugh said to Corinna. 'And we'll take Penny – on the leash, of course. It'll be quite safe.'

'Let's hope the nightingale doesn't make her feel any more sentimental,' said Fran. 'I'd forgotten how emotional bitches get at times like this.'

'She's unusually sensitive,' said Hugh, with a touch of pride.

After supper there was something on television that May wanted to see and Baggy and Fran joined her. The others strolled around outside, watching the last of the sunset, which for some time had been flooding the Long Room.

George, remembering June's remark about happiness, said, 'I wonder just why we're all so happy in this place.'

'Oh, we're just country starved and lapping up nature,' said Robert.

June said nothing. With one arm through Robert's and the other through George's, she knew exactly why she was happy.

The nightingale began to sing even before the sun was set.

Next morning it was finally agreed that Fran, May and June should all go to the station to meet Mildred. May tried to get out of it but her mother persuaded her – 'Do let's start off on the right foot, May darling. I wonder if Baggy and Robert would care to come?'

'Damn it, she doesn't need a whole reception committee,' said May. 'And there wouldn't be room in the taxi.'

'I do hope it will be on time,' said Fran anxiously.

It was early and they arrived at the station ten minutes before they needed to. A surprisingly cold wind was blowing and the train was late.

'Mildred, of course, has bewitched it,' said May and then mentally rebuked herself. Bitchy remarks of this kind were pointless and they upset her darling mother.

'Here it is!' said Fran enthusiastically.

A dozen or so people got out of the train, most of them fairly young women, hatless and mini-skirted. Certainly none of them was Mildred.

'She hasn't come,' said June.

'No such luck,' said May. 'Look!'

Mildred was descending at the far end of the long platform. She was wearing a large white straw hat trimmed with green ribbon and a white cotton frock printed with buttercups and daisies. It had a tight bodice and a full skirt which reached to her ankles. On her small feet were green leather ankle-strapped shoes.

June said, 'Mother, she *can't* dress like that – not in this day and age.'

'Wait till you see her latest evening outfit,' said Fran.

'Well, evenings are different. I wouldn't mind wearing that dress in the evening. It's really very pretty.'

'She hasn't seen us yet,' said May. 'Trust her to walk in the wrong direction.'

'I think she's going to the guard's van,' said June. 'Yes!'

A large trunk was being lifted on to the platform.

'My God, she's come for life,' said May.

Mildred now turned, saw them, and came running towards them swinging a little white wicker basket which looked as if it might house a dove. It was her handbag.

Fran thought, 'Well, she runs better than I do. I suppose that's the difference between being sixty-nine and seventy-two.'

June said, 'Ought we to run too?'

'A brisk walk will suffice,' said Fran.

They met her less than halfway and there was much embracing. Then June managed to get in, 'Aunt Mildred, how pretty you're looking.'

'Yes, it's not a bad little cotton dress,' said Mildred, spreading out her skirt and hitting May with her wicker handbag.

'I meant you, too,' said June, with sincerity. No one could have denied that Mildred Lane was pretty. Her white hat, worn on the back of her head and suggestive of a halo, revealed her still genuinely fair hair, bobbed and hanging against her cheeks. (So had she worn it in her youth, so would she always wear it.) The blue of her eyes was barely faded. (It was her habit to hold them very wide open. At their best they looked starry; at their worst, just a little mad.) Her unlipsticked mouth had a childish softness. Only in profile was her jawline revelatory of age.

She said, 'Dear June, how well you're looking – and so plump. May needs to put on weight. Your face is far too thin, May dear.'

'I'll get a porter,' said May.

Mildred's trunk was too large to go into Tom's taxi but it was eventually lodged in the open boot, where it stuck out precariously. By this time Mildred had annoyed Fran by saying, 'How funny it is to see you in the country! I always think of you as a very towny person.'

But at least Mildred was in a good mood. On the drive home she became quite lyrical. 'Oh, the woods, the lovely woods! How one longs to plunge into them! Is there a dog I can take for walks?'

'Not in woods,' said May. 'Some of them are full of pheasants and strictly preserved. Anyway, Penny's out of action.'

Penny's condition was then explained by Fran, very fully. Mildred said, 'Poor sweet lamb. Well, I must keep her amused.'

Fran instantly decided Mildred should have nothing to do with Penny. Then she pulled herself up. Why shouldn't Mildred have a share of Penny? Perhaps she was fond of dogs? If so, Fran didn't know of it but she did vaguely remember a puppy they'd shared as children, quite amicably. How exquisitely pretty

Mildred had been as a child. And surely she had then been...
perfectly normal? Anyway, I got her asked here, thought Fran,
and it's up to me to make her visit a success. She smiled warmly
at Mildred and said, 'What fun it's going to be, having you here.
I shall enjoy showing you the village. And we can take some
trips, to several nearby towns.'

'Let's leave that till later,' said Mildred. 'What I need most
now is solitude, solitude under a wide sky.'

At the Dower House, Baggy and Robert came out to greet
Mildred, Baggy having decided to please Fran by what he
thought of as 'doing the civil' and Robert having been asked, by
June, to be on hand. Mildred, her blue eyes at their widest, said
to Baggy, 'Why, Mr Clare!' (Baggy afterwards told Fran, 'She
seemed amazed that I was still alive.') To Robert she said brightly,
'How's the writing?' somehow making it sound like a hobby, not
a profession. Although she favoured the Dower House with a
long look she made no comment on it, and that very fact was
somehow an adverse comment.

Robert and Tom, the taxi driver, tackled the job of getting the
trunk upstairs while Mildred was shown the two front rooms.
She said she found them gloomy. Shown the Long Room, she
said it must get very hot. (Damn it, thought Fran, the front
rooms *are* gloomy and the Long Room does get hot. There's
usually some truth in what she says – but why say it? I suppose
she's ultra-honest, and most of us aren't.)

May excused herself, to get busy with lunch. 'You show Aunt
Mildred her room, will you, Mother?'

Fran was glad to; May would be spared Mildred's comment –
which was 'Quite pretty but what a small wardrobe.' Well, one
could hand on the 'Quite pretty' – improved to 'How pretty'.
Fran left Mildred to do her unpacking.

Downstairs, Baggy, Robert and June were talking – of course about Mildred. 'Oh, stop it,' said Fran. 'And that goes for me, too. We're all working it up. She hasn't done or said anything outrageous.'

May, coming in from the kitchen, said, 'She will. Let's all take to drink.'

'Not for me,' said Fran. 'I'm going to give the creature some exercise.' She knew that the conversation over pre-lunch drinks would continue to be about Mildred, and everyone, including herself if she stayed, would get a kick out of it.

Walking Penny, she tried to take her mind off her sister and, finding this impossible, concentrated on charitable thoughts. There was no doubt Mildred was much loved at her Bayswater boarding house; Fran had seen that for herself. Two elderly gentlemen paid gallant attention, a twittering spinster acted almost like a lady's maid, the proprietress could not do enough. Unfortunately Fran was convinced that they all had an eye to the main chance; Mildred had twice saved the boarding house from bankruptcy. And charitable thoughts about Mildred's generous behaviour at her boarding house came up against Fran's distinct resentment that Mildred should be so rich. Their parents, knowing that Fran was well provided for, had left all their money to their younger daughter. Fran had fully acquiesced in this but felt entitled to be a mite peeved that, while her annuity remained exactly the same (with the cost of living per-petually rising) Mildred's investments had gone up and up. And no credit to Mildred, who considered money barely mentionable. George had for years handled her affairs.

Fran took Penny to the end of the lane, then returned her to safe keeping, refilled her water bowl and fed her a few com-forting chocolate biscuits. Penny, who had already had a very good breakfast, ate them as if famished. Fran fed her some more, then came out and firmly closed the door on her. A loud rustling of tissue paper could be heard from Mildred's room. No doubt unpacking was still proceeding.

Fran rejoined the group in the Long Room. May was standing with a billowing sheaf of dresses over one arm. She said to Fran, 'I went to take your dear little sister a drink and she handed me this lot for "someone to press".'

'Oh, dear! Can Mrs Matson do them?'

'I can't let her loose on these materials – some of them are lovely.' May might dislike her aunt but pretty materials deserved to be protected. 'Oh, I don't really mind ironing them. It's just the calm way she takes it for granted that infuriates me. Do have a drink, Mother, and get your strength up to face her at lunch.'

Fran said, 'Let's all make up our minds that there'll be nothing to face. May, dear, you *will* control yourself?'

But when Mildred eventually sailed downstairs it was Fran who had to control herself for, accompanying Mildred, was Penny.

Mildred said, 'The poor baby was whining piteously so of course I had to rescue her.'

'But I told you –' Fran broke off. Penny was already out of the French window and into the lilac grove.

Robert, as well as Fran, went after her, only managing to catch her because she misguidedly ran into the little sundial garden.

'Idiot creature,' said Fran lovingly, picking up the now grovelling Penny. 'Robert, will you go back and explain to Mildred *fully*? If have to do it again I shall lose my temper. Tell her about Penny's delicacy and – oh, everything. I'll go and shut the creature up.'

Fran took her time, soothing Penny with more chocolate biscuits and then going to wash melted chocolate off her hands. Returning to the Long Room she found Penny still under discussion.

Mildred was saying, 'In spite of all you've said, Robert, I still think Nature knows best about these things.'

Robert, with noticeable patience, said, 'Well, setting aside Penny's special case and the difficulty of finding homes for mongrel puppies, let me remind you that she's Hugh's dog and it's up to him to decide when she mates.'

'"Hugh's dog",' said Mildred. 'What ominous words! I well remember his misery over the last one.'

'But that was when he was a little boy,' said June.

'People don't change, dear.' Mildred turned to greet Fran. 'Well, has the poor prisoner been shut up by her jailer?'

Fran was exasperated. 'Damn it, Mildred...!'

'Lunch!' said May loudly, opening the door to the kitchen. 'We're ready, Mrs Matson.' It would have been a pleasure to hear Fran lose her temper with Mildred, but May knew how upset her mother would be about it afterwards.

Lunch began. May, June and Robert addressed polite questions to Mildred who answered with chilly brevity. Fran said nothing; she was too annoyed with Mildred, and annoyed with herself for being annoyed. Baggy, deciding that he had not yet lived up to his intention of 'doing the civil' to Mildred, said, 'I believe you live in a boarding house – or should I say a private hotel? (He was pleased with that touch of civility.) My wife and I spent nearly a year in one, once, when we were between houses. I hope you find the food more satisfactory than we did.'

'Oh, I expect so,' said Mildred. 'But I never notice what I'm eating.' She continued to spoon up one of May's most exquisite cold soups.

Baggy shot a quick glance at May and caught her eye. She gave him a fractional wink, to which he responded with a feeling of great pleasure. In spite of the fact that May was unfailingly kind to him he found her, as he had never found June, a little formidable. The exchanged wink gave him a sense of assurance, somehow incorporated him more fully into the Dower House family, made him an accredited member of the gang, as opposed to non-gang Mildred. So warmly happy did he feel that he again treated her to 'the civil' and at last succeeded in getting a conversation going. Mildred, in fact, became slightly coy, and there was a general easing of tension.

Still, Fran was glad when lunch was over and Mildred went to get ready for her walk. She returned swinging a very small silk handbag by its drawstring. Fran, whose irritation had been dwindling, now softened completely. With genuine – if momentary – affection, she said, 'Oh, Mildred, we used to have little bags like that when we were children. Didn't Mother call them "Dorothy bags"?'

'I don't remember,' said Mildred coldly.

Fran sighed. Probably her remark about the Dorothy bag had been taken as an implication that the bag was old-fashioned. Well, it was more than that; it was archaic.

'We'll start you on your way, Auntie,' said June. 'And you can see our cottage.'

'Just at the moment I only need *woods*, dear,' said Mildred.

'I'll show you how to get to them quickly,' said Robert. 'And then go back home and do some work, June.'

They all escorted Mildred out.

'Isn't our lilac lovely?' said June.

'Just past its best, isn't it?' said Mildred, then sneezed delicately.

'Perhaps it gives you hay fever,' said Robert. 'I'll take you through the park.'

May called after Mildred, 'Tea's at four-thirty.'

Mildred called back to May, 'Oh, I never know the time. Watches won't go on me. I've too much electricity.'

Fran called, 'Well, come back sometime.'

'If only she wouldn't!' May whispered. 'Mother, she's worse than ever. She's impossible.'

'I know, I know,' said Fran. 'But I give you my word that nothing she says is *intended* to annoy. She simply speaks what comes into her head, like a child.'

'She's not in the least like a child,' said May. 'Children can be brutally frank but they can also be enthusiastic. They like lots of things. She never praised anything at all. My God, she even sneezed at the lilac.'

Fran laughed. 'I don't *think* that was intended as a comment.'

'I hadn't realised the lilac was past its best,' said June. 'How I shall miss it when it's over.'

'It'll come again next year,' said Baggy kindly.

May put her arms through his. 'How marvellous you were at lunch, Baggy. You're as good as George at stringing old Mildred along. Well, we're free of her for an hour or so, though it'll take me all of that to press her dresses. Come and talk to me while I do it, June.'

Fran went to see Penny. Baggy went to his room intending to take a nap. Settling in his armchair – he seldom lay on the bed during the day – he felt pleased with himself. What was that phrase May had used? Ah, yes, he remembered it. He returned the wide grin of his felt frog and mentally told it, 'George and I will string her along together.' He would not have admitted that he talked to his frog, even mentally. He merely thought thoughts at it.

Upstairs Fran, having brought 'the creature' into her bedroom, stood at the window looking out. She could see Mildred, minus Robert now, tripping gaily through the park. At least, Fran hoped she was tripping gaily, undistressed by the contretemps before lunch. She was certainly tripping, and swinging that absurd Dorothy bag. What would she be thinking about them all? But here Fran pulled her thoughts up. Mildred would only be thinking about Mildred.

13

Fran was wrong. Mildred, after Robert left her to make her own way, spent some little time thinking about them all and feeling disappointed. But apart from her irritation with Fran about Penny, nothing said or done had actually distressed her. She was disappointed simply because nobody had provided any food for her imagination.

From her childhood, the chief pleasure of her life had been to tell herself stories about people. She had always been secretive about this, partly because she had as a child vaguely equated 'making things up' with telling lies, and even more because she was guiltily conscious that the most pleasurable stories were erotic in content. She was possessed of, and by, a powerful imagination of a very freakish kind in as much as it was entirely focused on her own conception of people; she had no interest in what they might be feeling, and therefore no insight into it – hence her complete lack of realisation when she was being annoying. She did not try to please or displease and had no idea that she was an instinctive displeaser or why she was.

In her youth she, herself, had been the heroine of all her stories. (The heroes had been actors, other celebrities and, quite often, unknown men whose faces, seen on a bus, in the street, in a newspaper, had attracted her. Once she had seen a man driving a four-in-hand and made use of him for weeks.) But for many years now she had found it difficult to imagine about herself, because she liked her heroines to be young, and to think of herself as young not only put a strain on her imagination but also made her conscious that she wasn't young. So she bowed out of her imaginings and was always on the lookout for attractive and inspiring younger people. Television had provided good material but no longer did. Girls' skirts were too short, men's hair too long. Actors and celebrities weren't what they'd once been. She was also in need of new settings for her stories and had counted on the Dower House to provide them.

Well, so it might, she told herself, tripping towards the woods. And it was absurd to be disappointed just because the company at lunch hadn't been inspiring. How could she have expected it to be? She had sometimes thought that June might be used as a romantic heroine (if on the old side) but her perfectly happy marriage to Robert was dull. May wasn't in the least romantic and had no right to be married to such an attractive man as George – though Mildred admitted that May handled him sensibly and had long ago congratulated her on this, saying how wise it was to accept that some men had to have many women in their lives. George, ah, George! He was a rake – a word Mildred loved. She'd have no hesitation in imagining his rakish adventures if she could lay eyes on some exciting girl.

Fran and Baggy… would it be interesting to imagine them falling in love with each other? It would not. In the days when Mildred had been her own heroine Fran had often played a part in the same story, a subsidiary part and coming out of things pretty badly. But Fran, now… no, highly unromantic. Baggy had been nicer than Mildred had expected. Would it be possible to imagine a romance between Baggy and herself? The idea startled her so much that she stopped dead, to consider it. But no, it wouldn't do: that shapeless old man. It was, however, interesting that she had momentarily considered imagining about *herself* again… rather exciting.

She reached a small wood which, Robert had told her, contained nightingales. But it was too tangled for easy walking. She went on until she came to a wood where the walking would be easy. And here she would take a rest. But she soon found that this wood didn't invite sitters. There was no grass beneath these old, heavily leafed trees. It didn't occur to her to wonder what kind of trees these were; she simply knew they weren't the kind she wanted. What she did want were lithe, young trees with the sunlight filtering through their rustling leaves. She also wanted something she thought of as a mossy bank.

For some minutes she continued walking without pleasure. Then she saw sunlight ahead and shortly came, if not to a mossy bank, to a place where the trees were thin and there was grass which invited her to sit on it. She sat, and spread her flowered skirt around her. She must, she felt, surveying her small green shoes, look very like an illustration to a fairy tale. But her imagination no longer functioned in fairyland. She let her thoughts drift where they willed.

Would they be missing her at her hotel? (*Of course* it was a hotel, not a boarding house.) Most of them were staying on, in discomfort, during the redecorations. Such dear, devoted people, they all counted on her – but alas, such dear *dull* people; it was years since any of them had offered food to her imagination. At this time of the afternoon most of them would be taking a nap, as she normally would herself. It would be pleasant to fall asleep in this place – could one describe it as a 'glade'? A glade was even more romantic than a mossy bank. She lay down, closed her eyes and smiled, imagined her serene face under the afternoon sunlight, imagined how she would look to anyone coming out of the dark wood.

And then a really valuable memory stirred, a memory of a daydream she had made use of again and again when she was a girl. It had begun when she went for a picnic all by herself in some woods – where? That didn't matter. She had thought of

163

herself as a nymph, and there had been a creature…a faun, a satyr? Ah, now she remembered, it had been the great god, Pan. She hadn't used that daydream for years and years – and now it was potent again. And it was about *herself*, an ageless self just as Pan was ageless. She must on no account open her eyes; that would break the spell. She must lie there *waiting*.

Pan would be ruthless. He would tear her clothes off. No, clothes were unsuitable. She mentally removed them, allowing herself only the kind of clothing suitable for a nymph… wisps of chiffon, a few leaves. Then she removed even those. She would lie here naked, under the sun. A hot wind blew from the cool forest, Pan was coming, there was no escape. He was here, above her.

It was no use. She couldn't sustain the daydream. She was suddenly conscious of the hard ground and something crawling over her instep. She sat up and felt dizzy, not from bliss but because lying flat on her back always did make her dizzy… something to do with blood pressure but her doctor assured her it was normal for 'a woman of your age'. The remembered phrase hit her unpleasantly.

Dizziness passed. She removed the caterpillar from her ankle. It had been a mistake to think about *herself* as a nymph, to have wasted such a wonderful resurgence of imagination. But perhaps it wouldn't be wasted. She might revive it if she could think of a suitable nymph. Perhaps when she saw Corinna at the weekend… Up to now, Mildred's imagination had refused to be interested in Corinna and Hugh; a romance between two innocents was just plain dull. But it would be all right to have an innocent nymph, seeing that Pan would be anything but innocent. Yes, Corinna as a nymph (terrified) was a distinct possibility.

But it would probably be better to concentrate on George – and she'd want to, once she'd seen him again. He would be wonderful to imagine about, if only she could find him some beautiful woman. Perhaps she'd see someone on television or – yes, this was an idea – he might have a glamorous secretary. Mildred tried to visualise her and tried to visualise George in his city office; it would be an imposing place such as tycoons on television favoured. Soon he would say a few last charming words to the secretary (the romance between them should, as yet, only be budding) and then stride out to a powerful car – Mildred had been told that he almost always made the journey by train but she preferred him in a powerful car, tearing through open country. Dear George! Dear rakish George! She would wear her newest dress for him tonight.

It would have pleased her to know that he was, at the moment, thinking of her.

He had left the City early and come to Piccadilly to do some shopping, his first purchase being an expensive box of liqueur chocolates for 'poor old Mildew'. She was undoubtedly a nuisance but probably not as black as she was painted in family discussions – and he could be as down on her as any of the others. In the mellow mood induced by spending money on her he decided she was merely a slightly dotty old lady, more to be pitied than disliked.

Wondering if he should also buy chocolates for Fran it occurred to him that he never thought of *her* as any kind of old lady, merely as an intelligent and most likeable woman – and Fran was three years older than Mildred and, though she looked young for her age, she didn't look as young as Mildred did for hers. But there was something freakish about Mildred's preserved youth, and the word 'preserved' described it well. It was a sort of frozen youth. Perhaps she suffered from a new disease, deferred age, and would suddenly crumple and decay. He must tell May that – but on second thoughts, he wouldn't, as it might not awake May's tolerance but simply increase her dislike for Mildred, which wouldn't add to anyone's comfort. He finally dismissed his wife's aunt from his mind with a valedictory thought that early and frequent rape might have made a different woman of her – and why she couldn't have come by it, or a respectable equivalent, he simply couldn't imagine, seeing that she must have been a beauty. Something odd there. He'd once asked Fran about it but got no change out of her.

Regretfully, he decided against chocolates for Fran; it would detract from Mildred's. The same applied to May and June; anyway, the three of them were always thinking about their weight. Personally, he thought May ought to put on a little; her type of prettiness needed to guard against skinniness. June was just right at present. He had only recently realised that she could sometimes look quite voluptuously beautiful. He wished she could have more money to spend on clothes. Now that they lived so close to each other May never bought any clothes for herself without buying the equivalent for June, but they were only wearing simple summer dresses. He would have liked to see June in something rich – and she would conveniently be having a birthday sometime this month. He'd discuss it with May.

Coming out of Fortnum and Mason's at the back, he made his way to Piccadilly past the side windows. There was an amber negligée which would look well on June. He'd have liked to buy it but it might not be much use to her in the country. Still, he'd describe it to May. What else should he buy today and for whom? He was in the mood for spending but rather lacking in ideas. He didn't need anything himself and, anyway, he only got a kick out of spending money on other people. It was his form of gratitude for happiness and he was at present extremely happy. For that matter, he'd been happy ever since they'd moved to the country but the happiness had increased, most noticeably, just lately. Why, exactly? Summer weather?

Today was delightful, even in London, and would be more so when he got back to the country. Not that he had any particular longing to get out of town. He felt kindly disposed to the jostling crowds in Piccadilly, particularly to all the girls in their preposterously short skirts which made one long to pat their bottoms – merely as a friendly gesture; he was conscious of no sexual drive behind the thought. Indeed, he had been conscious of no extra-marital sexual drive behind any thought for months. Most peculiar, especially considering that he had, at the moment, an enchantingly pretty secretary who, though equipped with a steady boyfriend whom she intended eventually to marry, had managed to indicate that she was capable of driving a tandem. George, while liking her very much, had never felt a flicker of temptation. That kind of thing was *out*. And not simply on May's account. When moving to the country he had only sworn to himself that no more goings-on should take place under her nose. He hadn't sworn that the close season would operate in London.

Odder still was the fact that his mood today strongly resembled feelings he was apt to have when about to start a new affair. At such times the happiness that was normal for him was increased in a way which never failed to astonish him. Exhilaration and, surprisingly, peacefulness combined to achieve a sense of *complete rightness* – never did he feel in the least guilty. Not, that is, just before or during the affair. He had felt retrospective guilt – also prospective guilt, for he had always been certain there were other affairs ahead. Now he felt no such certainty and he had no desire to.

167

Perhaps he was settling down, getting middle-aged; but if so, he had no sense of loss. He had never felt more contented. Summer, the country to go home to, the two households… what a success it had been, linking up with Robert and June. Yes, everything was *right*.

Rightness, for George, was the equivalent of God's will to the religious. If he felt it about a state of mind, he accepted it unquestioningly. If it applied to a course of action, he was grateful for such guidance. He considered himself a shrewd businessman but he frequently made decisions which had nothing to do with shrewdness. He just saw them as 'right', knew he had been given the go-ahead. Later, he had been known to say to himself, 'My God, I must have been psychic.' But he didn't really believe that. It was simply that he had the knack of recognising 'rightness'.

The only thing that wasn't 'right' this afternoon was that he had an itch to spend money and didn't know what to spend it on. Then he sighted Hatchards. Of course! He could take home a present of books for the two households. That wouldn't detract from the 'special favour' of old Mildred's chocolates. She could share in the books – though, according to Fran, Mildred seldom read a book. 'You see,' Fran had explained, 'books aren't about *her*.'

He spent a happy half-hour in Hatchards, using his flair for knowing which books were likely to interest which members of the family. Then, heavily laden, he took a taxi to Liverpool Street Station. For once he didn't feel like joining convivial acquaintances in the buffet car ('rightness' was better savoured in solitude) so he found a quiet compartment and spent a pleasant hour glancing at the books he'd bought… a pity he didn't get more time for reading.

It was warm in the train, even on the non-sunny side. He was glad to get out on to the windy platform. Mysteriously, it was always windy, even when there was scarcely any wind; today, in the station yard, there was only a light breeze. Pleasant to see so many welcoming wives, children and dogs – though he hadn't any desire to be welcomed himself; he always enjoyed his solitary drive home. Not for the first time, it struck him how remarkable it was to see so many dozens of cars parked outside quite a small country station. Soon the supply of country properties suitable for commuters would run out. He wished they could buy the Dower House instead of renting it. But they'd got it for five years and could probably renew their lease. He drove back to it, with the car windows all down, feeling as benign as the early evening air.

As he entered the house he saw May coming from the kitchen with a filmy pink dress over her arm. He said, 'Hello! That looks very fetching.'

'Positively dreamy but don't imagine it's mine. I wouldn't be seen in anything so juvenile. Aunt Mildred will soon be delighting your eyes in it. I managed to get three of her four evening dresses pressed before tea but she *particularly* wanted this one. Just let me take it up to her and then I'll get you a drink.'

'I'll get *you* one.' He had noticed that she looked both flushed and tired. 'Shall I take it upstairs?'

'Oh, do. I simply must get some peace before dinner.'

He got the drinks and carried them up to the bedroom. The evening sun was shining on the windows, which stood wide open. There was enough breeze to stir the flowery chintz curtains and the air was both warm and fresh. He could smell newly cut grass; May had persuaded a retired gardener to come out of retirement for her.

She came in smiling cheerfully but obviously hot and tired.

'Lie down for a bit,' he told her, putting her drink on her bedside table.

'Yes, I think I will. I've got a couple of Matsons here. They'll dish up for me.'

She took off her dress and lay down in her slip, closing her eyes. George got out of his town suit, washed at the fitted basin, and put on a short-sleeved shirt and some thin slacks. He said nothing as he thought she might have fallen asleep, but eventually she opened her eyes and said, 'What sort of a day?'

'Pretty good. How about yours? Has the old girl been worse than usual?'

'Not really. And we got a nice long rest from her this afternoon. Then she strolled in saying she was gasping for tea an hour after it was cleared away. Still, that wasn't much skin off my nose.'

George looked at her closely. 'Then what was?'

'I suppose it's just sheer dread of having her here for a whole fortnight. She's never actually stayed with us before – one advantage of having no spare room in the flat. Oh, I'm probably being ridiculous but...'

She left the sentence trailing so long that he prodded her. 'Well?'

'I feel... a sort of indescribable horror of her. It's a bit as if she had leprosy or something – except that I'd feel sorry for a leper and I don't feel one bit sorry for her. I just feel she's a repulsive kind of menace. Go on, tell me I'm being fantastically silly.'

'Well, of course you are,' said George, kindly. 'And you're also being fantastically unlike yourself.' So much so that he felt worried about her. May did not go in for vague horrors. 'Now you take it from me that she's an annoying old thing but perfectly harmless. Do you know of any real harm she's ever done anyone?'

'Yes!' said May instantly, then avoided his eyes. 'That is, Fran's told me things.' Untrue, and most unfair to Fran who rarely said a word against Mildred. What would he feel, May wondered, if she disclosed that her first jealous suspicions of him had been awakened by 'harmless' old Mildred, who had thus forever deprived her of peace of mind? 'Oh, well, sorry to be a bore.' She sat up and drank her drink.

George sat down beside her and stroked her neck soothingly. 'Anyway, don't bother with Mildred this evening. Don't talk to her, don't even listen to her. Leave her to me.'

'You are kind.'

'Good. I *feel* kind.'

She was smitten by a tiny anxiety. George was never less than kind; kindness was the keynote of his character. But she had come to realise that he was especially kind when about to embark on an affair. (Not that, even mentally, she used that word. She still, in spite of bloody, bloody Aunt Mildred, thought in such terms as George's 'goings-on', 'nonsenses', still hoped that she hoped for the best.) She didn't believe the extra kindness was an attempt to lull her suspicions. She guessed he was lovingly trying to compensate for any unhappiness he might cause. She accepted the love lovingly – but was apt to become, as it were, alerted. Ought she to be alerted now? She doubted it. He surely couldn't have the time for nonsense, coming home every night and every weekend and with most days not long enough for all the work he had to do. This was kindness without strings to it, and she very much liked having her neck stroked. But she had to get ready for dinner.

She got up, saying, 'Well, you've done me a power of good. Bless you, darling.'

'Do you want another drink?'

'Not till we go down. I'll have to hurry. Keep a look out for Robert and June, will you?'

George went to a window. 'They're just arriving. June's got a lovely new dress. Golden satin.'

'*What*?' May dashed to the window. 'Oh, that! It's only one of the new satinized cottons. I've got a blue one, made the same way. We ran them up together.' This really meant that May had run them up while June kept her company.

'Well, wear yours tonight. I like my women to swish around in long evening dresses of satinized cotton or what the hell it is. Let's ask Fran to wear a long dress too.'

'I doubt if she's brought one. She doesn't like hiding those spectacular legs.'

Fran came out through the French window and went to meet Robert and June. She was wearing a long-sleeved white shift that just covered her knees, and heavy gold jewellery.

'Anyway, she looks very nice,' said George. 'Wonderful woman, Fran. Good God!'

Almost on Fran's heels came Mildred, in pink, frilled mousseline de soie, the waist up under her arms which dangled from little puffed sleeves. The dress reached to her calves and below it were frilled pantalettes and pink dancing sandals with crossed elastics. Ignoring the group now formed by Fran, Robert and June, she tripped over to the lilac grove, stood on tiptoe with her feet close together, and pulled down a spray to smell. The pose perfectly suggested an illustration to some long-ago child's picture book.

'I tell you, she's round the bend,' said May.

'Is she doing it for effect or just to please herself?'

'Well, she can't know we're looking at her and the others haven't noticed her. I honestly believe she just likes the thought of herself doing it. She's abnormal, George.'

'She certainly looks abnormally young. It's miraculous.'

At that moment she tilted her head farther back and the wings of silvery fair hair fell away from her cheeks, revealing her temples, cheek bones and jawline, all of which were strongly illuminated by the sunset. For an instant the delicate bones looked skull-like; the face, in the dramatic lighting, became that of an ancient woman. Then she lowered her head and the soft hair fell into position again.

'That was a painful moment,' said George.

'Looked like a zombie, didn't she?'

'Piling it on a bit, aren't you?' But the truth was that, although he had been stabbed by pity, he had momentarily experienced some of May's revulsion. There *was* something… uncanny, unnatural about Mildred's composite childhood and old age. But he pushed the idea away from him. 'Are we giving her champagne, as it's her first night?'

'Oh, sure. I knew you'd want to. I should think she'd get tight ever so cutely.'

'Well, put on your lush satinized cotton and let's go down.'

14

The following Friday Hugh was not able to get away from London until mid-evening and then he was minus Corinna. He had been to see her perform at her drama school, expecting that they would afterwards start for the country together. But he found she had been invited to some party given by a fellow student, to which she felt she ought to go; and though she offered to ask if he might come with her, he doubted if she really wanted him to, and he had no desire to. On the few occasions when he had met her friends at the drama school he had felt ill at ease with them. Besides, he wanted to get back to Penny. His Uncle George had, that morning, reported that she was doing a good deal of whimpering; also that three large dogs had been seen in the lane. Penny obviously needed consolation and a man to protect her when she was exercised.

The next available train was a slow one without a buffet car. Hugh planned to get a sandwich at Liverpool Street Station but did not get time for it; he barely caught the train. He hadn't even time to pick up an evening paper so, throughout the tedious journey, he had nothing to do but think. And he didn't enjoy his thoughts.

He was worried about Corinna. He had just seen her playing Celia in *As You Like It* and she had undoubtedly made a success; indeed, judging by the comments he had overheard, she had out-acted the Rosalind. He, himself, couldn't judge. He had always found it embarrassing to watch Corinna act. Earlier, he had taken it for granted that this was because she wasn't any good and he was distressed for her. But now she was obviously very good indeed, yet he was still embarrassed. Why? The nearest he could get to an answer was that he didn't like seeing her pretending to be someone else. Utterly unreasonable, of course; there must be more to it than that. Perhaps he was jealous of the men she acted with. He didn't feel he was but he did, somehow, resent them. They were all so ill-groomed. (He was rather particularly well-groomed; he felt this was expected of him in his Uncle's City office.) Perhaps Corinna liked ill-groomed young men.

Anyway, he now knew for certain that she liked 'Sir Harry' far more than she had ever admitted. What was more, she had given quite a false impression of him, making him sound like an old man to whom she was pleasant only in the interest of her work. Hugh had twice seen him act but only in classical, bewigged roles and had been unprepared for the barely middle-aged man with an extremely with-it hair cut whom he had met for the first time that evening. Corinna, at the end of the play, had come down to the auditorium of the school's little theatre to talk to Hugh, and Sir Harry had come to congratulate her on her performance. And if Corinna admired Sir Harry any less than Sir Harry admired her she was a better actress off the stage than on it – which Hugh simply didn't believe. She'd always had difficulty in hiding her feelings and was as bad at – to use their childhood's phrase – 'acting a lie' as at telling one.

What was she up to? Hugh didn't for a moment fear that she had fallen for Sir Harry. The idea was too revolting to contemplate and an insult to Corinna. But she hadn't been behaving with her usual transparent sincerity. Perhaps, thought Hugh gloomily, she's frightened of making me jealous. If so it was idiotic – and also worrying, for surely their joint ideal had always been perfect honesty with each other? And a Corinna who wasn't sincere wasn't really Corinna.

He began to think back. Had she been at all different lately? He hadn't seen much of her during the past week; she'd had a lot of evening rehearsals. But last weekend, surely she had been herself then? They had listened to the nightingale together, after that long discussion about Aunt Mildred. (Oh, God, *she* lay ahead of him.) He thought back to other weekends, Easter especially. How sweet Corinna had been about Penny. Oh, he was imagining things, because he was disappointed that Corinna wasn't coming down with him. After all, if she'd become a good actress on the stage she could have become one off it, and all her admiration for Sir Harry had just been cleverness. Perhaps she really did see Sir Harry as an old man. Surely she couldn't be attracted by that awful hair which looked more bitten than cut. Anyway, she'd be down tomorrow and they'd straighten everything out.

The train stopped. He remembered that he had to change – this train, as well as being slow and minus refreshments, didn't go all the way. The train he changed into was even slower, extremely jerky, and made alarming creaking noises. And when he finally arrived it was raining heavily, there was a shortage of taxis and the one he finally got didn't know the way to the Dower House so took longer and charged more than was normal – all very unlike the usual Friday evening journeys when he, Corinna and Uncle George all came home together looking forward to one of May's dinners.

The front of the Dower House was in darkness. Glancing up at the window of Penny's prison he thought, 'Well, they might have left the poor love a light' – but perhaps she'd be less restless without one. As he entered the hall he heard the television in the Long Room. He'd better let them know he was back before going up to Penny.

He opened the door so quietly that no one heard him. The room was in darkness except for the television screen, but he took in that his parents, his uncle and aunt, Baggy and Fran were there; and there was someone else, a young girl – or was it a child? – sitting on the floor, close to the screen. Good God, it was his Great-Aunt Mildred, in some kind of fancy dress. She must be madder, even, than his Uncle George had reported.

The person nearest to him was his mother who, that moment, turned and saw him. He sat down on the arm of her chair, kissed her, and whispered, 'I'm going up to Penny,' then hurried upstairs looking forward to an ecstatic welcome.

Would she bark or instantly recognise him and thump her tail? He opened the door quietly. No sound came from her; she must be very heavily asleep. Then he saw, by the light from the landing, that her basket was empty. Was she in the armchair? He switched the light on.

She wasn't anywhere – and as the room only contained her basket and the armchair for her visitors there was nowhere she could be hiding. He dashed to the window, a heavy, sashed window and open only a few inches, at the top. No danger there.

Could someone have taken Penny out? But surely not in this rain – besides, they'd all been in the Long Room, watching television. Perhaps Penny was with them. If she was with Fran, who was sitting at the back of the room near the door to the kitchen, he wouldn't have been able to see her. But wouldn't his mother have told him?

He went down to the kitchen, which for once was free of Matsons, quietly opened the door to the Long Room, and approached Fran. She looked up at him and smiled.

He whispered, 'Is Penny here?'

'No, she's upstairs,' said Fran.

'But she isn't. Her room's empty.'

Fran looked startled, then said, 'Ssh. I'll come out.'

They both went into the kitchen where Fran said, 'I simply can't believe I left her door open.'

'You didn't, darling. It was firmly closed. Could one of the Matsons have let her out?'

'There was only the official one here today, and I'm sure she wouldn't. She was saying only this evening when Penny was howling, "Better howl now, my girl, than howl later." Oh, I'm certain Mrs Matson wouldn't have done it.'

'Then what?'

For a moment Fran was silent. Then she murmured, '*Oh, no! She couldn't!*'

'Who couldn't?'

'Mildred. She *has* been moaning about the cruelty of keeping Penny shut up but I can't believe – Wait! No, don't come with me. Wait!'

Fran went back to the Long Room and made her way to Mildred who was still sitting on the floor. Stooping, Fran said quietly, 'Mildred, did you let Penny out?'

Mildred took no notice.

Fran knelt and repeated the question more loudly.

Mildred said, 'Ssh! I'm watching television.'

'The hell you are,' said Fran. 'Did you or did you not let Hugh's dog out?'

'Is Hugh back?'

'Yes,' said Fran. 'Mildred…'

Mildred interrupted her, 'Then you can tell him from me that it's time he knew the facts of life. His poor dog's craving to be mated.'

Fran, still speaking quietly, but very forcefully, said, 'Answer me. Did you let her out? And I warn you that, unless you answer, I shall slap your face.' Half a dozen times in her life Fran had slapped Mildred's face and it had always been a great success.

Mildred let out a shriek, 'George, George! Save me!'

George rose hastily. Owing to the noise made by the television he had no idea what the row was about but it seemed to him likely that the two small, elderly ladies were about to batter each other. He reached them quickly, saying, 'What is all this?' and turned the television sound down.

Mildred instantly clasped him round the knees, wailing, 'Don't let her hurt me – please!'

George, almost overbalancing on top of Mildred, said, 'For God's sake! Now stop it, Aunt Mildred. Nobody's going to hurt you.'

Fran said, 'I'm sorry, George, but they are, that is, I am – unless she tells me if she let Hugh's dog out. Now come on, Mildred, and be quick about it.'

Mildred clasped George's legs even tighter, murmuring into the knees of his trousers, 'No, no! She'll kill me!'

'Leave this to me, Fran,' said George and then tried to get away from Mildred. Failing to do so, he addressed the top of her head. 'All right, Aunt Mildred. I won't let her hit you. But if you don't answer her question you'll leave this house tomorrow and you'll never come into it again. Now: did you let Penny out?'

Mildred instantly released him, flung back her head and looked up at him with flashing eyes. This was magnificent. She was all the rebellious heroines she'd ever longed to be. And she was thrillingly defying her hero, George. 'Yes, I did!' she cried. 'And I'd do it again. And you, of all people, should understand.'

George, wisely ignoring the last sentence, said, 'How long ago was this?'

'It was after dinner. I happened to go upstairs and I heard her crying most piteously so I went in to comfort her. And when I left, the door didn't quite close itself so she followed me.'

'And you closed the door behind her so that none of us would suspect,' said Fran furiously.

'I don't remember. Perhaps the wind closed it. Anyway, she followed me downstairs and went to the front door. So I flung it open. I let her go free.'

'Into the pouring rain?' said Fran.

'As if that mattered. I sent her to find her mate.'

Fran reckoned up. 'She must have been out in that deluge for well over an hour. Have you any idea which way she went?'

'Certainly not. And I'm not talking to you any more. I'm only talking to George – and Hugh, yes, talk to Hugh. I'll tell him…'

'You will not,' said Fran. 'George, don't let her out of this room. Go on watching television, all of you. Leave Hugh to me.'

She turned the television up full volume – most suitably, gun fire came from it – then dashed towards the kitchen, just in time to intercept Hugh as he came through the door. She pushed him back into the kitchen, asking him how much he'd heard.

'Enough,' said Hugh. 'Fran, didn't she understand? Didn't anyone explain to her why Penny couldn't be mated yet?'

'We explained everything – all about Penny's smallness and nervousness, not to mention that one doesn't want a pure-bred bitch to have mongrel puppies. I told her again and again. Mildred's simply not normal – not that I usually admit that. Oh, my dear Hugh, I'm so terribly sorry.'

'I must go out and search,' said Hugh.

Fran glanced at the kitchen window. 'But it's raining harder than ever. You can't go out in this.'

'*She's* out in it. And Sarah warned me never to let her get wet through. Oh, God damn that crazy old hag.'

Angry though she was with Mildred, Fran winced at such a description. 'It's just that she's a bit childish, and wrapped up in a sort of dream world.'

'It's kinder to think of her as crazy,' said Hugh. 'Hell, my mackintosh is at the cottage.'

'Take George's. He won't mind.'

'And I must find a torch.'

They went into the hall. Fran, helping him into George's Burberry, said, 'But where are you going to look? Surely it's hopeless tonight?'

'I must do something. It's most likely she streaked for the Hall – she's apt to do that at any time. Anyway, there was no sign of her in the lane as I came home – and no waiting dogs. Perhaps the rain drove them away. Were there any earlier on?'

'I didn't see any when I took her out before dinner but we only went in the lilac grove. If she'd gone to the Hall, wouldn't Sarah have telephoned?'

'Penny might have taken shelter in some stable or outhouse. Anyway, I'm going to hunt.'

He found a torch and was testing it just as May and June came from the Long Room. Fran said hastily, 'Don't let Mildred out.'

'It's all right,' said May. 'She's now busy telling the men how right she was. Gosh, I was disappointed when George stopped you slapping her.'

June said, 'Darling Hugh, you *can't* go out in this downpour.'

'No arguments, Mother dear. And please don't wait up for me. Just leave the cottage door unlocked.'

As he hurried out May called after him, 'Hugh, wait! Have you had any dinner?'

He took no notice, beyond rather wishing she hadn't reminded him of food. It was at least nine hours since he'd had any… not that he was hungry.

He went some way along the lane, flashing his torch and calling Penny's name. But it was much more likely that she'd dashed into the park – unless, horrible thought, she'd got as far as the road and been run over. Well, if she had, it was too late to help her. He must concentrate on the thought of her alive and find her before she caught her death of cold. But suppose she'd been hit by a car and only maimed, was lying in the road suffering... he tried to put the idea out of his head. The park and Hall must come first. If he had no luck there, he'd walk all the way to the village, searching.

He turned into the park. Now that he was away from the dripping trees in the lane the rain was less heavy than he'd thought it was, but the grass was soaking wet. Of course he needed rubber boots. He'd get some at the cottage – and see if Penny, by any glorious chance, was sheltering in the porch. But she wasn't and, for once, his parents had locked both the front and back door. No rubber boots.

He went back to the park. The rain, praise be to God, had now actually stopped but there was a ground mist so thick that the beam of his torch only penetrated it for a few yards. He could not see the Hall at all, and in a few minutes he felt almost directionless. He looked back and could still see the roof of the cottage. He retraced his steps and got his bearings. It would be better not to make diagonally for the Hall but to walk in a straight line towards the first little wood. When he reached it he felt sure he would be able to see the Hall. Incidentally, Penny just might have gone to the woods as she was sometimes taken for walks there, as were Sarah's spaniels, it having been many years since old Mr Strange had preserved his pheasants.

Now that the rain had stopped the night was surprisingly warm. Hugh, striding towards the wood, felt stickily hot – except for his feet, which were most depressingly cold. He took off his uncle's very superior Burberry – he must try not to damage it

– and felt better, though he had never known air to seem so air-less. Ah, there was the wood, looming ahead of him. And believe it or not, the nightingale was singing. What a night to choose for it! Though, now he came to think of it, he'd once heard a song about nightingales in the rain. Perhaps it was pleased the rain had stopped.

Only last Sunday he and Corinna had stood here listening… Well, at least his anxiety about Penny had driven his worries about Corinna out of his head. But they'd come back, once he found his dog – if he ever did. Oh, of course he would, sooner or later but… Standing at the edge of the wood, with the nightingale giving a star performance, he made himself face the fact that Penny's chances were far from good. A delicate bitch, in her first season, exposed to such rain as there had been… and even if that didn't kill her, a too-early pregnancy might. It was going to be Bonnie all over again, only worse than Bonnie as she, herself, had come out of it all right. Oh, blast that crazy old Mildred! Even over Bonnie she'd made things worse, by prying into the misery he'd been trying to hide and then telling him to be a manly little boy. Loathsome Mildred!

He pulled his thoughts up, shone his torch into the wood, called Penny's name and whistled. He wasn't a very good whistler.

The nightingale stopped singing; perhaps it resented compe-tition. Anyway, he was grateful to it for giving his dog a better chance to hear him. If she did, surely she'd bark or whimper or he'd hear her coming towards him? He listened, silently. No sound came from the wood. He called and whistled again. Still he heard nothing in reply. She wasn't there. He'd have to go to the Hall, search the stables…

And then, just as he turned away from the wood… surely that was a whimper? Or had he imagined it? He called again but got no response. He achieved the most piercing whistle of his life. Yes! That was more than a whimper, it was a wail – but so faint, so distant. Again he whistled.

The nightingale, surprisingly, restarted singing, giving a performance worthy of Covent Garden. Really, he couldn't hear himself whistle. He banged his torch against the trunk of a tree and shouted, 'Shut up, you bloody bird.' All the talk about nightingales being timid must be rubbish. Still, it did at last stop singing.

And now the wailing changed to Penny's yap, though it was only a weak one. Oh, God, was she caught in some trap? He had never seen any traps and he doubted if there was anyone attached to the Hall who would set one. But did country people still set rabbit snares? Penny's yap seemed so far ahead that she might be beyond the wood, on some farmer's land. But at least she was alive.

There was a path through this wood, he remembered, but he couldn't waste time trying to locate it. He plunged in between the trees, swinging his torch from side to side though he was sure she was still some way ahead. Walking wasn't easy but the wood wasn't deep and fairly soon he came to a grassy clearing where he hoped to spot Penny, but there was no sign of her.

Beyond him now was a real thicket where it would be easy to miss her but he felt sure that her yappings, now continuous, were straight ahead. And surely they were nearer?

He struggled on through the thicket until he came out into the open again – as represented by a treeless mist. And now her yappings seemed near at hand, really close to him. He swung his torch into the mist. Why couldn't he see her? He stepped forward a few paces.

And then he stepped on air, found himself sliding down the bank of a mist-obscured pond, and only stopped sliding when he was knee-deep in water. The torch shot out of his hand and fell with a splash – and on its way, just for an instant, it showed him Penny. She was only a few yards away from him, her hind-quarters in the pond, her front paws scrabbling at the steep, muddy bank.

The torch was still shining at the bottom of the pond but it gave no useful light. Still, he now knew more or less where Penny was. He heaved himself on to solid ground and made his way towards her, calling endearments and encouragements. He couldn't see her but he knew when she was below him by the noise she made. He reached down, felt her scrabbling paws. She was nowhere near the top of the bank and he feared she might slip backwards into the water. He slid down the bank again, managed to get a fairly firm foot hold, got his arm under her behind and heaved her up. At the last second his foot-hold gave way and he slid down into the pond up to his thighs. He struggled out, frantically groping for Penny. Had she fallen backwards? To his enormous relief he found she was now on dry land – even if she and it happened to be sopping wet.

The torch now went out. Without its eerie glimmer he was in utter darkness. He hugged Penny, murmuring comforting words, tried to dry her head on his handkerchief. Much good that would do; every inch of her was soaked. He wondered if he could get her inside his jacket. Then he remembered he'd been carrying his uncle's Burberry. Had that gone into the pond when he fell? Holding tight to Penny he crawled to the place where he had first slipped down the bank – at least, he hoped it was the same place. He was in luck. He found himself on top of the Burberry. It must have shot off his arm.

He sat on the ground and wrapped Penny in it, patting it against her, hoping its dry inside would blot her a little. It wouldn't do much. She needed to be dried completely, given a warm drink, perhaps brandy. But it was all he could do for the moment.

How the hell could he get her – and himself – through the thicket in this pitch blackness? It had been none too easy making his way, even with a torch. He told himself his eyes would get used to the darkness – but not enough, he felt sure. Could he *crawl* through? It was conceivable, if he had both hands free to feel his way. But not if he had to carry Penny and he was sure she wouldn't be able to follow him. Even if he had remembered to bring a leash he couldn't have dragged her through the thicket. Indeed, he doubted if she could keep on her feet. He began to fear they'd have to stay where they were until daybreak.

How long would that mean? Recently he had woken up at 4 a.m. and there had been a glimmer of daylight then. But he doubted if, as yet, it could be much past ten o'clock. The thought of sitting here for six hours was sheer horror and might be fatal to the shivering Penny. He *must* get home. Would there, by any glorious chance, be a moon? No, not on a night like this.

He went on crooning to Penny and patting her until one of his pats came against something hard. He patted again, felt the shape of the hardness, remembering that he had seen his uncle carrying a small red torch. Could it be…? He fumbled his way into one of the Burberry's pockets. Heaven be praised, there *was* a torch: tiny, giving only a pencil of light but a fairly bright one. By contrast with utter blackness it was a blaze of glory.

He took a look at Penny's head, protruding from the Burberry. She, seeing his face, tried to lick it and he was almost sure he felt a feeble flick of her tail. 'We shall be all right,' he assured her, then struggled to his feet with her. Holding her in the crook of his left arm, like a baby, and keeping the torch in his right hand, he stepped into the mist.

Almost at once he was faced with the thicket and it proved worse, even, than he had expected. Eventually he found it best to proceed on his knees, forcing the lower shoots of the bushes aside with his head as well as with the hand holding the torch. He cheered himself on by remembering that the going would be much easier once he was through the thicket and that, in actual distance, the park was quite close – by daylight, and unburdened by Penny, he could probably have reached it in five minutes. But this thought didn't speed his gruelling progress through the thicket and he had begun to fear he was going round in a circle before he at last came to the grassy clearing.

Here he took a rest, setting Penny down. Undersized she might be but, when last on the bathroom scales, she had weighed thirty pounds; and though highly co-operative, leaning against him and not struggling, she was a dead weight and a cold one. But it was easier to carry her, once he could walk upright. He got through the clearing swiftly and then had the luck to find the path through the nightingale wood. From then on it was plain sailing – though Penny seemed to grow ever heavier – until, with relief, he reached the park.

And now the snag was that it had begun to rain again, so heavily that he hastily returned to the wood – not that the trees would for long protect him from this deluge. Should he wait or at once brave the walk back to the Dower House? It would take him ten minutes – longer, in fact, burdened with this ton weight of darling dog. He snapped the torch off while he thought; for some time its tiny beam had been growing dimmer.

If only he could go to the Hall! He was near enough to see its lighted windows dimly glimmering through the mist. But Sarah had made it so clear that she mustn't be called on. He'd better go home. At least Penny, wrapped in the Burberry, would be protected from the rain.

He snapped the torch on. But its bead of light was now no brighter than a glow-worm, and within a couple of seconds the so-miraculously-discovered little torch had finally burned out.

That settled it. He'd have to go to the Hall. If he tried to reach the Dower House he was liable to knock himself out against one of the trees in the park, especially in this dementing deluge. There were no trees around the Hall and he could reach it in two minutes; the lighted windows would help and as some of them were downstairs the household couldn't have gone to bed. Sarah, he was sure, would want to help, and he particularly wanted her advice about Penny. And surely her grandfather wouldn't mind in such circumstances?

Penny chose that moment to give a miniature whimper. Hugh whispered to her, 'We'll be under cover in a couple of minutes,' and then set off for the Hall.

The journey, if short, was drenching and even when he was under the pillared portico the rain was driving in. He hunted for a bell – and found one dangling from a foot-length of wire. No use trying to ring that. There was a knocker but he hated the idea of pounding on it. That really might alarm the old man.

He tried the front door and found it unlocked so he decided to go in, quietly open the door to the library, where Sarah was likely to be sitting with her grandfather, and see if he could attract her attention. Stepping over the threshold he, for the first time, saw the inside of the house.

The hall, dimly lit, struck him as suitable for a horror film. No, it wasn't romantic enough for that. There was a stone floor, far from clean, a damp-stained wallpaper, some bad murky paintings of fruit and slain animals, some moth-eaten antlered heads and a mammoth stuffed fish behind splintered glass. A wide staircase mounted into darkness.

The library, Hugh believed, was on the right of the hall; anyway, that was the room where he had seen light behind the drawn curtains. He went towards the double doors and quietly opened one of them. He saw a long, book-lined room lit only by a standard lamp. In the pool of light below this sat an old man in a brown velvet dinner-jacket. There was no sign of Sarah. Hugh was wondering if he should retreat when the old man looked up and said pleasantly, 'Hello, do you want something? Come in.'

Hugh went in. Penny surprisingly, put her head out of the Burberry and barked.

'Oh, have you brought back one of our dogs?' said the old man.

Hugh began to explain, became conscious of incoherency, stopped short and said, 'If I could just see Sarah, please –'

'Yes, of course,' said the old man. 'She's upstairs – some job she's working on. Is that the Dalmatian she had here? Too small but otherwise perfect, I thought. Were you just telling me she's been running loose while she's on heat? Bad business if she's got caught at her age.'

'And she's wet through. I'm afraid she may get a chill.'

'Sarah had better give her some warm milk and brandy.'

A door at the far end of the room opened and an elderly man-servant entered.

'Ah, my bedtime,' said old Mr Strange. 'It's always welcome. Now you go up and see Sarah. Turn left at the top of the stairs and hers is the third door. And take the brandy – if there is any. Don't often drink it myself now. Give it to him, Walter.'

Walter brought a decanter from the dim recesses of the room and handed it to Hugh, saying, 'There's only a little, sir.'

Hugh said it would do splendidly. Walter now helped Mr Strange to his feet; when standing, his great age was more apparent. Aided by Walter he moved slowly to the door at the far end of the room, then turned to say, 'You're from the Dower House, aren't you? Seen you walking with Sarah. Hope your bitch will be all right.'

'Goodnight, and thank you,' said Hugh, with feeling. That lion hadn't taken much bearding. Now to find Sarah's sitting room – she'd once told him she had one, that had been her grandmother's boudoir. Clutching Penny and the decanter he went back to the hall and mounted the stairs.

15

Turning left where the staircase branched, Hugh found himself in a wide corridor which was lit only by a feeble glimmer from the hall below. He could not see beyond the first door. And which side of the corridor would Sarah's sitting room be on? He walked slowly, hoping to see a crack of light under a door. Yes, there was one.

As he drew near to it he heard someone talking. Presumably she had some friend with her, which made him feel apologetic about barging in. But when he paused outside the door he realised that it wasn't talking he had heard but Sarah, in her 'unclenched' voice, declaiming Shakespeare. He recognised the Casket scene from *The Merchant of Venice*; Corinna, in the early days of her training, had played it – very badly, poor love. Sarah's voice was certainly improving:

> '*Myself and what is mine to you and yours
> Is now converted: but now I was the lord
> Of this fair mansion, master of my servants,
> Queen o'er myself; and even now, but now,
> This house, these servants, and this same myself,
> Are yours, my lord…*'

For the last two lines she had reverted to her 'clenched' voice. She broke off and said, 'Oh, blast!' Hugh knocked on the door.

She said, 'Come in,' and he entered what was certainly no sitting room, and saw her sitting up in bed supporting a large Shakespeare against her knees. 'Hugh!' she cried delightedly, then looked concerned. 'Whatever's been happening to you and Penny?'

'I'm most terribly sorry,' said Hugh. 'I'd no idea you were in bed.'

'Oh, that doesn't matter.' She sprang out of bed and came towards him. 'Let me have Penny. I suppose she got out. You both look half drowned.'

'Penny very nearly was. That pond beyond the nightingale wood…'

'Poor love, we'll have to get her dried.' Sarah dumped Penny, minus the Burberry, on the bed. 'You roll on the blanket, pet, while I get some towels.'

She dived through a door and came back with a couple of bath towels. As she approached, Hugh took in the astonishing garment she was wearing. It was of heavy cream silk, with long sleeves and a high neck; and tall though she was, it trailed for several inches on the ground. Hugh vaguely supposed she had gone to bed in some kind of house-coat.

Kicking the trailing inches out of her way, she said, 'Excuse this frightful nightgown. It was one of a dozen unused ones I found after my grandmother died. They'd been part of her trousseau but she'd fancied something more skittish and who could blame her?' She tripped, then added, 'They all need shortening – grandmother was nearly six foot – but they do keep my feet warm. Now, Penny, love – Here, you do one half of her while I do the other.'

Penny had not had the energy to roll and objected to standing up while she was dried.

'I think her legs are weak,' said Sarah. 'Well, let her lie on her side and we'll roll her over. The great thing is to get her dry underneath – that's where she's likely to catch a chill. Dalmatians have so little hair underneath.'

While they dried Penny, Hugh poured out his story. Sarah said she wasn't surprised about Mildred. 'That's a dotty old girl if I ever saw one. I suppose it's arrested development or something, and she's frightfully conceited. The way she dresses up! She was Little Miss Muffet the day I went to tea. Look, I'm going to get some more towels. And we'll light the fire – it is laid. You do it, will you? Matches on the mantel.' She picked up a torch from her bedside table. 'Light switches are few and far apart in this house. The linen cupboard's a couple of miles away but I shan't be long.'

Hugh, after an anxious glance at the far from lively Penny, went to light the fire. The small fireplace, with its art nouveau tiles and brass fire-irons, looked out of place in the high, nobly proportioned room with its elaborately moulded ceiling. But so did the faded pink and silver wallpaper and the elaborate bedroom suite, which was of some yellowish grey wood, much decorated with gold. The bed-head was of gilded canework.

He had got the fire to burn and was looking round the room when Sarah returned.

'This was my grandmother's room,' she said. 'The furniture's sycamore, used to be a lovely silver-grey, she told me. I moved in here after she died because it's the only room with its own bathroom. Grandfather used to be next door but, for a long time, he's slept downstairs. Now I'll go on drying Penny while you dry yourself. Go into the bathroom and take everything off – yes, everything, Hugh – and get yourself really dry. Here are some towels. I wish you could have a hot bath but our water's never warm at this time of night.' She got a woollen dressing gown from a wardrobe. 'This used to be grandfather's so it'll be large enough. And I should think you could get into one of my sweaters and my winter pants. Anyway, try. And don't mind if you bust the pants; they're full of holes already. Oh, and you can try my bedroom slippers – I do have big feet. Anyway, it's a nice thick carpet.'

She thrust the clothes on him and bustled him into the bathroom which, he found, was as Edwardian as the bedroom, all fancy tiles and once-gleaming plumbing. Now some of the tiles were cracked and the silvery metal was peeling off the exposed pipes. He got out of his wet clothes with relief, towelled himself, and found he could wear Sarah's pants and sweater but not her bedroom slippers, an ancient quilted satin pair, minus one rosette. He belted the tweed dressing gown and returned to the bedroom.

Penny was now lying in front of the fire on a dry towel. Sarah was pouring milk from a Thermos into a saucer. She said, 'Lucky I fancied hot milk tonight – well, it's been such a damn dispiriting day, and it's nice to have something to look forward to when you go to bed. This'll have to cool a bit, of course. And I'm not sure about the brandy. Most dogs hate the taste and if you force it on them they're liable to be sick. Anyway, I think she's going to be all right. She's stopped shivering and she's got quite a bit of warmth in her. Feel her.'

Hugh sat down on the hearthrug and stroked Penny's stomach. She whimpered, but with pleasure, not complaint. He was thankful that she'd outgrown turning on her waterworks when fondled.

Sarah stood by, blowing on the milk. When it was eventually offered, Penny gave it one delicate, suspicious lick, then drank it avidly.

'Poor lamb, now she'll have to wait while some more cools,' said Sarah, pouring out another saucerful and blowing on it fiercely. 'I wonder if she needs solid food.'

'I'm sure Aunt May's been feeding her handsomely.'

'Still, she might like some bread in the milk. I've got a loaf in my sitting room. And how about you? Did you get any dinner?'

'Well, no. But I can get plenty when I'm home.'

'Oh, I've masses of food. I often eat up here. You blow on Penny's milk while I see what I can find.'

She hurried out and very shortly returned with most of a loaf, some butter, jam, biscuits and chocolate, also some plates and cutlery. She then offered to go down to the kitchen for some cold meat but he dissuaded her. 'Bread and jam will be marvellous – if you don't mind me eating all your food. And Penny's drinking all your milk.'

'I have the milk more for company than as a drink, and now I've got you and Penny for company. I'll just take a slice of bread for her and then please tuck in.'

Penny made it clear that she preferred the milk without bread. She drank two-thirds of a Thermosful and then went to sleep.

'I swear she'll be all right,' said Sarah.

'But suppose she's been – well, caught,' said Hugh, through a mouthful of bread and apricot jam.

Sarah, after thought, said, 'I'd make a bet that she hasn't been. Bitches are very choosy and you'd be surprised how they can fend off unwanted dogs. And she's fond of the spaniels – she's always coying with Rufus. And I had them all in the wood, when the rain let up this afternoon. I bet she was on her way to the Hall when she picked up the scent of them and dashed into the wood. And if any dogs had chased her, I don't think they'd have left her.'

Hugh, comforted by food and warmth, began to feel hopeful. He leaned back in the armchair Sarah had made him take and held out his bare feet to the fire, saying, 'You've been marvellous to us both. Will it be all right to take her home now?'

'Not tonight – you might get her wet again. And why not let me keep her for a week or so? Your mad aunt might let her out again.'

'She might indeed. But how about the spaniels?'

'I can shut her up far away from them. Oh, I'll guarantee there'll be no accidents here. I never had one when we still had our bitches.'

'Well, if you really don't mind…'

'Love it, really. Do have some more to eat. I wish I'd a drink to offer you. Oh, the brandy!'

Hugh, who rather liked brandy after meals, said, 'I will, if you will.'

'All right, to keep you company. We'll have to use my hot milk cup and the Thermos cap. Oh, there's my tooth glass but that always smells of peppermint.'

'I rather fancy the Thermos cap.'

She poured the brandy out and they sat sipping it. Hugh decided it wasn't as good as the brandy his Uncle George sometimes gave him but it raised a pleasant glow. He said, 'When I've finished this I must take myself off. It must be midnight.'

'Not quite. We shall hear the stable clock. Oh, will Corinna be anxious about you?'

He explained about Corinna's party. (She'd be at it now, of course; it seemed much more than a few hours since he'd seen her.)

Sarah said, 'I might have guessed she wasn't here or she'd have come with you to hunt for Penny. Have a spot more brandy.'

'Hold hard, you'll have me tight,' said Hugh, unseriously. He prided himself on having rather a good head.

Sarah, having poured out the last of the brandy, settled on the hearthrug beside the sleeping Penny, with her tent-like garment spread around her. She had put on no dressing gown, and certainly none was needed over that vast, opaque night-gown of her grandmother's. He must remember to describe it to Corinna – also to tell her about hearing Sarah practising unclenching. He decided not to tell Sarah he'd overheard her; it might embarrass her. Poor girl, she must mind a lot about her voice – as if it mattered, once one got to like her. Had she been clenching since he arrived? Probably, though he hadn't noticed.

He listened now, as they chatted. She was talking quietly but undoubtedly clenching.

It struck him that never before had he heard her talk so freely. As a rule, she was apt to prod him and Corinna with rather humble questions and hang on their answers; he had known little more about her than that, orphaned early, she had been brought up by her grandparents. Now, as she volunteered information, he realised what an isolated life she had led. She had been away to boarding school but only for three years. 'Then I got ill and my grandmother decided I had outgrown my strength – whatever that may mean. So she kept me at home and got a governess – imagine! She was an antique but very highly qualified and she taught better than anyone at school had. Alas, the poor dear died when I was sixteen – and my grandmother died two years later, and my great-aunts died last year. Heavens, how I must be depressing you!'

But, curiously, it wasn't depressing. Indeed, when she rattled on about the difficulties of her present life, she was often funny – not deliberately funny, he was sure; it was her flat statements and lack of self-pity which gave things a comic slant. Still, her quiet, clenched voice made for a certain monotony. Once he caught himself on the edge of sleep. He finished his brandy and set the Thermos cap down. He'd make a move just as soon as she came to the end of her story of last winter's burst pipes.

He was awakened by a shaft of sunlight between incompletely drawn curtains. After a dazed few seconds he took in that the fire was out and that Sarah had now transferred herself and Penny to the bed. Both were fast asleep.

The shaft of sunlight obligingly showed the time by the clock on the mantel: 4.15.

Why hadn't Sarah wakened him? Presumably she hadn't had the heart to. He wondered how long she had gone on sitting by the fire. Probably not long; one soon got tired of sitting on the floor. It then occurred to him that if he could leave without waking her she might think he'd gone long before this. Not that it really mattered but it would be more, say, conventional to have cleared out while it was still dark. If one went before the sun rose, one had merely stayed until late at night. If one waited till dawn, one had stayed *for* the night.

He tiptoed to the bathroom for his clothes, which were nowhere near dry. He would, he decided, keep Sarah's woollen pants, which were now split in several places; he'd ask Corinna to buy Sarah some more. Should he keep the sweater on, too? And could he possibly go home in the dressing gown? That, he felt, would not be a good idea, supposing anyone saw him. No, he must face his damp suit and shirt – and very uncomfortable they felt, and his half-dried shoes felt worse.

Before leaving the bathroom he tore a sheet out of his pocket diary (damp) and wrote on it with its damp pencil.

> *Dear Sarah,*
> *Please do forgive me – why ever didn't you wake me up and sling me out? Thank you more than I can say. I won't worry you tomorrow but please do come over if you can spare a minute. Again thank you,*
>
> *Hugh*

He hoped that 'tomorrow' might imply that he was leaving during the night – as he would have been, had it been winter.

He tiptoed to the bedside table and left his note. Dear Sarah was sleeping with her beautiful mouth slightly open. She had an arm, in its voluminous sleeve, holding the quilt in position over Penny, the top of whose head was just visible. There was a suggestion of mother and child which Hugh found both funny and moving.

Now to get out of the room – and he must close the door in case Penny got out or some spaniel got in. The handle – china, painted with rosebuds – turned almost silently. The hinges squeaked only a little.

Out in the corridor he listened: no sound came from the bedroom, he didn't think he'd wakened Sarah. He hurried down the wide stairs.

The light was still on in the hall – probably Walter had left it on for him. He switched it off hoping this might give the impression that Sarah had seen him out. He couldn't, of course, bolt the door after him but, judging by the rusty state of the bolts, he doubted if they were ever used. He closed the door quietly.

It would be quickest if he went diagonally across the park but he would then be in full view of anyone looking out of back bedrooms of the Dower House – just the kind of thing old Mildew would do. He made for the wood and then turned a sharp right angle. From there, he hoped, various trees would screen him.

Apart from his damp clothes – and his damp shoes were soon damper – he enjoyed the walk in the sparkling morning. There were still troughs of mist but they were already pierced by sunlight. Clumps of trees, rising above the mist, glittered with last night's rain. Everywhere there was a curious mingling of mist and brilliance. Automatically, he wished that Corinna could see it all. And oh, the relief of knowing that Penny would be looked after – if it wasn't too late. But he felt it wasn't; Sarah's reasoning had been good.

As a token of gratitude to Fate, he wouldn't say one unkind word to Mildew. The silly old cow couldn't help herself. Really, it was pathetic. The sex-starved old woman probably felt that, in letting Penny out to mate, she herself would somehow be mating – though she might not know this was in her mind. Anyway, he'd be pleasant to her, he swore he would.

He had just sworn it when he saw someone come out of the lilac grove and run into the park. At first he thought it was Corinna; she must, after all, have come down by a late train. How angelic of her to come out to meet him! But no, it wasn't Corinna, though the short, fluttering negligée was very like one of hers. Good God, it was Mildew, and her feet were bare!

He dodged behind a clump of trees. Apart from the fact that he had no desire to see his great-aunt he felt it would embarrass her to see him. But she was coming quickly, doing a kind of running dance, and his cover was inadequate. In a few seconds she spotted him and, far from being embarrassed, ran eagerly towards him.

'Oh, poor Hugh,' she called out. 'Haven't you found her?'

He hastily assured her that he *had* found Penny and she was now safe at the Hall.

'There you are,' said Mildred blithely. 'I knew she'd be all right. Such a fuss everyone made last night but I *knew*. At the Hall, did you say?'

'Yes, Sarah's taking care of her.'

'Have you just come from the Hall now?'

He noticed the sudden excitement in her tone and said quickly, 'Auntie, ought you to be out with bare feet? You'll catch cold.'

'Dew never hurt anyone,' said Mildred. 'Don't try to put me off, Hugh. There's no need. You see, I approve.'

'Approve what?' said Hugh, anger already surging up in him.

'That beautiful dark girl's much more suitable for you than Corinna. And I'm glad you're not as saintly as I thought you were. But it shall be our secret. I promise you I won't tell a soul.'

'You can tell everyone in the world exactly what you bloody well like,' Hugh shouted, now in a state of blind fury.

Her blue eyes widened and she gasped, 'Oh, Hugh! Dearest Hugh!'

He was instantly contrite. He'd no right to swear at a dotty old woman, even if she did have a filthy mind. He said quietly, 'Sorry, Auntie. But you've got it all wrong.'

'Of course,' said Mildred, sounding as if humouring a child. 'I admire you for saying that. Any gentleman would. But it's all right, dear Hugh. In fact, it's very, very splendid.'

He started to speak but she interrupted. 'Ssh, dear boy.' She put her finger on her lips and looked roguish. 'We won't say another word about it. And now I must get on with my dabbling in the dew. I've so much to think about. But may I just say that I've never liked you so much? Dearest Hugh!'

To his dismay she dived at him and kissed him; it would have been on the mouth if he hadn't dodged her. Then she was on her way, flinging her arms wide, as if she were a liberated spirit.

He gazed after her in sheer horror. Surely she was mad enough to be shut up? But he'd never heard even the most tentative suggestion of it. And presumably she never got violent.

He found it obscene that she should believe that he and Sarah... Did she *really* believe they'd been sleeping together?

He would have been surprised to know that what they'd been doing was of no great interest to Mildred. What mattered was what she intended to imagine them doing. At last she had a new toy. She could take it for walks, think about it before she fell asleep. And she felt sure it would be a lasting toy; she tired of some of them so quickly. But Hugh, this splendid new Hugh who had shouted at her, and that dark handsome girl... she would think about them all the coming week and then take them home with her.

She wouldn't invent the first story yet. She was a little chilly in her fluttering negligée and she'd jabbed one foot on a stone. But this afternoon, she would take her thoughts about the passionate adventures of dear Hugh and dear Sarah for a very long walk.

16

In their taxi to Liverpool Street station the following Friday, George said to Hugh, 'Oh, a bit of good news. Your aunt rang up to say that old Mildred's going home tomorrow, instead of Monday. Some boarding house jollification she has to be back for.'

'Lucky us – and unlucky boarding house.'

'I gather they like her there. Well, she practically supports the place.'

'Then I suppose we ought to give her good marks for generosity.'

'If one didn't feel there was a catch in it somehow,' said George. He had only managed to keep his patience throughout the past week by turning on a bantering playfulness which frequently made him wince at himself, and he would be very, very glad to see the last of Mildew – that name, far from being outlawed, had increased in popularity.

Corinna met them at Liverpool Street. George thought his daughter looked tired. He asked if she'd been overworking.

'A bit, perhaps. And it's been so hot.'

'Well, a heatwave's better than the torrents of rain we had last weekend,' said George. 'And it'll feel cooler in the country.'

Once they were settled in the train Corinna retired behind an evening paper, hunting for the notice of some play. Hugh, failing to concentrate on his own paper, found his thoughts about her as unsatisfactory as on the previous Friday's train journey home.

He had expected her to arrive at the Dower House on the Saturday morning and had planned to tell her all about his adventures at the Hall; but she'd rung up to say she wasn't coming. May brought this information when she arrived at the cottage to find out if there was any news of Penny. (Hugh's report was true but distinctly curtailed; he had returned to the cottage without waking his parents.)

Corinna, it seemed, was to spend the weekend at Sir Harry's country house – 'Oh, his wife's there. It's all quite respectable,' May assured Hugh. He had barely taken this information in when Sarah arrived to ask him to lunch at the Hall. 'Grandfather suggested it. You must have made a good impression last night.'

'What, thickly coated with mud?' said Hugh. 'Not to mention dripping water all over his carpet.'

'Nothing could make that carpet any worse than it is. Anyway, please do come. It's so marvellous that he should ask to see someone. If you'd like to come back with me now we could take Penny for a walk together. She's as good as new this morning – she must have a surprising lot of stamina.'

Hugh went, had an ecstatic reunion with Penny, and quite enjoyed his – very bad – lunch. At least, he enjoyed the first half of it. The old man was gentle and only a little vague. Hugh began to hope that, eventually, it might be practicable to talk about the estate, hint that quite a lot, still, might be done about it. (George thought so and was most willing to give advice.) But long before the meal was over, Mr Strange became quiet and rather more than vague. He even forgot who Hugh was. When reminded, he was apologetic and came back to life for a few minutes, then fell silent and looked unhappy. Sarah rang for Walter, saying, 'Time for your nap, Grandfather.' When Walter came it seemed that Mr Strange would leave without even saying goodbye to Hugh, but he finally looked back and said, in a perfectly normal manner, 'So glad you could come. Come again.'

Sarah, giving Hugh a second cup of truly terrible coffee, said, 'That's how it always is. His mind has no staying power. It's… like clouds passing over the sun.'

Hugh then talked about the estate but, as always, Sarah insisted nothing could be done while her grandfather lived. 'We'll just have to go on as we are. At least we shall have a roof over our heads as I've recently had some work done on it. Once the roof goes, you're sunk. But it was a frantic expense and sometimes I think I ought just to let the house fall down. It *is* kind of you to take an interest.'

He had seen her again on the Sunday afternoon when, again, they had walked Penny. Then he'd sat with Penny while Sarah had exercised the spaniels. Penny was safely housed in a dilapidated room that had been a nursery, sunny but melancholy. He found himself thinking of his childhood, and Bonnie – and, of course, Corinna. He decided to return to London that evening as it seemed likely she would come back from her weekend, to be ready for her Monday classes. They could have a real talk.

But she didn't return on Sunday. And on Monday it was nearly midnight when she came back to the flat. Still, he hadn't been able to resist telling her all his excitements – about Penny lost and found, Sarah, the old man...

Corinna, of course, listened, and put in various comments, such as, 'That ghastly Mildred.' 'Poor darling Penny!' 'How very kind of Sarah!' but he gradually realised he had a polite, rather than an eager listener – indeed, he doubted if she took in his description of Mildred at dawn. Well, she was obviously tired. And no doubt he was being madly egotistical, doing all the talking. True, he'd begun by asking about her weekend but when she'd answered, vaguely, 'Oh, it was all right,' he hadn't pressed for details. Now he asked again and prepared to show real interest but she only said, 'It was a bit dull, really. Lots of people – tennis and whatnot. Lady Tremayne's very nice. Darling, I *must* go to bed.'

He had seen little of her during the week. Night after night she had come home late, owing to her half-term performances. He hadn't been invited to any more of these – she said she wasn't playing anything worth his seeing. He'd found it depressing, getting and eating his evening meal alone. But however late she came in, and over their rushed breakfasts, she was always pleasant. It was just that she seemed preoccupied, and unwilling to talk. Oh, perhaps it was simply that she'd been overworking; her father had said she looked tired. Anyway, the weekend was ahead of them – and, comfortable thought, Penny would soon be home. He'd had a postcard from Sarah that morning saying, 'Penny flourishing and can come out of purdah now. Come and collect her any time. Now that my grandfather knows you it'll be all right to come in and shout for someone.'

His train of thought was interrupted by ticket inspection. Then he put the evening paper down and his uncle began to talk about business matters. The firm was busy and George was thankful to find how much he could delegate to Hugh. It never ceased to surprise him that Robert's son should have a flair for business.

As often, it was hot on the train and they were all thankful when they arrived and found the platform, as usual, windy. They had cooled off considerably even before they got to the car. George, on the drive home, said, 'Wonderful how quickly one unwinds once one gets to the country.'

'Yes, indeed,' said Hugh, but he didn't today feel unwound; Corinna was still so unforthcoming. But it was pleasant to arrive at the Dower House, smell one of his Aunt May's good dinners cooking, think of having Penny back (perhaps he and Corinna would call for her that evening) and know that – glory be to God – Mildew would soon be gone.

Corinna said she must have a cool bath before dinner. Hugh, who had hoped for a little time with her, went to see his parents. George went to find May, as he always did on his return home, unless she came to meet him.

She was in the kitchen, stirring something on the stove. She said, 'Sorry, darling. I couldn't leave this.'

'No Matsons here?'

'Only the official one. She's turning down the beds. Isn't it bliss about Mildred? And she's going by a very early train. Do you want to give her champagne as it's her last evening?'

'I do not,' said George. 'When I gave it her on her first evening she said she'd never really cared for fizzy drinks.'

'Pity. I rather fancied celebrating – though it's hardly safe to, until she's actually gone. She could still burn the house down or something.'

'You and your "indescribable horror" of her – remember? The poor hag hasn't really done any harm.'

'She did her best to, over Penny. I shall have to stay with this sauce for a few minutes, darling.'

Mrs Matson returned. George, after enquiring about her mother-in-law and her daughter (Mrs Matson, senior, was feeling the heat; Miss Matson had gone pillion riding – 'You know these girls') went to wash. He then joined Fran, who was in a deckchair on the lawn outside the Long Room. She said, 'The lilac's a bit sad now, isn't it? I wish I'd looked at it more while it was at its best. You do know Mildred's going tomorrow?'

'I do indeed. And judging by the general relief, one feels the end of the world's been narrowly avoided.'

'Well, I *have* been a bit nervous. You see, I feel responsible, as I fished so hard for her invitation. And she really has got everyone down. The sad thing is that she doesn't mean to. It's just that she never gives a thought to anyone but herself. And now I feel ashamed because I've let myself gang up with the others. We're always getting together and saying things like, "Have you heard Mildred's latest?" "Have you seen Mildred's latest?"'

'Personally, I get a kick out of seeing her latest. What's she treating us to dinner?'

'Her pink frills and pantalettes. You've seen that outfit.'

'Disappointing. I hoped she'd still got something up her sleeve – say, Little Lord Fauntleroy or Lady Godiva.'

Mildred, frilled and pantaletted, tripped out on to the lawn. George beamed on her kindly, then said he must go and call for Robert and June.

Dinner had a champagne quality without the champagne. Everyone was particularly nice to Mildred, even May managed a few civil remarks. And for once, Mildred seemed appreciative and spoke of missing them all when she was back in London. Fran thought, 'If we'd tried harder to be nice, she might have been better. And tomorrow she'll be at that deadly boarding house while we're all enjoying ourselves here. Not that I must stay much longer.' There was quite a lot she wanted to do in London. She spent a few minutes thinking about this and only came back into circulation when iced coffee was being served. May remembered she'd bought some coffee wafers she wanted everyone to try and went to the kitchen for them.

Mildred then complained of the westering sun and asked if someone would draw the curtains. Robert, who particularly liked watching the sun set behind the Hall, rose resignedly. As he reached the west window Mildred, following him with her eyes, said, 'Isn't it funny how tall and thin Robert is, when June's short and plump? June's one of the *round* people – and George is, too. You know, George, I always think you should have married June

– somehow she looks *right* for you. But I can't imagine Robert marrying May. Robert…'

'You're talking nonsense,' Fran broke in sharply and then wished she hadn't. Her tone had helped to give importance to Mildred's words. And important they undoubtedly were. In little more than a split second Fran had taken in that George and June were looking at each other. June was blushing deeply and George… It was only later that Fran found a phrase to describe his expression. It was as if he had seen a great light.

Robert, having heard Mildred speak his name, turned from the window saying, 'What was that, Aunt Mildred?'

'I was saying that – oh, dear!' She broke off with a squawk of dismay.

Baggy, reaching for the cream jug, had knocked her glass of iced coffee over towards her, deluging her lap.

Fran sprang up. 'We must sponge it at once or it will stain.'

If there was anything in the world Mildred cared deeply about, it was her clothes. She gave apologetic Baggy one tearful glare and then allowed herself to be hustled upstairs.

Sponging the dress, Fran wondered if Baggy had knocked the coffee-glass over on purpose. It wasn't like him to be quick-witted but neither was it like him to want more cream. Anyway, God bless him.

'You're making me very wet,' wailed Mildred.

'Well, take the dress off and put on your dressing gown.'

May couldn't have heard, from the kitchen; the swing door always closed itself. And Robert had been drawing the curtains. Anyway, Mildred's idiotic words didn't much matter. It was June's blush and, even more, George's expression – it was then that the phrase 'as if he'd seen a great light' dropped into Fran's mind. Oh, perhaps she was exaggerating… but she was quite sure she wasn't.

'I shan't go down again,' said Mildred. 'I've got to finish packing.'

'It looks as if you'd barely begun,' said Fran, gazing round the untidy room.

'Well, I don't like packing. Usually someone helps me.'

'I'll help you,' said Fran. The helping proved to be doing the whole job, while Mildred issued commands. Fran made a bet with herself that she'd keep her temper and this wasn't too difficult as she found Mildred's absurdly unsuitable pretty clothes both pathetic and nostalgic. Even as a tiny, exquisite child Mildred had adored her clothes.

'Well, that's all we can do tonight,' said Mildred at last. 'But you'll help me in the morning?'

'I will indeed.' Fran visualised the glorious moment when that frightful trunk would be carried down the stairs.

'And now I shall go to bed. I must be fresh for tomorrow.'

'I expect you're looking forward to your newly decorated room and to seeing all your friends again.'

'Oh, yes, I've lots to look forward to,' said Mildred. At the moment she was looking forward to a bedtime instalment of her latest Hugh and Sarah daydream. Corinna would come into it tonight. Corinna would be jealous. And serve her right; she'd been most offhand before dinner.

Fran, returning to the Long Room, found Baggy alone, reading an evening paper. She enquired where everyone was.

'Corinna's in her room studying a part. Hugh's gone to call for his dog. May's doing something somewhere. The others have gone to the cottage for some serial on television. They could have seen it here but George said he knew I like to see the news. And very dull it was. Did I ruin Mildred's dress?'

'Oh, it'll be all right,' said Fran. *Had* he knocked the coffee over on purpose? She didn't dare to ask him in case he hadn't, hadn't even noticed anything. Mustn't risk putting ideas into his head. A pity. She'd have been thankful to talk it all over with him.

Baggy happened to be in the same position. He'd have welcomed praise for knocking the coffee over. Never in his life had he done such swift thinking followed by such decisive action. And he'd have liked to tell her how quickly George and June had recovered themselves. By the time Robert was back at the table and May had returned with the coffee wafers (rather good, they were) there had been nothing to see. But Fran might not have noticed anything. Mustn't risk putting ideas into her head.

Fran went to the television, which was on without sound, and twiddled for a programme they could enjoy. She found one about a young couple who were converting a flat. Baggy thought they were paying too much rent, Fran thought it was going to be uncomfortable. No flat ever seemed as comfortable as her own. She remembered that she'd promised herself a speedy return to it but now... She couldn't leave until she felt more at ease about George and June.

She would have been relieved could she have seen how normal and relaxed they – and Robert, too – appeared to be, watching television in the tiny cottage sitting room. They had enjoyed their cliff-hanger serial, in spite of the fact that their combined brains had failed to unravel the intricacies of its plot, and were placidly watching the programme Fran and Baggy were watching. But soon Robert remembered he had some notes to make and went up to his study. George took his place on the sofa, beside June, and after a moment put his arm around her.

June wondered if she ought to tell him not to, but didn't. She was quite sure she ought not to put her head on his shoulder, but did.

George said, 'Darling June.'

June said, 'Darling George.'

George said, 'Was it as much of a surprise to you as it was to me?'

'You mean, what Aunt Mildred said?'

'I mean, what you felt.'

'Oh, that wasn't a surprise,' said June. 'You see, I've always felt it.'

'Good God! Surely not always?'

'Absolutely always,' said June cheerfully. 'From the very first evening I met you. But of course it doesn't mean anything. I love Robert just as you love May. It was just… well, you're like Rudolph Valentino.'

'I'm *what*? I saw him in an old movie and he was ghastly. June, you don't really mean…'

'Oh, I don't mean you're like him that way. I think he was ghastly too. It's just that, for me, you're like he was for Mother. Exciting to think about but not in the least important.'

'Thank you very much,' said George.

'What?' said June, through a blare of television sound. George got up and turned the sound down.

'Oh, I wouldn't do that,' said June. 'I shouldn't like Robert to come back and find us sitting here in dark silence.'

'Robert would never dream of thinking… And if we keep the sound up, we shall have to shout.'

'Well, you can turn the sound off if you turn the lights on. Then it'll seem quite natural that we're sitting here talking.'

'I don't *want* the lights on,' said George, who found the room, lit only by television, exactly right for his mood. He went to the door, opened it, listened, then closed it again. 'Now stop fussing. Robert's typing away like a beaver. He won't be down for ages. Just a second, while I draw the curtains.'

'But we never draw them. What will Hugh think, when he comes back, if he finds them drawn?'

George, drawing them, said, 'He'll think far worse if he finds them undrawn and happens to look in.'

'But why?'

'Because this discussion has reached a stage where I have to kiss you.'

With great strength of mind June sprang up from the sofa and moved to a small chair which had hard, discouraging arms. For a few seconds she felt it was sinking under her or was she sinking through it? Then she and it came to terms with each other, also the room steadied itself. And she was able to speak firmly, though the firmness was more in the intention than in her voice.

She said, 'George, if you have any real affection for me, any true liking – and surely you must have, after all these years – I implore you to sit still and *think*. Please, George. Just for a few minutes.'

George gave her a loving smile and said, 'All right. I'll do just that.' It was, he decided, a very good idea indeed.

At the dinner table he had been in no doubt about the nature of the great light he had seen (he would have approved of Fran's phrase) as the result of Mildred's unpardonable remark. (Actually he had not only pardoned her but was even feeling grateful to her.) He hadn't instantly known he ought to have married June; he hadn't fallen in love with her or even felt violently attracted to her. He had simply known, without any shadow of doubt, why he had been so happy since the move to the country, why everything had felt 'right'. Of course! It was the presence of June. Dear June, *not* short and plump as Mildred had most libellously described her, but certainly round… and above all, *right*.

That had been enough for him at dinner. He hadn't looked ahead to possible delights or difficulties or both. He had simply

215

felt 'So that's that. Dear, darling June. And, oh you poor love, how you're blushing. Never mind. May's out of the room, Robert has his back to you. And there's nothing, nothing to worry about.' Well, if he'd really felt that, he must have automatically decided that this particular case of 'rightness' couldn't be allowed to develop in the way most similar cases had. Of course not. Even if June were willing, he couldn't allow himself to come between her and Robert or between her and May. Nor, in this particular case, could he allow himself so to hurt May.

Yes, indeed. Even though not consciously worked out, those must have been his underlying thoughts. But now, sitting in the small, dimly lit room, staring unseeingly at the silent television screen, he realised that just a few minutes alone with June had altered the situation. This was largely because he now intuitively knew what she felt about him. He was good at knowing what women felt about him; indeed, the main reason of his suc-cess with them was that he seldom showed an interest until he knew he had aroused one. (Perhaps it was only then that he felt the interest. He was no hunter; what attracted him most was mutuality of attraction.) And he knew now that, though darling June would verbally say 'No, no, no' she would physically say 'Yes, yes, yes' sooner or later.

He sneaked a look at her. She was sitting with her eyes closed in a certain way... really, one could only describe it as swooning. Those eyelids were already saying 'Yes, yes, yes'.

On which he suddenly felt, of all the unlikely things, fatherly. Poor love, this kind of thing was outside her experience. She must be protected. And he could do it. Quite a few times he had denied himself delightful women, and for less potent reasons than applied to June. Business reasons, even... husbands who were extra suspi-cious... wives who were not discreet... women he suspected of being clingers. Now he came to think of it, he had switched off his interest in Sarah, though it was that interest which had clinched his decision to take the Dower House, on a soaking wet day. Of course he could protect June. He was in control.

He said, 'Wake up, love.'

'I wasn't exactly asleep.'

'I've never seen you asleep.' Unwise remark, that; one would have to watch one's step all the time. 'Well, I've done what you asked. I've thought. And I promise you there's nothing to worry about.'

'How do you mean that?' said June warily.

'I mean it in the way you want me to. We're not going to risk hurting Robert and May.'

'It wouldn't be a risk, it would be a certainty.'

'Well, one *could* keep things secret.' Another unwise remark. 'But we're not going to try – that is, we're not going to have any *guilty* secret. What we feel for each other will be a perfectly innocent secret. And we're not going to be miserable about it. Promise me that.'

'I do promise. I can, now you're being so wonderful. Actually, I feel insanely happy. I can't remember ever before feeling quite like this.'

This time *her* remark was unwise, George reflected – while saying with equal unwiseness, 'Me, neither.' He then added firmly, 'It's going to be *fun*, darling June. Never anything serious, never anything hurtful, to anyone. God help me, I'll resign myself to being just your Rudolph Valentino.'

'Is there anyone I could be for you? Greta Garbo or someone?'

'I prefer my women in the flesh,' said George, thinking what very nice flesh June's was. The flesh of women who were almost, but not quite, plump was the nicest flesh in the world.

The front door was heard to open, followed by the tinkle of Penny's chain collar. June hastily turned the television sound up; then opened the door to the hall. Penny, at her most wriggle-some, dived into the sitting room.

'Don't let me interrupt,' said Hugh, then glanced at the screen. 'Oh, I'd like to see this.' He sat down and picked up the squirming Penny.

George said he must go, and went into the hall, followed by June. Out in the little porch he said, 'Goodnight, darling. See you tomorrow.'

'Not tomorrow – nor Sunday. You've got weekend guests.'

'Good God, I'd forgotten.' May had reminded him when she telephoned that afternoon – it had been an extra reason for being thankful that Mildred was leaving – but a lot had happened since then.

'May will have more than enough on her hands without us. And Robert and I wouldn't mix well with your business friends.'

'Can't say I feel like mixing with them myself.' But, really, he was quite glad they were coming. It would give him the chance to do some further sensible thinking.

He stooped to give her the usual goodnight kiss, but she drew back, shaking her head. He whispered, 'Nonsense, darling. We've got to get used to behaving in our usual way. Don't *worry*. Just leave everything to me.'

Anyone was welcome to see the kiss he gave her, his normal, brother-in-law's kiss. Unfortunately, he got no cooperation from her – no cooperation, that is, in keeping it normal. And it lasted longer than he had intended. Not much too long; he was pleased with himself about that, also pleased that it had ended just before Robert came down the stairs. They exchanged brotherly goodnights.

Dear, darling June! No wonder she'd tried to avoid a kiss. But all would be well, George told himself, striding back to the Dower House. He was definitely in control.

17

Hugh, after a disturbed night during which Penny success-fully established a claim to over half his narrow bed, was awakened by his mother saying, 'Sorry, darling, but Aunt Mildred particularly wants to say goodbye to you – in fact, she's here now.'

His great-aunt, suitably dressed for travelling in pale blue gingham, was already in the room. She said, 'Would you excuse us, dear June? This is a little *private* farewell.'

Hope she's not going to rape him, thought June, on her way downstairs.

Mildred, having closed the door, turned towards the bed. 'Dearest boy, I just wanted to assure you that I haven't breathed a word. Your secret's safe.'

'There *is* no secret,' said Hugh desperately.

'I know, I know, dear dark horse – that's my new name for you instead of Little St Hugh. How *is* dear Sarah?'

'She's fine but... No, Aunt Mildred! Please don't kiss me. I haven't shaved.'

'Nor had you at our last secret meeting. I find it most virile. Well, goodbye, my dear boy.'

She was now sitting on the bed, with her hands on his shoulders. Luckily for him Penny possessively interposed, pushing her nose into Mildred's face.

Mildred backed. 'Oh, dear! But perhaps she only meant to kiss me.'

'They're blowing the car horn for you,' said Hugh, inventively. 'You'll miss your train.'

Again she leaned forward, then saw that Penny was baring her teeth in a way which certainly wasn't a smile. 'Well,

I must just *blow* you a kiss.' She did so, then swung her white wicker handbag in a last farewell gesture and sped out of the room.

'God Almighty,' breathed Hugh sinking back on his pillow, which Penny took to be an invitation to wash his face.

He had barely recovered from both Aunt Mildred and Penny before he began to feel worried. Ludicrous as his great-aunt's suspicions were, was it conceivable that Corinna, too, might entertain them? Could that be what was wrong with her? It now occurred to him that her seeming disinterest in his night at the Hall could have been jealousy. Oh, no! He was just letting Mildew's nonsense put ideas into his head.

All would be well if he could have a real talk with Corinna. She must come for a walk with him. He sprang up. Penny firmly accompanied him to the bathroom.

He dressed and breakfasted hastily, then set out. June called after him, 'Don't forget we're leaving the Dower House to itself this weekend.'

'I know. I just want one word with Corinna.'

He found her in the William Morris dining room, struggling to arrange some beech leaves in a large stone jar.

'Mother wants us to have meals in here and I'm supposed to make it look lived-in. It'll certainly never look eaten-in; it hasn't had so much as a sniff of food since we came. Oh, hell!' The beech leaves had fallen over. 'What *is* it, Hugh?'

'I thought we might plan a walk.'

'Sorry. I've got to help Mother. And if I do get any free time I want to work on a new part.'

'What part?'

She hesitated, then said, 'Oh, I can't tell you about it now. Do clear out. I must get this room finished.'

222

He didn't feel convinced there was any part. Something was wrong with her and he really couldn't believe it had to do with Sarah. He was about to ask her point-blank when Fran came in, back from seeing Mildred off.

'Your mother's mad to think of using this room,' she said to Corinna. 'It'll take all the flavour out of the food. Besides, the decor calls for two parlour maids, if not for a butler.'

May, appearing in the doorway, said, 'Mrs Matson now says she can't carry all the food all the way from the kitchen. So we shall have to stick to the Long Room. It's awful the way we waste these front rooms. Oh, hello, Hugh.'

She didn't, Hugh thought, look any too pleased to see him. This weekend certainly wasn't going to be any fun. He made one last effort with Corinna. 'Perhaps you'll have some time tomorrow.'

'If I do, I'll come and get you.' She gave him a quick, curiously tentative smile.

He smiled back but he still felt both worried and aggrieved as he turned to go. His aunt, with her customary kindness, called after him, 'We shall miss you all. Well, back to normal next weekend.'

He called back, 'Lovely!' and hoped she was right.

Fran asked what time the guests were expected.

'Around midday,' said May. 'I must say I'd have liked a few days to recover from Mildred but George asked them before he knew she was coming.'

'I'm surprised he hasn't asked any business friends here before.'

So was May – and relieved. The wives of business friends were always potential dangers. She was glad to be able to say now, 'He doubts if he'll be asking any more. He says we've all the company we want with Robert and June so near. I must get back to the kitchen.'

'Anything I can do?'

'Only to be on hand in case the Harleys arrive early. And make sure George is around. I hope he's recovered from driving Aunt Mildred to the station.'

'He seemed particularly cheerful. Relief, no doubt.'

The Harleys, Graham and Sally, arrived punctually, a handsome couple in a handsome car. Graham, a new client of George's, was in his fifties, pleasant, extrovert and only a trifle too heavy. Sally, still in her early thirties, was so attractive that Fran watched George's reactions to her with both suspicion and hope. Should he be attracted it would be hard on May but not as hard as what *might* lie ahead of her – though Fran was now censoring her suspicions about June, assuring herself there was 'nothing in it'.

George, on this first meeting with Sally Harley, at once began using her as a touchstone for his feelings about June. He found Sally delightful, so pretty, so admirably dressed, so – to say the least of it – friendly. And so much younger than her husband; normally it would positively have been one's duty to meet her fully halfway. Now, the most that he felt was a faint wistful 'what might have been' – and every minute that he was free to live his own thoughts he wondered if there could be any chance of catching even a glimpse of June over the weekend. He had begun wondering that as soon as he woke up. He was no longer glad of two days in which to think sensibly. He just wanted to be with June – but not, in any way, harmfully. And he still felt in control.

Meanwhile, the weekend lay ahead and one had to be a decent host, also to do a little something for Sally Harley. He summoned up a fair line of banter (definitely higher grade than the playfulness he'd turned on for Mildred) but it was a strain; and he was thankful when, after lunch, the Harleys said they would like to be shown the neighbourhood. Banter could hardly be expected when he was driving the car.

Fran, too, was thankful. She had pulled her weight in the conversation at lunch – considerably better than Baggy and Corinna had – and would be glad to go off duty. Perhaps an afternoon nap? But when, after seeing the car off, she was on her way to the stairs, she ran into Baggy, returning to his room.

'Come in and talk a bit,' he suggested, then added quickly, 'unless you've something to do.'

'Not a thing in the world.' She waved farewell to her afternoon nap without too much regret. She had grown fond of Baggy and had seen less than she wished of him during Mildred's visit.

As usual she found his room cheerless. The brightest note was the felt frog, displayed on the divan. She patted it on her way to sit down and said, 'Lucky Fred. He doesn't have to face weekend guests. Oh, Baggy, I'm getting old. Nowadays I only seem to like family or really old friends.'

'Same here. And most of my old friends are dead.'

'So are many of mine. But I've replenished the stock a bit.' She then added, 'Doubt if I shall any more, though,' so as not to sound more fortunate than he was, but found herself thinking it might well be true.

'I dare say you're looking forward to getting back to your flat.' To his delight, the letter he had drafted for her had secured a slight reduction in her rent, since when he had taken an almost proprietary interest in the flat. 'It must be a nice little place.'

'Well, it's right for me. You know, Baggy, as I grow older I get more selfish and the best way of coping with that is to live a life where my selfishness doesn't hurt anyone.'

Baggy smiled. 'You're not selfish, Fran.'

'Oh, I am. And I'd be quite abominably selfish if I didn't pamper myself when I'm on my own. Then I can save up a bit of unselfishness to offer other people.'

'But how does the flat help?'

'Well, I don't have to consider anyone but myself there. I can get up when I like, go to bed when I like – quite often I have supper in bed and lie there listening to the radio or watching television.'

'Or reading all those Agatha Christies you told me about,' said Baggy, with amused reminiscence.

'I shall send you some as soon as I get back, and we'll write to each other about them.' Perhaps it would come near to approximating what he always hankered for: the shared pleasure.

'I shall like that. Tell me, Fran, is Mildred deliberately malicious?'

Fran looked at him quickly. Did the suddenness of his question indicate that he *had* taken in the effects of Mildred's remarks last night? But her eyes got no response from his – for though he had indeed hinted, he was not prepared to do more unless she met him halfway, so great was his fear of alarming her if she wasn't already alarmed.

As cautious as he was, she merely answered, 'No, Baggy. When she does any harm she doesn't know what she's up to. You see, she's never quite grown up.'

'Was she as bad when she was a child?'

'She didn't *seem* so bad. She was so pretty and tiny and delicate – then; she's strong as a horse now. Of course she was spoilt, but lots of spoilt children turn out all right.'

'I suppose she ought to have married,' said Baggy.

'Well, I did my best about that when we were girls. I had her to stay with me in Bloomsbury – where, I'm afraid, I was living a pretty variegated life – and introduced all the men I knew. She quite cut me out, with her prettiness, but then I think they found her too fancy.'

Baggy nodded his head sapiently. 'Men don't like affectation.'

'Actually there was one man… not that he intended matrimony but he did at least make a pass at her, one night when I'd left her alone in my flat. Oh, poor Mildred.'

'Did he frighten her?'

'No, she frightened him. He told me afterwards that she started to dance and pretended she was a nymph. He ended by rushing out into the night. I still feel guilty about letting her in for that. Do you think it did her any harm?'

'Depends if he rushed out before or afterwards,' said Baggy, feeling something of a dog.

'Oh, before, definitely. What I meant was… well, I wouldn't have liked to be rushed out on. Oh, dear.' Fran shook her head, laughing, then stifled a yawn. 'Sorry. It's that enormous lunch.'

'You'd better take a nap. I could do with one, too.'

After she'd gone he displaced Fred the Frog and lay down on his bed. Normally, he would have merely dozed in his chair but today he found it pleasant to think he was lying down when Fran was lying down; it gave him a sense of companionship. Funny to think of her as a girl, living a 'variegated' life. He didn't feel shocked about that. Must have been around the time he first met Mabel at the tennis club. Mabel would have been shocked – and so would he, then. One lived and learned.

He slept until the car returned and the unspectacular weekend continued its course. It never had any claim to fame in its own right but eventually almost every member of the Dower House family saw it as the ending of an epoch. And George came to feel that, if it hadn't happened, things might have turned out differently. He was none too sure about that but, anyway, he looked back on it as two wasted days.

By the time the Harleys left, after supper on Sunday, he had only one idea in his head: he must see June instantly. He had no plans as to what was to happen when he saw her. He just had to be with her – all the more so because it had now dawned on him that he would be away from the Dower House on Monday and Tuesday nights as he had to visit a client in the north of England. The thought of not seeing her until Wednesday evening was unbearable. He must see her *now*. He didn't even spend time in telling anyone he was going to the cottage. He simply went.

He found her, with Robert and Hugh, watching the news on television and only when it finished did Robert turn the sound down, before enquiring how the weekend had gone. George described it briefly, concluding by saying that the Harleys had given Corinna a lift back to London.

Hugh, with assumed nonchalance, said, 'Ah yes. I expect she has an early class tomorrow,' then got up and went out of the room.

'Working tonight, Robert?' said George hopefully.

'No, there's something I want to watch. Do you mind if I turn the sound up now?'

'No, no, go ahead,' said George. 'But I need some fresh air.' He turned to June. 'Let's see if your friend the nightingale's singing.'

'No, thanks, George. I want to see this thing that's starting.' She glanced at the window. 'Besides, it's begun to rain.'

Even the elements were against him. He said, 'I shan't be back at the Dower House until Wednesday evening.' Robert had now turned the sound up.

'What, George?' said June.

He repeated the information loudly, explaining why he would be away. June said, 'I see,' and Robert said, 'Right,' then they both concentrated on the screen.

George gave it up. 'I'll be off.'

He looked back after he opened the door and saw that June had turned her head and was smiling at him. It seemed to him a most melting, loving smile. Well, that was something to take away with him.

Driving to the station with Hugh next morning, he said, 'Your mother all right today? Last night I thought she looked tired.' He had thought no such thing but needed some reason to mention June, for the pleasure of it.

'Really. I didn't notice. She was blithe as a bird this morning.'

'Oh, good. Blithe, was she? Living in the country suits her, doesn't it? I've noticed she sometimes looks quite beautiful.'

'I've always thought Mother beautiful.'

'Yes, indeed,' said George heartily, now thinking it retrospectively. Idiot that he'd been not to have noticed it in well over twenty years.

They drove on through the fresh early morning air.

After a few minutes Hugh said, 'I see they're cutting the hay already,' then added with elaborate casualness, 'I suppose Corinna didn't send any message to me last night?'

'Not by me. She went off in rather a rush – it was a last-minute idea to go with the Harleys.'

Hugh tried to find comfort in that. But it was no use trying to pretend she'd been her normal self recently. He'd simply have to have it out with her as soon as possible.

But when he got back to the flat that evening there was a note saying, 'Sorry, I have to be out – spending night with Joan (you saw her in "As You") we're working on some scenes together. There's a dish of cold food in the fridge and I've made the salad. The coffee's all ready to perk.'

She had laid the table, put flowers on it and obviously gone to trouble over his supper – there were two kinds of cold meat, set out with more trouble than she was apt to take over their shared meals. Also there was a handsome peach on the table with a note beside it saying 'Eat me'. He smiled. Darling Corinna, she was simply busy, obsessed with her work. He relaxed and ate everything she had left him. He wished he could ring her up and thank her but he'd no idea what Joan's surname was, couldn't even place her in *As You Like It*...

He went to bed early and slept well. Last night he'd been kept awake by anxiety, plus Penny's usual bed-hogging.

As soon as he entered the flat on Tuesday evening he knew that Corinna was there. He heard music and could smell something cooking. The television was on in the sitting room but nobody watching. The kitchen, too, was empty. He tapped on Corinna's door.

She called, 'With you in a minute, darling. Get yourself a drink.'

He went back into the sitting room, poured drinks for them both and sat watching television. He felt cheerful. She had sounded her usual affectionate self. He'd simply imagined some crisis between them. Now everything would be all right.

But when, after a considerable delay, she joined him he was shocked by her appearance. Her delicate features were puffy, her eyelids swollen and red.

Hastily switching the television off he said, 'Darling, whatever is it?'

'Oh, God, my idiotic face! And I've been bathing my eyes for ages. No, don't come near me or I shall start again.' She seated herself on an isolated chair and averted her eyes.

'But what *is* it? Something gone wrong with your work? This new part?'

'There isn't any new part. That was only an excuse not to talk to you. Well, I've to get this said, so listen, please. It's over, Hugh – I mean, between us. It's finished.'

'Nonsense,' said Hugh. 'Now tell me what's wrong, quietly. Is it something I've done?'

'God, no. It's me, not you. I'm – I'm having an affair with Sir Harry.'

'Since when?' said Hugh, mainly conscious of fury.

'I went to his flat last night. It nearly happened last weekend when I stayed in his country place only I felt I couldn't there, not with his wife in the house. But I more or less promised to, then. Oh, darling, I've fought and fought about it...'

'Well, one can't fight against a grand passion, can one?' said Hugh satirically. 'Tell me, is it simply in the interest of your career?'

'No. Oh, Hugh, I'm trying to be honest about it – with myself as well as you. I suppose ambition does come into it but there's more to it than that. You see, I'm not good like you.'

'God damn it.'

She sprang up. 'I'll have to turn the oven down.'

During the few minutes she was gone his anger abated a little, partly because he was reminded of the night he had moved into the flat, when her mother's casserole had been in the oven. Since then, her own efforts at cooking had been minimal. He found it both ludicrous and pathetic that she had chosen this night to offer him a good dinner.

Returning, she said, 'I did mean to break it gradually, after dinner. Are you hungry?'

'Ravenous, naturally. Oh, darling, don't be idiotic.' He found himself laughing.

She was surprised but relieved – and then insulted. 'What's so funny?'

'That you should think I'd want to eat. Now listen. You said that you're not good, like I am. Has my so-called goodness any-thing to do with this? That first night in the flat we agreed that if either of us felt the need... Do you remember?'

She did indeed and had often reminded herself of it. But the need would have to come from him – as it had from plenty of other men. Never, never would she tell him this. She simply said, 'I know. It's all my fault. Ambition – and finding I wasn't as hopeless at acting as I thought I was. And then getting carried away… Oh, it's mainly that I've been living in a different world from our world.'

'I wish you'd told me before it happened, given me a chance to – well, put up some competition.'

'I almost told you last week, that night you were so taken up with Penny and her troubles, and how you spent the night with Sarah. I was angry about that.'

'But, good God, you surely didn't think…'

'No, no. But I was angry because of what Aunt Mildred thought. It was insulting – to me.'

Hugh looked dazed. 'But you scarcely seemed to be taking it in.'

'I was taking it in all right *and* thinking about my own problem. And I suddenly felt I'd have to decide things on my own. But it did make a difference, Hugh; you and Sarah, and Aunt Mildred thinking whatever she did think. She wouldn't have thought it if you hadn't fallen asleep in Sarah's bedroom.'

'But I couldn't help falling asleep.'

'You shouldn't have given yourself the chance to. You ought to have taken Penny home as soon as she was dry.'

'But it was pouring with rain.'

'Anyway, Sarah ought to have wakened you. But of course she's been after you from the beginning.'

'That's a bloody lie,' said Hugh, furious again.

'Well, *I* think she has – though I daresay you've never realised it. Oh, I'm sorry. Perhaps I'm using it as an excuse. But I *was* angry, especially about Aunt Mildred, and I was muddled. And Harry managed to see me every day last week and he's, well, he's so dynamic.'

'What a delightful thing to be when you're pushing fifty.'

Corinna flushed. 'He's nowhere near fifty. And he's terribly attractive, whatever you like to think.'

'I like to think about him as little as possible. Is this…"affair" was, I believe, your description, to be a prolonged one?'

'I don't know.' She was none too sure she'd been a success. 'Anyway, one's got to learn not to take these things too seriously.'

'How right you are. I'm beginning to get the knack of it already.' He was, indeed, shocked at his lack of sorrow. Would he feel differently when he stopped being angry or was it that she had already become for him a different person? If he grieved it would be for a memory, not for an actual girl.

She said, 'I didn't mean that I'm not taking *us* seriously – what I've done to you. I suppose you'd laugh if I said I still love you.'

'Does that by any chance imply that you'd like us to go on as we were – say, after you've had a few years on the loose?'

Vaguely, she'd hoped for something very like that but she instantly denied it. 'Of course not. But I'll always care for you.'

'As a cousin, no doubt. Well, at least your mother will be pleased. When shall we give her the glad tidings?'

She gave him a piteous look. 'Hugh, I can't bear it, that tone in your voice! It's not *you*.'

'Well, you're not exactly you, my dear,' said Hugh. 'Still, I'm sorry that I'm taking it so badly. Don't start to cry again or your poor eyes will disappear entirely.'

'I know but…' She gulped, then fished down the neck of her dress for a handkerchief.

'Look,' said Hugh briskly. 'We'll eat now, whether we want to or not. And we'll try to be matter-of-fact. There's a lot we'll have to discuss. How much are you going to tell your mother and father?'

'Need I tell them anything? I was hoping you and I could... sort of slide apart.'

'They'll have to know why I'm clearing out of the flat.'

'But must you? Surely we can go on sharing it? Things needn't really be any different. After all, it isn't as if we've ever...' She blushed painfully and went off to the kitchen.

He finished his drink before following her, wondering if he could face staying on at the flat. The alternative would be some boarding house or bed-sitting-room, dreary and almost certainly expensive. It would help her with her parents if he stayed on. And, as she'd said, things needn't really be any different. Oh God...

He suddenly felt to blame for everything. Of course he ought to have slept with her. 'And don't think you held off out of saintly idealism,' he told himself. 'You're not good, you're just a vegetable. You didn't want to sleep with her, not until you're well enough off to have a solid conventional marriage. You're just a citified little gent wearing a spiritual bowler hat.'

She called from the kitchen. 'I've some hock in the refrigerator, if you'd like to come and open it.'

He called back, 'Right.' Dear idiot girl, how could she feel this was an evening for celebration? But no doubt the hock and the special food had been a last loving gesture. She'd intended to feed him before breaking his heart. Not that it showed any sign of breaking. He'd felt anger, he'd felt guilt, but not one flicker of real grief.

When he went into the cheerful kitchen she was laying the table. Looking up brightly she said, 'How was Penny?'

And he was instantly quite shattered with grief. He said, 'Tell me something, please. Did you know all this was going to happen when you gave her to me?'

'No! I swear it.' But even as she said it, she doubted it. Hadn't she thought of Penny as a compensation not for Bonnie but for what might lie ahead?

Hugh, with an effort, smiled. 'Well, at least I've got the custody of the dog. Where's the corkscrew?'

It was, strangely, a relief to feel what he was now feeling. If one could suffer, one wasn't quite a vegetable.

18

George, driving home from the station on Wednesday evening, asked himself if ever in his life he had felt as happy as he did now. He decided he hadn't – not even when he had first fallen in love with May. He had certainly been happy then, but the happiness had been... well, a sort of charming light-heartedness, plus the solid satisfaction of knowing that he and Robert had found two delightful sisters who would make ideal wives and everything was set fair for a shared future. They had almost always gone out as a foursome and had a wonderfully *jolly* time. Robert and June had been more romantic than he and May but that was merely a matter of temperament. George considered himself to be quite as much in love with May as Robert was with June and had never imagined himself capable of any deeper feeling. What was more, he had gone on loving May and had never embarked on an affair without assuring himself that it 'didn't count'. Now things were very different.

What he now felt for June certainly 'counted' and yet he still loved May and didn't want to hurt her; nor did he want to hurt Robert. Everything must be done to protect them both – short of giving up loving June. There now, he'd thought the words 'loving June'. Up to now he'd only admitted to himself that he 'wanted June' and had tried to press his feelings into the mould which usually contained them for his affairs. Well, this time it couldn't be done. He thought, 'I love June,' and thought it so loudly that he actually seemed to hear the words shouted. Then he drove extremely fast.

Being, as well as a man in love, an admirable driver, he soon slowed down and then became more than usually conscious of the beauty of the countryside. High wooded slopes, water meadows; a great estate with a fine house, smooth lawns, swans on the lake…he had admired them countless times before but only with his eyes. Now, in some extraordinary way, he felt at one with them; and when he reached a more intimate countryside, he was equally at one with the fields, farms, cottages and pretty villages. He found everything delightful and, though familiar, astonishing.

He must, he decided, be more romantic than he had ever suspected himself of being and he'd better pull himself together before he reached home. With so much protecting to do he was going to need tact, skill and firmness. He must, as he'd told himself on Sunday, remain in control. And in the interest of remaining it he would now play the Devil's Advocate about his feelings.

Was he not exaggerating them, mainly because, since coming to live in the country, he had been entirely respectable? (Most unwise, really.) He'd known June over twenty years without feeling anything like this. She was the same woman, he was the same man. How could they change so spectacularly just because dotty old Mildred made an idiotic remark? If she hadn't, he'd probably have gone on for the rest of his life feeling nothing more than a brother-in-law's affection for a pleasant sister-in-law. Well, all he could say, then, was 'Thank God for Mildred' – which must surely be the first time anyone had said *that*.

It was no use. He stopped arguing with himself, simply looked forward to seeing June. It was the sort of mindless concentration with which a very thirsty man looks forward to a long drink.

Arriving at the Dower House he found May in the hall, picking up fallen rose petals. She asked if he'd had a good trip.

'Excellent, excellent,' he said, for the moment unable to remember anything about the trip. Ah, yes, of course. 'That reminds me, there's something I want to ask Robert – about a quotation. My host was surprisingly literary. I'll just have time before dinner.'

'Robert's gone to London – some journalists' dinner. He won't be back till late. I said you'd meet him.'

'Yes, of course. June's all alone then.'

'She's coming to dinner. I asked her to come early.'

'I'll call for her,' said George.

'Do, and give her a drink.'

George, pleased with his luck, hurried out; but June was already emerging from the lilac grove. He could only go and meet her halfway across the lawn. He looked into her eyes and said 'Darling June'. She quickly averted her eyes and said 'Darling George' in a tone anyone was entitled to hear. Normally he would have kissed her after an absence of three days – or wouldn't he? He did that sort of thing spontaneously, not according to any decided protocol... strange that he would never again be spontaneous with June – when there was any chance of their being observed.

Fran came from the Long Room with Penny, who greeted George enthusiastically.

'She much prefers men to women,' said Fran. 'Still I shall miss the creature.'

'You're leaving us?' George sounded concerned, as indeed he was; he now saw no chance of being alone with June before dinner.

'On Monday – and I ought to be gone by now. I'm only staying on because Prudence and Dickon will be home for the weekend.'

'Yes, of course; it's their half-term holiday.' Well, at least he could *look* at June, June in her golden dress. He said, 'I love you in that dress, June' – quite unexceptionable as a remark, he assured himself, while taking great pleasure in saying it.

'May gave it to me.' June had told herself to wear some unobtrusive frock – and ended by putting on the one she liked herself in best. And now she felt herself blushing. She stooped and patted Penny.

Fran had seen the blush and was torn between wanting to give George and June a few minutes alone together, and wondering how she could prevent their getting them, now or later. Not that anything she could do would make any difference, really. No, that was being defeatist. Perhaps she ought to talk to June, if only to put her on her guard.

She was to feel that more and more during dinner. Really, it was astounding that two mature people should allow themselves to look so moonstruck – and George the last man one would have expected to be indiscreet. Fran thanked God that, for once, May was minus all three Matsons (owing to something known as the Horticultural Outing) and therefore much occupied in serving the meal; though even so...

There came a moment when Fran caught Baggy's eye and was instantly sure that he was fully aware of what was going on. Now she would be able to talk to him freely. It might not help but would at least be a relief.

She seized the first opportunity, after dinner. May had turned the television on, saying there was a programme George liked, and he and June had settled down to watch it. Fran said, 'Baggy, could you spare me a moment? There's one last little problem about my lease.'

Baggy, knowing that her lease had been settled long ago, was fully aware of what she was up to. He said, 'Ah, yes,' portentously and led the way to his room.

The minute they were together there, Fran said, 'Oh, Baggy, how long have you known?'

'Only since that night when Mildred dropped her brick. There wasn't anything *to* know before that.'

240

'I was *almost* sure you knocked Mildred's coffee over deliberately. That was brilliant of you, Baggy.'

'Much good it'll have done in the long run,' said Baggy gloomily. 'Of course I did it to stop her saying any more, for Robert and May to hear; but they'll know soon enough now.'

'Is there anything we can do? If I talk to June, will you talk to George?'

'I've been thinking about that, myself. But I'm afraid it would make no difference; anyway, with George. He's been hit by something that's never hit him before. The truth is that he *should* have married June. May's a good, kind woman and the soul of efficiency but there's something lacking: a sort of softness, I think. When I lived with June I was far less comfortable than I've been here, but I was never lonely. There was… enough warmth to go round.'

Fran said, 'Whatever May lacks – and I do know what you mean – she's capable of intense suffering. And she adores George – and June. And Robert adores June and thinks the world of George. They're all tied up together. Oh, God, it doesn't bear thinking about. But I don't believe anything irrevocable's happened yet and it may never happen. After all, they're not a couple of kids, or Tristram and Iseult or someone. Anyway, I can't believe that June…'

Baggy shook his head unhelpfully. 'George always gets what he wants from women, as you probably know. Does May know it?'

'She never admits to knowing it, just blames herself for unjustified jealousy. Now listen: if we're going to put up any kind of fight we've got to act quickly. I shall talk to June tonight. Oh, I shan't admit to taking it seriously. I shall just say they're being silly and they'll upset Robert and May. And you talk to George. Even if we can't persuade them to end the whole thing, at least they can be more discreet.'

241

Baggy looked shocked. 'Do you mean they could have a *secret* affair?'

'Well, it wouldn't be easy in the circumstances, but I suppose… Oh, Baggy, try not to be too upset. These are such permissive days, lots of husbands and wives… Still, it would be dreadful. Anyway, the *first* thing is to get them to be more circumspect, because once May and Robert notice what's happening, much of the damage will be done, even if things go no further – as they mustn't, Baggy; let's concentrate on that. Now come on. I shall ask June to come up to my room.'

'I don't guarantee to talk to George. I might make matters worse.'

'Well, it may be enough if I talk to June. Come on, anyway.'

But they found the Long Room empty. May, coming in from the kitchen, said George and June had gone to see if the nightingale could still be heard.

'We'll go too, Baggy,' said Fran.

'Yes, do,' said May. 'I'll be up in the sewing-room, if anyone wants me.'

She was, Fran knew, making a dress for Prudence to wear at the weekend. How like May to be occupied at this vital time – and how fortunate that she was.

Baggy, after May had gone, said, 'We can't chase after them.'

'It won't look like that. It's perfectly natural that we should want to hear the last of the nightingale; Robert says it's due to stop singing any day now. Please come, Baggy. Even the sight of us in the distance might… well, act as a bit of a brake.' She opened the French window. Penny, left behind by George and June, shot out and headed for the lilac grove. 'Oh, dear. Still, I expect she'll only go back to the cottage. I wonder if that's where they've really gone.'

Baggy, unwillingly accompanying Fran across the lawn, stopped walking. 'If they have I'm not going in after them.'

'Of course not, unless the door's open and the curtains are undrawn as usual. Then it would seem natural for us to go in. Let's just see – and then play it by ear.'

'What?'

'It's just an expression. Means act on the inspiration of the moment.'

'Very unsafe thing to do,' said Baggy, now most unwillingly going with her into the lilac grove.

Under the interlaced branches it was already dusk, though the sunset had barely begun. Fran, who prided herself on knowing her way about the grove's maze-like twists, found the dimness confusing and took several wrong turns, but did not admit this to Baggy. They walked in silence, their footsteps making no sound on the grassy paths. Somewhere ahead of them the tag on Penny's chain collar tinkled.

After a few minutes Fran gratefully saw daylight ahead, then realised, only seconds later, that it came not from beyond the grove but from the sky above the little enclosed garden. They would have to turn back. But simultaneously with deciding this she got a clear view of the garden and stopped dead, as did Baggy.

Standing beside the sundial were George and June, clasped in each other's arms – looking, Fran thought, for all the world like some long-ago Academy painting. One expected George to be in knee breeches.

As simultaneously as they had stopped, Baggy and Fran started up again, in reverse. Mercifully only a few steps took them round a twist in the path where they could not be seen from the garden – not, Fran thought, that there was any likelihood of their being seen, even had they remained in view. That embrace looked as if it would be going on a long, long time. Probably it would only break when the participants had to come up for air.

This time Fran took no wrong turnings and had Baggy out of the grove in a couple of minutes. They emerged into the full light of sunset.

Baggy, in a choked voice, said, 'Oh, Fran!'

'Wait till we're indoors,' said Fran, then noticed that his face was ashen. There were some deckchairs only a few yards away. She urged him towards them. 'But sit down for a few minutes first.'

He shook his head. 'No, I'd rather go in.' Then he walked fairly steadily to the Long Room. 'I shall be all right if I lie down for a bit.'

There was a Victorian one-ended sofa near the west window. Baggy was fond of it because it reminded him of a horsehair sofa he had known as a child, also the back gave him better support than that of any modern sofa did. He settled there now, after putting a newspaper between his shoes and May's chintz upholstery.

'I'll get you a drink,' said Fran. 'Brandy, whisky?'

'Whisky. I don't like brandy. I'm all right now. It was just that… It was so shocking.'

Fran hadn't felt that. It had seemed to her both ludicrous and moving: the absurdly romantic sundial, June's outspread golden dress, the ecstatic mingling of the two figures… one couldn't quite be shocked at such rapture. Still…

'Just a minute,' she said and went into the hall. She could hear the whirring of May's sewing machine upstairs. It would be safe to talk.

She went back, got Baggy his drink, and sat down beside him. 'Try not to worry too much,' she told him. 'Even if the worst comes to the worst, May and Robert may never find out.'

'Of course they'll find out, and so will the children.' Baggy's voice was now angry as well as weak. 'And I'll tell you something, Fran. I'll not stay here and watch it. I'd give my life if I could save them all from what's coming – truly, I would – but staying here won't help them. And I can't face it. I'll have to go, at once. I suppose I can find some boarding house.'

'But you'd hate that, Baggy.'

'I know, but where else can I go?'

'How about a little flat like mine?' Of course the idea was preposterous but she hoped it might be stimulating, cheerful. To her astonishment she saw a flicker of eagerness in his eyes.

'Do you think I could get one – somewhere near you, perhaps? I wouldn't be a burden.'

'Of *course* you wouldn't.' She hoped heartiness would hide her dismay. Poor, darling Baggy, always wanting to share life with someone, he would be a burden of burdens. But it couldn't happen, of course it couldn't, and she must go on cheering him up. 'We'd have lots of fun – often lunch together.'

'And I could telephone you in the evenings.' A chuckle, if a faint one, emanated from Baggy. 'When we're both lying in bed reading Agatha Christie.'

'Lovely,' said Fran, who hated being telephoned in the evening. It invariably interrupted one's favourite television programme.

'Seriously, Fran, would there be any chance of getting a flat in the block you live in?'

'I'll find out the minute I get back.' *Oh, no*! She couldn't have him in the same block. Already she felt a dead weight of liability for him. But she mustn't let him see. She said brightly, 'You're looking better. Shall I help you to your room now and into bed?' Good God, it was beginning already. She'd probably end up as his full-time nurse.

Baggy said, 'Not yet. I'd rather lie here for a while and do some thinking – about ways and means. I can afford the rent you pay but… well, it needs planning. Just leave me on my own for a bit. And put the lights off, please, so that I can watch the sunset. I don't often get the chance to. Never like to hang around in this room after dinner.'

'You won't lie here worrying about George and June?' Damn it, she oughtn't to have reminded him of that.

But he took it in his stride. 'Not now, not till I've done some thinking about the flat. You see, I want to leave here quickly. Anyway, there's no point in worrying when I can't do anything to stop them. And I felt so *ill* when I saw them. One's got to try and protect oneself a bit.'

'Yes, indeed,' said Fran, switching the lights off. 'Well, you've certainly got a glorious sunset. Now leave the door open and my bedroom door, too. You just call when you want me to help you.'

He thanked her as she went, then lay back looking at the golden sky. Already the first stars were coming out, where it paled to blue above the dark Hall. Wonderful how Fran had cheered him up. Actually, he'd liked the sound of that one-room flat ever since she'd first described it – though it might be better if they found a rather larger flat and shared it; more economical for them both and quite respectable at their ages. Well, well… what was it Mabel used to say? 'A door never shuts but another opens.' Mabel would be grateful to Fran now. He heard her open the door of her room… yes, she'd remembered not to close it. She'd come if he called her. It was a comfortable thought.

It wasn't a comfortable thought to Fran, as she propped her door open. She'd have liked to go straight to bed. Not that she could, so early; May would think she was ill. She'd just lie down on the bed – but if she did that, she might fall asleep and not hear Baggy call. She must settle for just sitting down.

She sank into the armchair with too much abandon; her back gave a painful jerk. She moved cautiously. It proved to be a warning rather than a rick, but one would have to be careful. And now the open door was causing a through draught. Hoisting herself up she went to close the window. From here she could see the break in the lilac grove that indicated the little sundial garden but she could not see down into it. How could George and June be so reckless? Though, poor loves, if they wanted each other as much as that... But there was such a thing as being too permissive, she told herself sternly, and one must concentrate on protecting May and Robert. Incidentally, what reason could Baggy give for leaving? He'd probably blow the gaff on everything.

She went back to her armchair and thought about Baggy in London. He'd be astounded at what he'd have to pay for a cleaner, if one could be found. Soon she'd have to find one herself. One ought to be able to cope with cleaning a tiny flat but one was, after all, well on into the seventies. (Usually she thought of herself as barely out of the sixties.) She felt old, old, old – and then made a valiant effort to stop feeling it. 'You're fantastically young for your age,' she told herself, 'and if that poor old man's got the guts to start a new life, you'll jolly well help him. Anyway, stop worrying about it and about June *and* George. There's nothing more you can do tonight, so relax.' Oh, God, another worry had wriggled its way into her mind: Penny was somewhere out on the loose. She hadn't given the creature a thought since seeing that tableau by the sundial. Ought one to go out and find her? Well, one couldn't – in case Baggy called. And surely Penny would come to no harm – she wasn't on heat now. She'd either return to the Dower House or go to the cottage or, at worst, the Hall.

And there was no traffic anywhere near. But, really, if another catastrophe happened to Hugh's dog…

Penny, in actual fact, was having a particularly pleasant evening. She had located George and June in the sundial garden not long after Baggy and Fran had turned tail on seeing them; and, far from turning tail, she had wagged her tail ecstatically and then proceeded to break up the clinch. Having almost completely outgrown her original nervousness, she was fast becoming a confident, loving dog who considered that endearments should be exclusively bestowed on her. So she instantly stood on her hind legs and pushed her way between George and June. They capitulated.

'She doesn't like people to kiss,' said June. 'Silly Penny! There's enough love for everyone.'

Since then George and June had been sitting on the white painted seat with Penny stretched across their laps. She was more comfortable than they were; they found her painfully bony.

The conversation had been loving, vague and repetitive. Again and again June said, 'What *are* we going to do?' and George, in various ways, assured her it would be all right. He also, repeatedly, called her 'my dear love', which he had never called anyone before. (May was 'darling', 'sweetheart', even 'dearest' but never before had he felt a positive need to say 'my dear love'.) June, also again and again, said it mustn't go on, and George told her that it must – 'Just give me time to plan. We can meet at the flat – when you come up to London for shopping.' 'But May would always come with me – determined to pay for everything – and Hugh and Corinna might come into the flat.' 'Well, we'll manage here. We can go for walks. Perhaps we can find a hut in the woods. We *could* go to the cottage now.'

At this June said firmly, 'We could not. And it'll soon be time for you to go to the station to meet Robert.'

'I'd forgotten that. Let him take a taxi.'

'He'd wait for ages first – and he'd be anxious. George, I still love Robert.'

'I know. I still love May. It's what you told Penny: there's enough love for everyone.'

'That's exactly how I feel, really.'

George, whose arm was around her, clasped her closer. She dropped her head on to his shoulder and looked up at the sky, now pale with dusk. From where they were sitting, the house was invisible and the little circular garden seemed to her a secret refuge from the world. Idly she quoted, 'A garden enclosed is my sister, my spouse', then added ruefully, 'Not a fortunate quotation, seeing that my sister is your spouse, and she'll be wondering where we are.'

'May will not be wondering where we are. She'll be making jam.'

'Which, in this case, will be a dress for my daughter. Oh, George, do you realise how *good* May is?'

'I do, indeed,' said George soberly. 'And so's Robert. I suppose I *shall* have to think about meeting him. Anyway, this creature's elbows are crippling me. Get down, Penny. Give her a shove.' They dislodged the unwilling Penny.

June, rising, said, 'I know what I ought to do: get Robert to take me right round the world. He's always wanted to go round the world – it was he who put the idea in Mother's head. If only I had a lot of money!'

'I do have quite a lot of money,' said George. 'And it's at your service. But not for that.'

He drew her towards him but Penny instantly intervened.

'Just as well,' said June. 'I'll take her back to the cottage and try to get my thoughts in order before Robert comes home. You'll have to say goodnight to May for me.'

George saw them both back to the cottage, then shut Penny in the kitchen and took June in his arms. But he did not kiss her lingeringly. He was suddenly inhibited by the thought that he was in Robert's house. Ludicrously conventional, he told himself but still… things weren't going to be easy.

It was now too dark to risk losing his way through the lilac grove. He went by way of the park. There was still a faint golden glow beyond the Hall. It had been a benign sunset, not one of the lurid ones that Robert found inspiring. Not that, as yet, he'd been sufficiently inspired to start work on that projected Gothic novel. It was to be hoped that he soon would and that the work would utterly absorb him. Yes, indeed.

George opened the gate which led from the park to the Dower House front garden. There was a light upstairs in May's sewing-room. No light yet in Baggy's room so presumably he was still in the Long Room. Perhaps he'd enjoy a drive to the station. He and Robert could chat on the return journey, George having no desire to chat with Robert. Sad, that. George, who had an enormous respect for his younger brother's work and intellect (no head for business, though) usually enjoyed a quiet talk with him.

Surprisingly, the Long Room was in darkness. George switched the lights on and then saw that Baggy was asleep on the sofa. Most unusual; unless there was a family gathering or something special on television he was almost always back in his room by this time. George felt a wave of affection for him. Funny, he couldn't remember ever before seeing his father sleeping. Poor old dear. Actually, he looked younger than usual, so relaxed and faintly smiling. Very, very peaceful…

George, feeling a sudden catch at his heart, hurried to the sofa.

A few moments later he was out in the hall, calling loudly for May.

19

Baggy's death came as a shock but not a surprise, to everyone but Fran. If she had ever known that his heart was weak she had forgotten it, and there had been no mention of it during her visit. She remembered his saying that he had been afraid he might not live long enough for his deed of gift to Robert to be satisfactorily completed, but she had taken that to be the superstitious fear she herself would have felt in similar circumstances. Now she learned that his tenuous hold on life had been generally accepted, also that he had visited the local doctor. This transpired only after his death as he had asked that the visits should be treated as confidential.

Well, if he had to go he had chosen a good moment for it, Fran told herself. In his state of health he obviously could not have lived on his own in London and had he even mentioned the idea it would have caused trouble. Either he would have brought what was happening between George and June out into the open, or he would have given the impression that he wasn't happy at the Dower House, in which case Robert and June would have felt that they ought somehow to have kept him with them. She could only hope that his new interest, impracticable though it was, had given him some happy thoughts, and she hung on to the fact that he had died with a smile on his face.

So exit the living Baggy; and May, with her usual efficiency, made sure that the dead Baggy's exit from the Dower House was remarkably swift. Her main reason for this was that Prue and Dickon were due home on Friday. She telephoned Dickon on Thursday morning suggesting they should stay at school for this particular half-term holiday but he firmly declined. He was, however, willing that they should spend Friday night in London – 'We'll go to a concert – more respectful than a theatre and, anyway, we *want* to go to this concert.' May therefore, with determination which overcame all opposition, achieved the minor miracle of arranging for Baggy's cremation – at some distance – to be on Saturday morning.

Fran, on hearing this, said, 'But didn't the children feel they should go to the funeral?'

'I should hope not,' said May. 'And anyway, June and I wouldn't have permitted it. It took us ages to get over Father's funeral when we were young. I wonder that you took us.'

'His family expected it,' said Fran. 'In *my* family, women didn't go to funerals. They stayed at home and pulled up the blinds and got a meal ready.'

'And we'll stick to that ruling,' said May, beginning to plan the food.

Fran said, 'Goodness knows, I hate going to funerals but I do rather feel I ought to show respect.'

'Who to? Some officials you've never met before? Darling Mother, I won't let you go.'

Fran was glad to be overruled. She had never been to a funeral without feeling that death took a step nearer. And the older one grew, the less ground death had to cover.

Eventually, George, Robert and Hugh went, the two brothers driving off after the hearse soon after breakfast, Hugh travelling direct from London. Prue and Dickon arrived home mid-morning, by which time May had sorted Baggy's clothes, which were to be sent to a deserving charity, and was finishing the turning out of his room.

'Oh, don't come in here, darlings,' she said, when her son and her niece routed her out. 'This room feels depressing.'

Dickon said, 'We've been thinking we might use it as a studio.' He looked round critically. 'Pity it's not large enough for sculpture.'

'Couldn't you do some small sculpture?' said May.

'Nowadays, dear Mother, small sculpture is a contradiction in terms.'

Prue, picking up Fred the Frog, said she wouldn't mind having him but was frustrated by the entrance of Fran who, after greeting her grandchildren affectionately, firmly claimed Fred the Frog for herself. She said she wanted him as a memento of Baggy. This was true; but she also wanted Fred in his own right.

'I must see about lunch,' said May briskly. 'Now, no one's to stop in here brooding.'

No one had the slightest desire to, though Dickon gave one backward glance and said to Prue, 'Remember coming in here that last night of the holidays? Poor old Baggy.'

Prue said, 'Where's Mother?' at the same moment that Dickon said, 'Where's Penny?'

'They're both at the cottage,' said Fran, who had just come from there.

'Mind you bring your mother back in good time for lunch,' May told Prue, 'or Dickon's favourite cheese soufflé will go flat.'

Fran took Fred the Frog up to her room and then stood at her window looking out at the sunless day. The lilac grove was at its worst now, with all its heads of blossom shrivelled and brown. She felt it was in keeping with her mood.

She had gone to the cottage soon after Robert had left for the funeral. It had been her intention to speak frankly to June, except that she didn't intend to disclose that Baggy had known as much as he did. That would have troubled June unnecessarily. But as things turned out, she hadn't troubled June at all. She had found herself incapable of it. The main reason for this was June's manner which had been... poised, aloof? Perhaps 'assured' was a better word. As a rule, June gave the impression of feeling that others knew more about everything than she did. She was humble when criticised and always vaguely apologetic for being what she had once described as 'rather a muddle'. This morning she had been surprisingly clean-cut and, though sincerely sorry about Baggy's death, she had shown no emotion about it. She had, however, shown emotion about Robert.

'He's so terribly upset,' she told her mother. 'He feels we ought to have gone on having Baggy with us. Not that we could have – he was longing to be with George and May, anyway with George. Robert knows that but... I think he feels guilty because we've been so happy on our own. And there are other things besides Baggy troubling him.'

'Such as?' Did this mean Robert knew about George?

'Well, he can't get started on his novel. And he's so tired of reviewing. He was tired of that in London but he quite enjoyed it when he first came down here, and he did particularly good work. Now he's tired of it again. So he feels guilty about that *and* about his novel *and*, now, about Baggy. Robert's always so hard on himself. But I shall cope. I've just got to work things out.'

Would a wife talk like that when on the brink of being unfaithful to her husband? But perhaps it had already happened and June was feeling triumphant rather than guilty. Fran had known women to acquire supreme self-confidence as the result of a consummated love affair. Well, if June *had*, there was nothing to be done about it. And if she hadn't it didn't sound as if she was going to. And either way, Fran decided to hold her tongue. Speaking frankly might easily do more harm than good and she didn't really want to admit she knew anything at all – especially now she would so soon be leaving and wouldn't have to witness whatever lay ahead. The Monday evening train which took her grandchildren back towards their school would take her back towards her flat.

And, standing by the window, she realised just how desperately she was longing for that flat. Age, in Baggy's case, had craved company. Age, in her case, craved solitude – anyway, some good, solid dollops of it. Oh, the bliss of being on her own for a while! What joy to escape from the tyranny of regular meals, particularly and most ungratefully May's superb meals which caused one to feel full, take afternoon naps and put on weight. She reminded herself how often she disliked having to go out to buy food, and then cook it, or get to some restaurant in the pouring rain. Well, she needn't do either, for a long, long time. She could live on tea and toast. No, tea and starchless rolls.

A delicate smell of cooking cheese wafted up through the open window. She sniffed it with pleasure. Well, three more days of the fleshpots.

The funeral contingent arrived back in the early afternoon, George determinedly cheerful, Robert determinedly ungloomy but noticeably quiet. George reported one touch of light relief: Mildred had turned up for the funeral, looking like Mary Queen of Scots on her way to execution – 'Somebody asked if she was the widow. By the way, Fran, she said she was looking forward to having you back in London.'

Fran sighed. 'Well, we all have our crosses. Anyway, it was nice of her to go all that way for the funeral.' But it was hard not to believe that Mildred had just seized an opportunity for dressing up.

Hugh, though feeling genuine regret for his grandfather, was now mainly troubled by the thought of the weekend ahead of him. Since Tuesday he had only had one conversation with Corinna, during which she had asked him to tell her mother she wouldn't be coming down – 'Just say I'm busy.' She had then added, 'Perhaps I'll write and tell her about us but I may not get the time. If I do write, she'll speak to you about it. If not, you needn't say anything unless you want to.'

Since he had gone direct to the funeral, only now did he deliver Corinna's message to his aunt. May said, 'I know. Spare me a minute, Hugh darling. In here.'

He followed her into the William Morris drawing room which no one but she ever used. There was an elegant desk where she did her household accounts.

'This came this morning,' she said, taking a letter from a pigeon hole. 'You'd better read it.'

The letter read:

> *Darling Mother,*
>
> *Thank you for writing about Baggy's death and for saying I mustn't go to the funeral. It would have upset me terribly. Sorry you couldn't get me on the telephone. I never seem to be in these days. Poor old Baggy – but it's lovely to know he went so peacefully.*
>
> *I think I ought to tell you that Hugh and I have broken off our engagement – if we ever really were engaged. No quarrel or anything. It's just that I want to concentrate on my work. And anyway, we're not right for each other. I'm not nearly good enough for Hugh. But of course I shall go on being fond of him.*
>
> *I won't be coming for the weekend or for quite a while now as I've got a tiny job in Sir Harry's new play. Only an understudy but it's a miracle to get a job at all – and be allowed to take it while one's still a student. Sir Harry managed it for me. Later on I'll come down just for a Sunday. Be as nice to Hugh as you can – but I expect he'll*

like it best if you just leave him alone. Love to you all, and
I am so sorry about Baggy.

Corinna

'Well, that's that,' said Hugh, handing the letter back.

'I suppose you wouldn't care to amplify at all?'

Hugh shook his head. 'I think she's covered the ground pretty well.'

May doubted it. For some time she'd had her suspicions about 'Sir Harry' and now felt they'd been more than justified. But she had once said she would welcome anything that prevented Corinna from marrying Hugh and she hadn't changed her mind. She said now, 'I won't pretend I'm sorry this has happened but I am sorry for you. And if there's anything in the world I can do to help... But she's probably right in saying you'll prefer to be left alone. Would you like me to tell the others and warn them all, even your mother, to lay off you? She'd understand.'

'Yes,' said Hugh. 'That would help quite enormously.'

'Then I'll do it at once. Oh, Hugh darling, do please believe I'm truly fond of you.'

Hugh smiled. 'I know. It was just those idiot grandchildren you were against. Well, you won't have them now.'

'Unless Prue and Dickon want to marry. They do seem completely satisfied with each other's company. Perhaps I ought to separate them.'

'Oh, I wouldn't put ideas into their heads,' said Hugh.

'Anyway, I don't think I'd *dare* separate them. They'd consider it such an impertinence. Oh, I've probably got another nightmare ahead of me.' She put Corinna's letter away and then added, 'Gloomy in here, isn't it? I sometimes think this house is just the Long Room for eating in and a lot of bedrooms for sleeping in.

And I still haven't got the right line on the conservatory. Well, I'll go and see your mother now.'

'I'll come too, and whisk Penny out for a walk.'

At the cottage, June greeted Hugh with, 'Sarah's just been here, wanting you particularly – you can catch her if you're quick. Take your mac; it keeps on trying to rain.'

'All right,' said Hugh, defending himself from his dog's ecstatic welcome. 'Come on, Penny.'

He set out after Sarah, but her stride was as long as his and she was almost at the Hall before he got within shouting distance. Then she turned and came to meet him.

She was wearing her grandfather's old Burberry which was highly unbecoming to her. It occurred to Hugh that he had never yet seen her in any becoming clothes – except the tent-like silk nightgown, which had made her look a little like a madonna. He had often remembered that.

Her voice as she greeted him managed to be both harsh and tragic. 'Oh, Hugh, I'm so terribly sorry to bother you when you've just come from your grandfather's funeral, but I simply must talk to you.'

'Right,' said Hugh. 'Talk away. What's the trouble? Is it *your* grandfather?'

'Goodness, no. He's been particularly well. He wanted me to ask you to dinner tonight but you probably won't want to come.'

Dinner at the Hall would be a way of escaping from his family. Even if May muzzled them all he was going to feel embarrassed. He said at once, 'I shall be delighted to come. Now tell me what's upset you.'

'I meant you might not want to come after I've told you I've had a letter from Corinna and though she says it's not my fault in any way – not that I'd have thought it was if she hadn't mentioned

258

it but now… What I mean is, has what's gone wrong between you anything to do with that night you fell asleep in my room?'

'Nothing whatever,' said Hugh, convinced he was speaking the truth. Corinna had only used that incident as an excuse for following her own inclinations. 'Now take it calmly, Sarah. We'd better go indoors and discuss it quietly.'

'If we go indoors, Grandfather may grab you. We can sit down over there.'

There was an ancient seat built round a far more ancient oak. They sat, with Penny and the spaniels milling around them. Hugh, after a moment's silence, said, 'I'm going to tell you something I shan't tell the others, so please keep it to yourself. She's chucked me because she's got someone else. And besides that, she finds me dull.'

'I don't believe it. She says wonderful things about you in this letter. She says how good you are.'

'I'm not, of course. Anyway, goodness can be extremely dull.'

'Not to anyone who's lived in my family. You wouldn't believe what most of the men have been like – even grandfather, when he was young. To me, goodness is the most exciting thing in the world.'

'Not my dreary kind of goodness. Anyway, please believe that you hadn't anything to do with what's happened. And I can't think why Corinna should write to you.'

'She meant to make it easier for you, and I think she meant to be kind to me, only it hasn't worked out that way. She's made me feel terribly guilty.'

He was suddenly so angry with Corinna that some of his anger overflowed on to Sarah. He said, 'Oh, don't be idiotic Sarah,' then added more kindly, 'I swear she's only trying to excuse herself. May I see the letter?'

'No!' said Sarah, blushing furiously. 'I mean, well, it's private.'

He could interpret that blush. Corinna, no doubt, had handed him over with her blessing. As if to confirm his guess Sarah went on, 'She's got it all wrong. I never for one moment hoped… One can't help liking people but I'd never have tried… Never, never.' She turned away, took an outsize handkerchief from the Burberry's pocket and blew her nose loudly.

Hugh, waiting until she had recovered herself, knew that in spite of feeling resentfully disenchanted by Corinna, he still loved her. And in spite of both liking and admiring Sarah, he did not love her at all. But he also knew that he would, almost certainly, end by caring enough for Sarah to marry her and help her save what little could be saved from the wreck of her family's fortunes. He saw this not in any moment of clairvoyance but as the result of his common sense. He was well aware that he had a great deal of common sense. Goodness and common sense, what could be duller? But dear Sarah would appreciate both. And then he found himself remembering her asleep in bed with one arm round Penny and knew he was already fonder of her than he had realised.

She put her handkerchief away and said, with her jaw tightly clenched, 'I'm making an outsize fool of myself. I do apologise.'

Hugh, placing his hand on hers, said gently, 'Unclench, Sarah.'

May, on her return from the cottage, told George about the break between Hugh and Corinna. He asked if June was upset about it.

'Only because she thinks Hugh will be. She agrees with me that it's for the best. So does Robert.'

'Oh, he was there, was he? He said something about going for a walk.'

'He came in just before I left, looking very down. June was hoping hot buttered toast for tea might cheer him up; I'll make some for us. And I must tell the others about Hugh's troubles.'

'They're Corinna's troubles too. She must have hated hurting him. Any idea what she's up to?'

'Your guess is as good as mine,' said May, deciding to keep her own guess to herself.

After tea, George said he would go and cheer Robert up. The truth was that he could no longer stay away from June. Even if he couldn't get a moment alone with her it would be something just to be with her.

As he entered the cottage Robert came out of the sitting room, said, 'Hello, see you later,' and went upstairs two at a time. George stared after him in astonishment.

Robert, his fair skin flushed, his blue eyes alight with excitement, had looked and also sounded on top of the world.

'What's up with Robert?' said George, entering the sitting room.

June was seated by the little fire she had lit to welcome Robert, on this cheerless day of intermittent drizzle. She gave George a loving look and said, 'You may well ask. Did you ever see such a change in a man? I've just convinced him that we ought to go round the world.'

It had been George's intention to take her in his arms the instant they were alone together; not since Baggy's death had he had the chance to. But he was now so stunned by her words that he could only say, 'You can't be serious.'

'Couldn't be more so. We've just worked it all out. We can sell Baggy's house now. And he's left us far more money that we expected – thanks to your making him leave everything to us. And Robert's sure he can get a series of articles commissioned. He's full of ideas for them already.'

George sank heavily on to the sofa. He found June's bright manner both chilling and convincing. She wasn't putting on an act. And rarely had he seen her so self-confident. All he could find to say was, 'But us, June?'

Her manner softened. 'George darling, you know we couldn't go on. It was… just a silliness, caused by crazy old Aunt Mildred's nonsense. Why, you said yourself, here in this room…'

'I never said it was a silliness. Anyway, that was at the beginning. Later, that night in the garden…'

'You still must have known it couldn't go on.'

'I knew it couldn't *not* go on. So did you. Be honest, darling.'

She would have liked not to be honest, not to admit that even for one moment she had felt… but it wouldn't be fair. So she said, 'I know. I did feel like that, for a while. But I stopped feeling it after Baggy died. And it wasn't anything to do with the difficulty of keeping it secret. I simply didn't want it any more. It didn't seem real – compared with death. Death's so terribly real.'

'Isn't love real?'

'Real love's real – what I feel for Robert. When I saw how stricken he was about Baggy I knew just how he'd feel about us, if he'd known. Oh, George, let's thank God we weren't found out. We've been lucky. I could almost be grateful for Baggy's death because it brought me to my senses.'

George said, 'I shall always love you, June.'

'You'll do no such thing.' She spoke gently but very firmly. 'And you don't love me now, any more than I love you. What happened was a mixture of fondness and sudden physical attraction – just a flare-up. Perhaps it hit you harder than it hit me because you weren't prepared for it – whereas I've had this silly thing about you for ages. A sort of crush, really – I told you. Well, I'm over that now and I do beg you to help me to forget it all and of course to forget it yourself. Otherwise, how can Robert and I ever come back here?'

For a moment he looked at her in silence. She was wearing a very ordinary cotton dress which reached barely to her knees. He noticed that her legs, though pretty, were just a trifle plump. They always had been, he remembered, even when she was a girl. May had inherited her mother's admirable legs. Oh, yes, May had definitely been 'the pretty sister'. So of course he'd made a beeline for her. Strange that it had taken him over twenty years to find out his mistake. He now knew that he loved June as he had never loved any other woman. He also knew that if he convinced her of this she would remove herself from his life for ever. Ironically, the best proof of his love he could give her was to reassure her that it didn't exist.

He said at last, 'Oh, my darling, sensible June. Of course you're absolutely right. I know that, really.'

She flashed him a smile. 'Oh, thank you, dear George. I was so afraid you might – well, pretend it really mattered, even try to turn me into one of your lady friends.' She looked mischievous. 'Not that I officially know anything about them. Oh, George, I'm so truly fond of you.'

He, too, smiled. 'But I'm not your Rudolph Valentino any more?'

'I should hope not. It was about time I outgrew that school-girlish nonsense.' But she was going to miss Rudolph Valentino. Perhaps, provided George never found out, it would be all right to revive him – later, of course; though even now… She pulled her thoughts up, stopped smiling fondly at George and said briskly, 'Well, there's nothing more we need say, is there? I mean, Robert will be back any minute. He only dashed upstairs to find some travel book.'

George said, 'I'll wait and have a word with him, God bless him.'

Again she smiled her thanks. He smiled at her in return, then sat watching the firelight flickering on those very dear only slightly too plump legs.

Dinner was late, by request, May having overdone what she thought of as the funeral tea. She had also gone to town over dinner, as she invariably did when Prue and Dickon came home from school. They eyed every course with faint amusement but always accepted second helpings.

The dull day had relented to the extent of a few pale greenish-gold streaks beyond the Hall. As Hugh was dining there he and Corinna could be freely mentioned – with considerable sympathy but only Prudence thought the break was a pity. Asked why, she said, 'Well, they looked so nice together. But I always did say they were star-crossed.'

Dickon said, 'I gather only Hugh was star-crossed. Corinna was a star-crosser.'

'You can't use "star-cross" that way,' said Prudence.

'Why not? If you can double-cross, you can star-cross.'

Nobody agreed with him and he didn't really agree with himself. A very foolish remark, really, on the edge of his besetting facetiousness.

After that, the main topic of conversation was the projected trip round the world. Robert now had qualms about going.

He'd had, it seemed, an extraordinary experience while hunting for an atlas. 'I got a queer, oblique view of the Hall, through my little round window – I seemed to catch it unawares. And I suddenly knew exactly how to begin my novel. Ought I to stay here and work on it?'

'No,' said Fran, decidedly. 'Let the idea run after you. I'll tell you something about going round the world, Robert. Sooner or later you feel homesick and *that's* the moment you should begin your book. You should write about things when you're missing them.'

Robert was impressed. 'You're right, Fran. I've been too happy here to want to escape into a book. I've been shockingly lazy.'

'You've never been lazy in your life,' said June. 'And kindly remember this is going to be a holiday.' But she felt it in her bones that he would be writing like mad in some faraway hotel bedroom, while she did her sight-seeing alone. Not that she'd mind, as long as he was happy. She was still haunted by the thought of how unhappy she might have made him.

George was wondering how he could contribute to the trip. Those two mustn't squander too much of their money. And he still hadn't decided what he could give June for her birthday on the last day of the month. For a moment he cherished the idea of giving her real pearls and telling her they were imitation. But May took a pride in being able to recognise real pearls.

June was asking her mother about her own recent travels. Everything she was told excited her. She said, 'I still can't believe it's going to happen – and it's all thanks to dear Baggy's wonderful generosity.'

Fran felt something approaching a shiver. It wasn't, so much, Baggy's generosity that had made the trip possible as Baggy's death. She remembered his saying he'd give his life if he could prevent what lay ahead. She half thought one could get taken up on that kind of offer – by God, or Fate or one's own innermost self. Superstitious nonsense, no doubt; and Baggy's last thoughts had probably been about living, not dying – living in a one-room flat close to hers, God help her. But still… she hoped he wasn't earthbound, regretting his bargain and still hankering for that one-room flat.

Robert was now telling Prue and Dickon that they ought to listen to the nightingale. 'Though you may be too late. They stop singing around the middle of June.'

'We'll go tonight,' said Dickon.

May looked anxiously at her son. Was there a budding romance? She said she would come too. But they welcomed the idea so eagerly that she decided not to bother. She really had a great deal to do this evening, planning the Dower House bedrooms Prudence and Hugh would use while their parents were away.

George got up to refill wine glasses. Burgundy tonight, to go with May's wine-dark casserole; she had vaguely felt that a dark dinner was suitable for the occasion. June put her hand over the glass and smiled her refusal. George found this symbolic. Ah, but she would come back, and next year they would listen to the nightingale again. And he could keep his love for ever, provided he kept it to himself. He even felt a surprising satisfaction. Good God, for once in his life he was going to behave well!

He travelled on around the table and smilingly refilled his brother's glass.

HESPERUS PRESS

Under our three imprints, Hesperus Press publishes over 300 books by many of the greatest figures in worldwide literary history, as well as contemporary and debut authors well worth discovering.

Hesperus Classics handpicks the best of worldwide and translated literature, introducing forgotten and neglected books to new generations.

Hesperus Nova showcases quality contemporary fiction and non-fiction designed to entertain and inspire.

Hesperus Minor rediscovers well-loved children's books from the past – these are books which will bring back fond memories for adults, which they will want to share with their children and loved ones.

To find out more visit **www.hesperuspress.com**

@HesperusPress

SELECTED TITLES FROM
HESPERUS PRESS

Author	Title	Foreword writer
Adler-Olsen, Jussi	*Alphabet House*	
Alcott, Louisa May	*Good Wives*	
Alcott, Louisa May	*Jo's Boys*	
Alcott, Louisa May	*Little Men*	
Alcott, Louisa May	*Little Women*	
Arlt, Roberto	*Mad Toy, The*	Colm Tóibín
Austen, Jane	*Lady Susan*	
Austen, Jane	*Love and Friendship*	Fay Weldon
Austen, Jane	*Sanditon*	A.C. Grayling
Bannalec, Jean-Luc	*Death in Pont-Aven*	
Baum, Frank L.	*Emerald City of Oz, The*	
Baum, Frank L.	*Glinda of Oz*	
Baum, Frank L.	*Marvellous Land of Oz, The*	
Baum, Frank L.	*Wonderful Wizard of Oz, The*	
Benson, E.F.	*Mapp & Lucia*	
Biggers, Earl Derr	*Love Insurance*	
Börjlind, Cilla and Rolf	*Spring Tide*	
Brinton, Sybil	*Old Friends and New Fancies*	
Bronte, Charlotte	*Professor, The*	
Cather, Willa	*O Pioneers*	
Collins, Wilkie	*Frozen Deep, The*	
Conan Doyle, Arthur	*Poison Belt, The*	Matthew Sweet
Conan Doyle, Arthur	*Tragedy of the Korosko, The*	Tony Robinson
Conrad, Joseph	*Heart of Darkness*	A.N. Wilson
Dickens, Charles	*Chimes, The*	
Dickens, Charles	*Haunted House, The*	Peter Ackroyd

Author	Title	Foreword writer
Dickens, Charles	*Holly-Tree Inn, The*	
Dickens, Charles	*House to Let, A*	
Dickens, Charles	*Mrs Lirriper*	Philip Hensher
Dickens, Charles	*Mugby Junction*	Robert Macfarlane
Dickens, Charles	*Round of Stories by the Christmas Fire, A*	D.J. Taylor
Dickens, Charles	*Seven Poor Travellers, The*	
Dickens, Charles & Collins, Wilkie	*Perils of Certain English Prisoners, The*	
Dostoevsky, Fyodor	*Notes from the Underground*	Will Self
Eliot, George	*Janet's Repentance*	Kathryn Hughes
Eliot, George	*Mr Gilfil's Love Story*	Kirsty Gunn
Fitzgerald, F. Scott	*Popular Girl, The*	Helen Dunmore
Fitzgerald, F. Scott	*Rich Boy, The*	John Updike
Flaubert, Gustave	*Three Tales*	Margaret Drabble
Forster, E.M.	*Arctic Summer*	Anita Desai
Forster, E.M.	*Obelisk, The*	Amit Chaudhuri
Gara, Nathalie and Ladislas	*Welcome to the Free Zone*	Norman Lebrecht
Garnett, David	*Lady Into Fox*	John Burnside
Gaskell, Elizabeth	*Mr Harrison's Confession*	
Gaskell, Elizabeth	*Moorland Cottage, The*	
Gibbon, Lewis Grassic	*Spartacus*	
Goethe, Johann Wolfgang von	*Madwoman on a Pilgrimage, The*	Lewis Crofts
Goethe, Johann Wolfgang von	*Man of Fifty, The*	A.S. Byatt
Greene, Graham	*No Man's Land*	David Lodge
Hastings, Milo M.	*City of Endless Night*	
Hawthorne, Nathaniel	*Rappaccini's Daughter*	Simon Schama

Author	Title	Foreword writer
Hiltunen, Pekka	*Cold Courage*	
Hiltunen, Pekka	*Black Noise*	
James, Henry	*Diary of a Man of Fifty, The*	David Lodge
James, Henry	*In the Cage*	Libby Purves
James, Henry	*Lesson of the Master, The*	Colm Tóibín
Jonasson, Jonas	*Hundred-Year-Old Man Who Climbed Out of the Window and Disappeared, The*	
Kafka, Franz	*Metamorphosis*	Martin Jarvis
Kafka, Franz	*Trial, The*	Zadie Smith
Keilson, Hans	*Comedy in a Minor Key*	
London, Jack	*Before Adam*	
London, Jack	*People of the Abyss, The*	Alexander Masters
London, Jack	*Scarlet Plague, The*	Tony Robinson
London, Jack	*Sea-wolf, The*	
Montgomery, L. M.	*Tangled Web, A*	
Montgomery, L.M.	*Blue Castle, The*	
Nokes, David	*Nightingale Papers, The*	
Parks, Tim	*Talking About It*	
Puenzo, Lucía	*Wakolda*	
Roberts, Elizabeth Madox	*Time of Man, The*	
Roth, Joseph	*Hotel Savoy*	
Sackville-West, Vita	*Heir, The*	
Sade, Marquis de	*Betrayal*	John Burnside
Sade, Marquis de	*Virtue*	
Safier, David	*Apocalypse Next Tuesday*	
Shaw, Bernard	*Adventures of the Black Girl in her Search for God, The*	Colm Tóibín
Starobinets, Anna	*Living, The*	

Author	Title	Foreword writer
Stevenson, Robert Louis	*Dr Jekyll and Mr Hyde*	Helen Dunmore
Stjernström, Peter	*Best Book in the World, The*	
Thériault, Denis	*Peculiar Life of a Lonely Postman, The*	
Tolstoy, Leo	*Confession, A*	Helen Dunmore
Twain, Mark	*Diary of Adam and Eve, The*	John Updike
Vallgren, Carl-Johan	*Merman, The*	
Von Kleist, Heinrich	*Marquise of O–, The*	Andrew Miller
Walpole, Horace	*Castle of Otranto, The*	
Wilde, Oscar	*Canterville Ghost, The*	
Wilkie Collins	*Frozen Deep, The*	Andrew Smith
Woolf, Virginia	*Memoirs of a Novelist*	
Zola, Emile	*For a Night of Love*	A.N. Wilson